A WITCH APART

A WITCH APART

THE WITCH NEXT DOOR™ BOOK FOUR

JUDITH BERENS

LMBPN Publishing
PMB 196, 2540 South Maryland Pkwy
Las Vegas, NV 89109

First US edition, September 2019
Version 1.02, December 2020
ebook ISBN: 978-1-64202-470-8
Print ISBN: 978-1-64202-471-5

Thanks to the JIT Readers

Larry Omans
Jeff Eaton
Dorothy Lloyd
Jeff Goode
Deb Mader
Peter Manis
Paul Westman

If we've missed anyone, please let us know!

Editor
SkyHunter Editing Team

DEDICATIONS

From Martha

To everyone who still believes in magic
and all the possibilities that holds.
To all the readers who make this
entire ride so much fun.
And to my son, Louie and so many wonderful friends who
remind me all the time of what
really matters and how wonderful
life can be in any given moment.

From Michael

To Family, Friends and
Those Who Love
To Read.
May We All Enjoy Grace
To Live The Life We Are
Called.

ONE

"Hey, is that him?" Lily Antony pointed through the windshield of her 2002 Winnebago Adventurer at the man who stepped toward them with a light in his hand. It grew to illuminate his dark face and a thick, pointed beard and dark eyes below a navy-blue watch cap.

"Oh, yeah." Beside her, Romeo Stephens gripped the steering wheel a little tighter and nodded. "That's him." The light flickered quickly in his palm—once, twice, three more times—and a streak of white shimmered from the crewmember's hand to designate a magical path from in front of the RV to the freighter's docking ramp. "And that's the signal."

"Do you mean we can finally get off this boat?" She looked at him slowly and smirked.

He chuckled and started the engine. "Three weeks sloshing around on the Atlantic and trying not to lose my mind cooped up in here? You know, I think I'm gonna miss it."

"Ha. Right."

The Winnie's headlights clicked on and revealed the metal deck of the cargo freighter, the captain of which they'd basically bribed to let them drive aboard for passage from Trinidad and Tobago to France. That had been three weeks before, which had culminated in a very long twelve hours of doing nothing but sit in the Winnie until they could resume their road trip. They had both been impatient to continue but had to wait for night to fall over Brest so they could get off the ship without anyone asking too many questions. This time, their journey resumed in Europe.

"It's a good thing we slept during the day, right?" Romeo tapped the gas gently and eased them along the deck through the narrow strip of space recently provided by the day's unloading into the cargo yard.

"Well, yeah. That's a plus." Lily took a deep breath. "I'm simply glad we're moving again." For the entire journey from South America to France, the Winnie had been in the same position on the freighter—wedged between two huge stacks of light-blue containers. "Honestly, I constantly imagined those things would crash down on us when the waves got big."

"Ilya said that storm was like rockin' a baby to sleep." Slowly and quietly, they moved through the other rows of containers.

She raised her eyebrows him. "Oh, Ilya, huh? You guys finally become friends?"

With a chuckle, he shook his head. When they reached the end of the docking ramp, they drove past the man with the dark cap and pointed beard. She smiled from the passenger seat and raised a hand in farewell. Ilya met her gaze briefly but seemed more interested in her companion. The men shared a nod of understanding before the Winnie bounced a little over the rivets on the deck and they entered the space between the ramp and their landing in Brest, France.

"You still didn't answer my question," she pointed out.

He shrugged. "Yeah, well...I guess it turns out we don't hate each other."

"Because..."

"Because I also beat Zander at cards. And darts. And then I gave Ilya a chance to win his money back."

"Seriously?" She snorted. "That's what ended the battle?"

"It wasn't a battle, Lil. I was a werewolf on a cargo ship with a crew of witches—"

"And a ferret."

Romeo glanced quickly away from the maze of the half-full cargo yard to catch her gaze. "Why does that matter?"

She laughed. "I only know one other witch who used a familiar. But that ferret was way more than a pet."

"Huh. I always thought ferrets were smart on their own, anyway."

Lily nodded slowly. "They are. But did you wonder at all over the last three weeks how Kruzjic showed up in front of the Winnie almost every time we stepped out of it?"

He shrugged. "Cameras?"

"Ferret."

"On the ocean?" He laughed. "Okay. I guess I'll hafta take your word on that."

"Well, we can turn around right now and go ask. You know...one last bet before we're officially done with the *Atlantic Maiden*." She gestured over her shoulder with her thumb and after a brief moment of silence, they both laughed.

"Ferret familiar or not, the captain was keepin' an eye on us. Like I said. Werewolf on a freighter full of seafaring witches."

"Actually"—she smoothed her blonde hair back from her forehead—"I think he was more worried about what I might do."

He laughed divided his attention between her and the cargo yard as his gaze flicked from one to the other in turns. "What?"

"Yeah. We paid him enough in gold coins. Okay, a hefty price. And I put up a few wards on his cabin or room or whatever. I made one little comment about the oranges going bad, and I'm very sure he expected me to mess with his wards and screw our deal up."

"Because of oranges?"

She grimaced. "Yeah, I know. At least he's cautious."

"Sure. Maybe that's a good thing."

"Well, the guy brought us here in one piece." She folded her arms and leaned her head back against the head-rest. "You've never been to France, have you?"

Romeo smirked. "Not even a little."

"That's not... You can't be a little in a different country."

"But what if you're standing on the border and you only have one foot in France and, like...one in Germany?"

She stared at him. "Do you know what this sounds like?"

"What does it sound like?"

"It sounds like a conversation we would've had in middle school."

"I think it was a conversation we had in middle school."

"Okay, so we've both made my point." She turned her head to the window to look out over the twinkling lights that appeared in the darkness as they finally finished their slow exit from the cargo yard and out onto the road. "Let's talk about how we'll get into Bucharest."

"We'll drive." When she rolled her head against the headrest to shoot him an exasperated look, he grinned. "Don't worry about it, Lil. I mapped out the entire thing."

"Of course you did."

"It'll only take us seven hours a day for four days. That's not too bad for passing through five countries. Have you ever been to any of the others?"

"Only France." She smiled. "That was a good trip with my mom. I think it'll be better with you."

Romeo batted his eyelashes and cocked his head. "I'm so flattered."

It was hard to slap his arm across the Winnie's huge center console between them but Lily did it anyway. "Or not."

"Aw, come on." He laughed and wiggled his eyebrows. "I'm glad my first time's with you."

"Oh, jeez." She grinned and rolled her eyes before she looked out the passenger-side window at the streetlights and the few other vehicle headlights that moved past them through the darkness. *I really hope he's not disguising the truth inside that joke right now. We've never actually had that conversation.*

After five minutes of driving in the dark and the unfamiliar silence, Romeo sighed. "Okay, does it feel really quiet to you?" He glanced quickly at her, raised his eyebrows, and sent her a playful grimace.

"Not really." She shrugged. "I spent the last three weeks as the only woman on a cargo freighter full of men who spent at least half their time drinking, gambling, smoking, yelling at each other, and playing Rammstein nonstop. I had to soundproof the Winnie on the third night."

He chewed the inside of his cheek and considered that statement. "It wasn't all Rammstein—"

"Okay, but it was all death metal all the time."

"What? That's not even the right—you know what? Never mind." He shook his head like she'd made an awful joke.

"Not death metal?"

"Not really." He smirked at her. "How bout a middle ground with playing different music right now? It feels like we're sneaking around when there's not even a little noise."

"Romeo. We kind of are sneaking around, remember? That's why we took almost a month longer than we really had to. No paper trail with plane tickets or hotels. We have the Winnie and my mom's gold coins. Yeah, I know, that's weird to say. And we have everything we need to bribe our way to a different continent, monetarily or magically." She winked at him. "But yeah, if you wanna play music, that's fine."

"That would be awesome."

She chuckled and located his phone in the cupholder in the center console, where both of their devices had been since before they'd found all the magicals imprisoned beneath the so-called healing temple of Ichacál. She hadn't forgotten the passcode to his phone—five-four-five-nine—and quickly pulled up his extensive and ridiculously eclectic music collection. "All right. Here we go."

The opening of "The World at Large" by Modest Mouse played through the Winnie's updated stereo system and he immediately laughed.

The music gave her another excuse to zone out for a while while he drove, and now reality had sufficient time to sink in. She took a deep breath.

This might actually be it. Canada, Mexico, Guatemala, and now we're in Europe, of all places. Okay, Mom. You said things were getting dangerous. I'm ready. No matter who else I have to fight between here and Romania, I'm coming to find you.

TWO

By the time they reached Paris a little over six hours later, the sun had barely risen. Lily's eyes drooped heavily as she stared out the window at the city she thought she'd remembered so well. "It looks so different."

"Oh, yeah?" Romeo's mouth stretched wide with a huge yawn, and he blinked against the morning sunlight that winked at them from between the buildings. "How's that?"

"I don't know. It seemed...bigger last time I was here."

He chuckled. "That's kinda what happens when we're not kids anymore, right? And you were here with your mom last time. This time, we're trying to find her."

"Maybe." She retrieved her sunglasses from her purse on the center console and slid them on against the sunrise. "I have kind of a bad feeling about being here."

"Huh. The only thing I'm feeling is tired." He rested his upturned hand on the center console and sent her a few glances as they drove down Rue de Rivoli. "Maybe we need to rest."

"Shouldn't we try to stay up? Get used to the time change? 'Cause I'm sure I'd sleep all day."

"Nah. We can set an alarm." He wiggled his fingers and with a smirk, she took his hand.

"Okay. So where does one park their RV for a quick nap in Paris?"

Romeo shrugged. "I have no idea. By this point, though, we're fairly good at finding where we need to be."

Fifteen minutes later, they pulled the vehicle into the parking garage of a shopping mall on Rue Saint-Didier. He shut the engine off and sighed. "So, my list of total pros on this part of the trip is still growing." He turned his head against the headrest and grinned at her.

She unbuckled her seatbelt and shifted toward him in her seat, her eyes widening in exaggerated excitement. "Oh, do tell."

"Okay, ready? First, your excellent idea to cast that translating spell on me."

"Of course, it was excellent." She laughed. "Neither one of us would've survived the *Atlantic Maiden* if we couldn't understand the crew. I think most of them were Portuguese."

"Well, yeah. That part was important." He smirked. "I don't really need words to kick someone's ass at darts, but it did get Melbón to whip up a little more legroom in this baby for me."

Lily stared at the bottom of the dashboard in front of the passenger seat. She raised both legs and kicked them around in all the open space. "Didn't he simply remove the glovebox?"

"Well, yeah. But there's some kinda nice curving design to it, right?"

She looked at him with a sideways glance. "It almost doesn't look like he took the glovebox out."

"Okay, you're moving this way off topic." He chuckled, stood from the driver's seat, and walked backward across the living area. "I was saying how much I like being able to understand and speak other languages. For instance, this lovely garage right here"—he gestured with an exaggerated wave toward the window behind the couch and the cement structure beyond it—"I know is the Beautiful Leaves Shopping Center. And I don't even have to ask. Reading the French names in Canada was hard enough."

Lily shook her head and followed him across the RV. "You must be thrilled."

"I am, actually. Second pro of this trip? No one's gonna pin us down as Americans."

"Yeah, everyone pegged us right away in Mexico. It's a different flavor when it comes to the French, I think."

He nodded and stretched both hands out and she took them. "I really hope you plan to glamor our license plate every time we reach a different country."

"I really don't think that matters."

"Why not?"

"Um..." She squinted at him, but he was completely clueless when it came to the politics of where they were and where they were going. "Literally every country we'll go through is in the EU. People travel around here all the time."

He drew her into the narrow hallway behind the tiny kitchen and bathroom and scrunched his nose. "I don't know if I want everyone to think we're French."

She laughed. "There's nothing wrong with the French."

"There's nothing wrong with us, either. But we're still incognito, aren't we?"

"I'm reasonably sure that's because we're tracking my mom, who we now know for a fact is imprisoned by seriously messed-up witches trying to siphon magic out of anyone and everyone they catch." She raised an eyebrow. "Not because we're Americans."

When he moved her through the bedroom door, he took a breath to speak and paused. "That too."

Lily rolled her eyes and chuckled. "Are those the only two things on your list of European Road Trip Pros?"

"Definitely not." Romeo stopped on her side of the bed and drew her toward him. She slid her arms around his waist. As she hugged him, feeling way too heavy and tired, he tucked her blonde hair behind her ear. "Number three. I did not expect them to drive on the right side of the road here."

She fought back a laugh. "Instead of the left? Or instead of the wrong side?"

"They're synonymous, Lil."

"Uh...we're not in the UK." She couldn't hold a giggle back. "Most people in Europe drive on the right side of the road. Please tell me you knew that."

He licked his lips and squinted at her. "Is that a trick question?"

"It wasn't a question."

"A trick request, maybe?"

"Oh, my God." She leaned away from him and grinned while she stared into his wide green eyes flecked with gold. "Did you think the entire continent was like the UK?"

"I mean...no." He pressed his lips together and frowned, and she burst into laughter.

"You did."

"It's not that rare a misconception." He shrugged but managed a chuckle at her amusement. "Not everyone can go to a seriously fancy high school or take random trips to Paris with their mom for fun. You know, one guy I worked construction with in Charleston thought British was a different language. Granted, he still spoke Gullah, so maybe for him it was."

"You haven't really built yourself a very strong case."

"Hey, I've never been here before, okay? And I definitely never thought I'd be ferried across the Atlantic on a freighter of...what? Portuguese magicals?"

"That doesn't have anything to do with you thinking everyone in Europe drives on the left side of the road."

"Well, consider me informed." Romeo tilted his head and laughed. "Do you wanna hear what else is on my list or not?"

"You mean there's more?"

He squinted at her and poked her below the ribs.

"Hey." She squirmed and slapped his hand away, laughing.

"One more thing so far." He yanked her back toward him to hug her again. "And I'm very sure you can't find some kinda rebuttal to this one."

"Oh, okay..."

With his hands on her hips, he sat on the edge of the bed and drew her closer. She climbed into his lap, wrapped her legs around him, and draped her arms over his shoulder to play with the dark, loose curls at the nape of his neck. "Number four," he said, holding her gaze. "We got to bring the Winnie."

Her mouth fell open before she summoned a playful smile. "That's your final pro?"

"Yep. You can't argue with that one, can you?" She laughed but didn't have anything to say. He slid his hands down her thighs and squeezed. "It would've sucked if we had to leave our adventuremobile behind. 'Cause I'm really starting to like the way we fit in this bed." In one quick motion, he held her against him and flopped sideways onto the comforter.

Laughing, she rolled away from him and settled onto what had been his side of the bed for the last six weeks. She propped her head up in her hand and waited for him to scoot himself up until he'd reached her pillow and copied her pose. "That sounds like a good list." She smirked.

"I thought so."

"I do have a rebuttal, though."

"You do, huh?"

"Yep." She sighed. "That was actually two different items."

He squinted at her, his lips pressed together in what might have been an effort to hold back laughter. "Come here." His hands snaked out to grasp her around the middle, where he poked her a few times and began to tickle her.

Laughing, she tried to fight him off and finally managed to shriek, "Stop!" He grinned. "That's not how you get someone to agree with you, you know. Or take a nap."

"I don't think we'll have any problems." He winked and she laughed again. "Come here."

When he flopped his head onto the pillow, she rolled onto her other side and scooted back toward him. His warm, heavy arm around her waist made her sigh, and she snuggled closer against him. "Did you set your alarm?"

"Yep."

"Good." He hugged her a little tighter and she closed her eyes. "One more pro for the list."

"Oh, yeah?"

"Yeah." She settled her arm over his and laced her fingers through the back of his hand. "This."

THREE

The alarm on Romeo's phone screamed two hours later and jolted Lily out of her deep sleep.

"What are you—" She stopped, sat bolt upright in the bed, and her favorite attack spell crackled with red energy at her fingertips, her arm outstretched toward the mirror on the wardrobe across from the bed. "Oh, jeez." With a sigh, she reabsorbed the spell and nudged him beside her.

He groaned, sat up as quickly as she had, and snorted. "I don't remember setting it that loud." He snatched the device off the built-in table on her side of the bed, tapped it, and plunged the Winnie into relative silence again.

She still tried to catch her breath but tasted the smoke and ash that always came with the dreams or the visions or any interaction she had with the black shadow-bird. A little disoriented, she rubbed her cheeks and shook her head.

"Are you okay?" he asked.

"Yeah." She turned to look at him and took a deep

breath. "I had another dream."

"About your mom?"

"She looked even worse than the last time. Skinnier, I think. And she was..." She frowned and shook her head again as she struggled to pull out the memory of her dream and separate it from her emotions. *Otherwise, I won't get anywhere with this.* "She was falling. The bird had dropped her and was diving after her, but she... I think she made it drop her."

"Man." He searched her gaze and sighed slowly, then rubbed his nose. "You think it's a warning?"

"Yeah, maybe. Or some kinda call for help?" She shrugged. "I wish I knew what that stupid shadow-bird actually is. It's part of her. I know that much."

"Do you still think she left that image of it under the healing temple?"

"That man Joseph said that was where they'd kept her." Lily smoothed her hair away from her forehead. "And the shadow-bird's been...what? Trying to protect me? Warn me? It has to come from my mom. But, having said that, I don't understand why I dream about it carrying her away and dropping her from a bajillion miles up in the sky."

Romeo caught her hand and gave it a gentle squeeze. "You'll figure it out, Lil. I've tried to put it together too, but..." He smirked. "The truth is, no one knows your mom like you do."

"Yeah. That's why this is so infuriating." She frowned at him but quickly offered a conciliatory smile and gave him a peck on the cheek. "I'm gonna go brush my teeth."

He laughed. "Again?"

She shrugged. "It's only the...smoke." Wiggling her fingers in front of her mouth, she wrinkled her nose and slid off the bed. "I dunno why that's always a thing, either."

"Okay." He ran his hand through his curls and stopped to scratch his head vigorously. "Do you wanna go see Paris when you're done?"

"That's not even a real question." She winked at him before she stepped through the narrow bedroom doorway, down the short hall, and into the tiniest bathroom ever invented. Once she'd retrieved her toothbrush and toothpaste from the holders mounted on the wall, she turned the water on and scowled at her reflection. "It tastes like Grandpa's ashtray."

"What was that?" Romeo called from the bedroom as he jammed his feet into his sneakers.

"I'm only talkin' to myself." Lily stared into the mirror. *And maybe trying to talk to Mom too. If this is her trying to talk to me, she should've written some kinda secret code for dreaming about shadow-birds too.* A bright flash illuminated in her eyes, and though it seemed impossible, she saw the wide wingspan of the black bird made of smoke grow larger and larger within her own pupils. The wings flapped once, and she had the overwhelming expectation of seeing two huge wings spring from her own eyes and overtake her.

You can find everything you need to know by looking into the eyes.

The words of her mom's last note—which she had dug up from a hole in the ground outside the healing temple of

Ichacál—burst through her head as the glistening black wings of the shadow-bird she'd thought she'd seen in her own eyes disappeared entirely. The smoke taste remained in her mouth, and she grimaced.

"After everything else," she muttered, "there's no way I'm seeing things." Quickly, she squirted toothpaste onto her toothbrush and scrubbed away at her mouth while she glared at herself in the mirror.

"Seeing what, now?" Romeo passed the open bathroom door with raised eyebrows.

She simply shook her head and gestured to her foaming mouth.

With a smirk, he shrugged and turned toward the kitchen. "Do you want coffee now or do you wanna try to buy something while we're out?"

"It doesn't matter to me." It came out garbled around the mouthful of toothpaste and she paused to spit in the sink. "I'm basically wide awake now anyway. I think." Once she'd rinsed her mouth out and splashed her face, that statement felt more like the truth despite the ashy aftertaste that still lingered faintly.

"All right. First order of Parisian business, then. Do you think we can find a decent cup of coffee in this city?"

Lily put up her toothbrush away and stepped through the bathroom door. "Seriously?"

He laughed and rolled his eyes. "I'm not that clueless. Although I'm not sure how French coffee compares to what we had in Córdoba. That was supposed to be, like, the throne of amazing coffee."

"Well, I'm sure a café in Paris can hold its own." She

stepped quickly back into the bathroom so she could tie her hair back in a ponytail. That done, she turned the light off and moved out into the living area. "Is there anything else you wanna see while we're here?"

He stuffed his phone back into his back pocket and eyed the ceiling. "I think the only things I know about Paris are the Louvre, Notre Dame, and...yeah. Cafés."

She snorted. "We can probably only manage one of those. Notre Dame's on the other side of town, and I'm not sure the Louvre's such a good idea, actually."

After a moment's pause, he studied her. "You're thinking about what happened in Las Cruces, aren't you?"

"Yeah. It was stupid enough that they threw you out simply for being a werewolf. I promised I'd drop it until after we find my mom. But if that happened again..." She frowned and folded her arms. "Honestly, I don't know if I could drop it a second time."

"Fair enough." He stepped toward her and put his hands on her waist. "I'm not exactly excited to go through that again, either." He touched her cheek and stooped to leave a soft, gentle kiss on her lips. "As much as I like watching you get all fired up about magical injustices."

"Oh, whatever." Laughing, she pushed him away and turned down the short hall. "I forgot my shoes. Then we can go."

He chuckled and watched her while he tried not to let the humiliating memory of that particular discrimination in the Las Cruces Museum of Art impact him full-force again. Yes, Lily had promised to drop the whole ordeal until they found her mom—on the condition that he let her fight against it once they found a way to fight. With the poisonous wolfsbane that treated a werewolf's allergy to magic—and the Council's misperception that all were-wolves were "wild animals" incapable of controlling their impulses within the magical community—maybe they did really have a chance. But for now, the Louvre was off the table. There were more important things to focus on.

"Hey, what about the Eiffel Tower?" He spread his arms and grinned as she headed back through the hallway in her flats.

"Yep. That's also in Paris."

"No." He laughed. "I meant we could go there, right? I can't believe that wasn't the first thing that came to mind."

She tilted her head in thought. "Yeah, that would actually be fun. And I bet we can find a good café between here and there." She went to the front and took her purse from the center console.

Romeo's eyes grew incredibly wide. "I'm gonna see the Eiffel Tower. For real."

"Don't look so excited." Lily chuckled and caught his hand as she walked past him to pull him with her toward the Winnie's side door. "It's not like you get to climb it or anything."

They stepped down the two steps and out the side door before she turned to lock up quickly.

"Can you actually do that?" he asked. "Climb all the way to the top?"

She turned to face him. "No, only to the second floor."

He snorted. "That's no fun."

FOUR

"Okay, this is way better than being cooped up on that ship." Holding Lily's hand, Romeo gazed with wide eyes at the tall rows of buildings that lined the street, interspersed with streetlamps and green, leafy trees and the cars and pedestrians that flowed in either direction. In the center of the street was a wide median lined with trees and a few statues, where people sat on benches, played in the grass, or stopped to cross the traffic. When they moved onto Rue Mignard and then Rue de la Tour, the streets narrowed between the tall white buildings on either side.

"This doesn't feel claustrophobic to you?" She gazed at the tops of the buildings and felt a little dizzy. "It feels so much like being on that ship between those giant stacks of containers." He shook his head and smiled, and she laughed. "I will say that the weather in France beats Mexico any time of year."

"Any time? Really?"

She shrugged. "So far, it's not raining. And it's not a desert. So I'm happy."

"Yeah, I dunno if all these scooters would do very well on those mountain roads anyway."

"They're everywhere." She snorted. "Still, the Winnie didn't really travel on mountain roads, either."

"It did for a short distance."

"Before all the village witches teleported us." She wiggled her brows and smiled at a mother who pushed a stroller with two toddlers inside while a third walked beside her and held her hand. "Teleporting doesn't really count as travel."

"It did with them."

Lily studied the rows of scooters parked on the one-way street between all the cars and alongside the recessed doorways on the ground floor of the long, high buildings. "Do you wanna rent a scooter?"

"What?" Romeo shook his head. "If I'm riding anything with two wheels, it's a motorcycle."

"Do you know how to ride a motorcycle?"

"No."

She laughed. "A scooter's probably better to start with, then. Don't you think?"

"Lily, I feel like I'd break one of these things."

"You'd be surprised how much weight they can carry."

He raised an eyebrow. "Yeah, without going over ten miles an hour." When she looked away from him with a broad smile, he grinned.

They walked for about twenty minutes until they reached a traffic circle at the end of Rue de la Tour. The intersecting streets were lined with storefronts—shops and restaurants and businesses. "Are you hungry at all?" she asked and took his hand with both of hers this time.

"I don't think I've ever said no to that question."

"Excellent. Come on."

It took them a while in mid-morning traffic to cross Rue Vineuse and Rue Benjamin Franklin before they finally made it halfway around the traffic circle to the median between Rue Benjamin Franklin and Avenue des Nations Unies. Red tables and chairs were positioned outside the restaurant's entrance. The front door stood between a bright red awning with white lettering. "Raspberry Creperie?" He raised an eyebrow and studied the front windows.

"Did I tell you that translating spell of mine works with reading too?"

He looked at her and frowned. "You didn't need to. That much was obvious when Rosalía sat down with your spellbook and didn't know how to read English."

"Or Latin." She laughed. "I kinda stepped in it with that one."

"Nah. She's fine, Lil."

"Oh, I know she's fine. She proved that much with everyone else in the temple. And she did a great job of teaching her people what she knew." She shook her head. "I only meant I should've tested that spell before I decided to play magical interpreter."

"Well, now you know." He winked at her and glanced at the restaurant sign again. "So this is..."

"Crêperie framboise Passy Trocadéro." *At least it sounds like I'm saying it in French.*

"Yeah, I still heard Raspberry."

She laughed and pulled him closer to the front door. "We'll go with that, then. Let's find a seat outside."

The front door opened and a young woman stepped out with a huge smile. "Table for two this morning?"

"Yes, please." Lily nodded. "Are you seating people outside?"

"Of course." The woman collected two menus and silverware, then gestured toward the empty red tables and chairs. "Take your pick."

"How about over here?" Romeo walked toward the corner table closest to the restaurant.

"Please." The server nodded and followed them to the table. "Would you like anything to drink?"

"Two coffees with cream." Lily held two fingers up, then realized how odd that was because thanks to her spell, everyone thought they spoke the same language.

"Of course." The woman set their menus down, glanced from one to the other, and moved into the restaurant.

"Why didn't you simply say latte?" Romeo smirked at her with a raised eyebrow.

She frowned. "I actually ordered in French. Coffee with cream."

"That sounds like English."

"Because you—" She sighed but couldn't help but laugh. "It's a latte. I promise."

"Okay." Romeo smiled at her and scooted his chair a little closer.

She eyed him sideways. "We can trade seats if you wanna look out at the road instead."

"That would be pointless." He put his arm around her and pulled her closer to almost kiss the corner of her mouth. "We're in Paris, Lil. If I'm gonna be anywhere with you, sitting outside at a café in front of the river with a giant French monument on the other side, I don't wanna miss any opportunities."

She laughed and tucked her hair behind her ear. "Opportunities for what? You actually listed everything."

"Well, yeah. All those. And you can't say Paris isn't the perfect place to tell you—"

"Two coffees with cream." Their server returned with small white cups on saucers and a covered bowl of sugar cubes.

"Wow. That was fast." She smiled at the woman. "Thank you."

"My pleasure. Have you decided what you'd like to order?"

"Um..." She scanned the menu and looked at her companion. "Does anything look good?"

"Yep. Forest crepe, please."

"Sure."

"I'll have the salmon crepe." She nodded, and they both handed their menus to the server.

She tilted her head at them and her brown ponytail fell over one shoulder as she grinned. "I simply have to say you two are lovely together."

Lily laughed.

"See, Lil?" With his arm still around her, he squeezed her shoulder. "We're literally in the perfect place."

"Where are you from?" the woman asked.

"Germany."

"Italy."

Their server frowned and Lily gave Romeo a playful look. "And we're meeting in France."

"I thought you were local. Your French is very good."

"Thank you." She inclined her head in acknowledgment.

"We've practiced for this." He winked at her again, and the server clasped the menus to her chest and grinned at them.

"I'll have your food right out." She turned and disappeared inside the building.

"You were gonna say something before she showed up out of nowhere." She picked up the sugar spoon and pointed it at him.

He shook his head and shrugged. "It went right outta my head."

"Okay. So you're from Germany, huh?" She spooned three sugar cubes into her coffee, bit back more laughter, and pretended that this was the most natural conversation in the world. *It kind of is, though. I never thought I'd admit that.*

"Well, someone in my family's from Germany. I think."

"You know, I heard a story somewhere..." She sipped

her coffee, closed her eyes in appreciation, and opened them and nodded at his drink. "Where we're heading. Romania? I heard a story that apparently, that's where werewolves really come from."

Romeo almost snorted his latte all over the table. "Man, this coffee's good. And that's ridiculous."

"Really?" She laughed.

"Yeah. That's like saying all witches come from England or something."

"Well, what if they did?"

He paused and swallowed another sip. "Do they?"

"I have no idea." They both laughed.

"Is there any reason you picked Italy?"

Lily gazed out over the traffic circle, the cyclists, and the pedestrians moving down the street toward the walkway taking them across the Seine. "I dunno. Maybe because it's the next on the romance-language list. Romanian is too."

"Seriously?"

She chuckled. "Yep. I've only been to France, though. Last year, I was convinced my mom was planning a trip to Italy for my birthday. It kinda seems like a moot point now, though."

"Your birthday's in September, Lil. You still have, what? Six weeks until then."

"Right..." She took another sip of coffee and focused on him. "I have no idea how long it's gonna take to find her. I really thought she'd be at Ichacál."

"She was."

"I know. But not when we got there." She put one more sugar cube into her coffee and stirred again. "If we find her before my birthday, I don't even care about another trip. I'm serious. I'd even settle for her trying to train me in some kinda new magic and kicking my butt on the sparring mat."

"You sparred with your mom?"

"Sometimes."

"That's...actually not surprising." He found the thought intriguing, but when he saw a tiny frown crease the space between her eyebrows, he set his cup on the saucer. "It's not gonna take us six weeks to find her."

"We left Charleston over a month ago."

"And you realize how many places we've been since then, right?" He began to count on his fingers.

"You really don't have to—"

"All the way from South Carolina to Montreal. And a creepy magical bar underground. Plus, a park in the forest and back again."

"Romeo—"

"Two." He touched his second finger and she laughed. "From Montreal, which is basically New York in the US, all the way through any number of states to Colorado. Three. Into the desert, then Mexico, then virtually every state in that country."

"Oh, my God." She turned to look at him with wide eyes and grinned. "We did not go through every state."

"Wait a minute. I'm not done."

"Come on."

"Four. We went out of the desert and into the jungles

of Veracruz and Chiapas and into Guatemala. Next, we drove the Winnie—"

"Into South America. I know. That was a long drive too."

"Two continents, Lil. Continents. In a little over four weeks. And another three weeks smuggled onto a freakin' freighter across the ocean."

She snorted. "We weren't smuggled."

"Okay, your mom's gold coins bought our way in. That's irrelevant."

"How are gold coins irrelevant?"

Romeo laughed and leaned back in his chair. "I'm trying to make a point. We've done more in less than two months than most people do in their entire lives."

Lily clicked her tongue. "Well, most people's moms don't get stolen by witches trying to take everyone else's magic and...who knows what else."

"You're Lily Antony." He wrinkled his nose and gave her a playful smile. "There's only one of you."

"Huh. Sometimes, I wish there were more."

He paused and stared at the table. "Now that's an interesting idea."

"Romeo..."

"What exactly would that look like?"

She snapped her fingers under his nose and he laughed. "Something tells me you're not imagining multiple versions of me casting spells or solving riddles or finding my mom."

He smirked. "I could've been. You don't know."

"Uh-huh." She couldn't help but chuckle at the

devious smirk he sent her.

After another sip of his coffee, he leaned back in the chair again and laced his fingers behind his head. "The world couldn't handle more than one of you. And I mean that in the best way possible."

"Well...thanks." *I don't think I could handle more than one of me, either.* Spinning her coffee cup slowly between both hands, she looked across the street and the traffic circle again. A woman in her early thirties walked briskly across the road on the other side of the circle, then crossed into traffic to jump onto the round median in the center. A few car horns honked but she didn't seem to notice.

"It looks like jay-walking's a thing in France too, huh?" Romeo sipped his coffee.

"I guess so." Lily squinted at the woman. "I don't think most people look that terrified to cross the street, though."

"Yeah, she does look a little—"

The woman glanced at her chest and touched a small pendant at her throat. It flashed a light, almost silver-blue, and she glanced at the oncoming traffic one more time before she miscalculated her step off the median to cross the street again. The closest driver braked sharply and thumped his horn, but the woman merely jogged across the road and onto the sidewalk in front of the restaurant.

She passed them quickly and turned to look over her shoulder before she stumbled into a red chair and shoved it against the table. When she jerked to see what she'd hit, a tiny sob escaped her, and Lily realized she was crying.

"Hey, are you—" Before she could finish asking the question, the woman set off at a half-jog past the rows of tables outside the creperie and around the side of the building down Avenue des Nations Unies. Her hurried footsteps were lost in the sounds of traffic and other pedestrians and the loud, boisterous cry of a toddler not interested in minding his parents.

"That didn't look good." Romeo met her gaze and raised his eyebrows.

"No, it didn't." She leaned forward in her chair to try to see more, but they were seated on the left side of the patio and the woman had disappeared around the right side of the building.

"She's a witch, though. I know that much," he added

"Yeah, I saw it too." She took another small sip of coffee. "I wonder what—"

She ducked when a huge black shadow darted toward their table, only to disappear again with a loud hiss. This time, though, there was no lingering taste of smoke in her nose and mouth, only an intensely bad sensation that triggered a wave of goosebumps down her arm. The surprise of it made her choke on her drink.

"Hey, are you okay?" Romeo lowered his head toward her and put a cautious hand on her back.

"Yeah, I..." When she stopped coughing, her eyes were watering. "Tell me you saw the giant shadow."

"The bird again?"

She nodded. "It—"

A shrill scream came from behind the creperie, instantly followed by the sound of shattered china. They both whirled in their seats to see their server standing outside the restaurant door, their orders spilled over her feet and the cement. She glanced at them with wide eyes, and the scream came again. It wasn't hers, however.

"That is definitely not good," he muttered. The couple stood from the red patio table.

"Nope."

FIVE

The server looked at them like they'd completely lost their minds when they sprinted between the red tables and chairs toward the other side of the restaurant in the direction of the woman who'd been so clearly distressed. When they rounded the corner and found the small alleyway between the back of the restaurant and the next long row of tall buildings down Avenue des Nations Unies, they stopped.

"Oh, my God." Lily closed her eyes briefly and swallowed.

The witch hadn't managed to get very far and lay in a pool of what might have been blood if it wasn't light-purple and shimmering like some kind of gel. Her eyes—completely white—were wide open and stared vacantly at the thin sliver of blue sky above her in the alley.

"What the hell does something like that?" Romeo muttered.

"I have no idea."

A group of teenagers came down the sidewalk on Avenue des Nations Unies toward them and of course, slowed to peer down the alley and see why the couple stared so intently into it. "Hey, check that out." One of the boys slapped his friend's chest.

"Woah, that's...is she dead?"

A gasp on the other side of her made Lily turn. Their server stood beside them with her hands clamped over her mouth. "That's a—" She spun and ran back toward the restaurant, probably to tell her boss about the very strange tragedy that had occurred behind the establishment.

"Leave her alone."

At the sound of Romeo's voice, two of the teenagers who'd started to step into the alley looked up and scoffed at him. "This is some kinda trick, man. What's all that purple crap?"

The other kid snickered. "I bet this is some kinda new art exhibit. Or a—" He turned into the alley, paused, and his mouth fell open.

"Dude, what the hell is that?"

The shimmering purple gel around the woman's body trembled now like someone had slapped a huge pile of Jell-O. The first snaking tendril rose from the pool and flickered in all directions as if it possessed a life of its own.

The teenagers stared and on the other side of the alley, Lily saw another handful of people stop to watch the show. She took a step back and gave the werewolf's arm a cautious squeeze. "I think we should get outta here."

"Do you know this...whatever this is?"

"No. But if a whole group of people comes to see what

happened—like I have a feeling they will—we're gonna get caught up in the middle of it."

They stepped away from the alley to the very edge of the sidewalk and watched the crowd grow in tandem with the myriad of purple tendrils that flickered like a macabre flower garden around the dead woman's body. "None of these people are magicals," he muttered.

"I know. I'd do something about it if I could, but there are way too many people for me to use enough magic to catch all those creeper things at once." Another woman screamed, which could have been either from the sight of the dead body or the fact that the purple tendrils now climbed up the back of the restaurant and the end of the long, tall building at the other end of the alley. Cars and scooters began to slow too. "Come on." She led him around to the restaurant's front patio.

Their server and either the manager or the owner stepped swiftly outside again. "I'm telling you, Maurice. In the back alley. It's the creepiest thing I've ever seen."

Neither of them looked at the couple, who simply placed twenty-five euros on the table and assumed that would be enough to cover the brunch they never managed to eat. She saw a man across the street speak into his phone and stare at the growing crowds on either side of the alley. Two black SUVs barreled around the traffic circle. Sirens blared and lights flashed as they pulled up alongside the shops on the other side of Nations Unies.

"Okay, if the French police see this…" Romeo glanced from the cars to the crowd. "Why won't people leave that stuff alone?"

"Romeo, if you'd never seen magic before in your life, do you really think you'd simply keep walking and leave it to...I dunno. The authorities?" He shrugged. "And I don't think those are police."

"What?"

She nodded toward the four men who jogged across the street toward the restaurant and the alley. Two of them approached the crowd on this side, where over a dozen people now tried to catch a glimpse of the steadily growing tendrils that looked more like a forest of magical purple fungus where they swarmed over the dead witch's body. The other two men—definitely not dressed like the police —walked swiftly around the red patio tables and chairs toward the other side of the alley on Rue Benjamin Franklin. One of them sent Lily a curt glance before they rounded the other side of the restaurant to address the onlookers.

She grasped her companion's wrist and snapped her fingers. A silver light flashed from her hands and washed over them in under a second.

"What's that?" He glanced at her fingers clamped around his wrist.

"Only a precaution."

"Against what?"

"All right, people. Can I have your attention over here, please?" A man's loud voice echoed from the right side of the alley, eerily echoed by another man's voice saying almost the same thing on the left. "What a day, right? Let me tell you all what'll happen next." A bright, dark-blue flash spilled around the sides of the restaurant and down both streets. It washed over the young couple too, but her ward repelled it easily with a sharp flash of the same silver-blue light that faded almost immediately.

In the next second, everything in a square only a block away from the Seine was completely silent. There were no screams or gasps, no shouted questions, and no struggles to see the odd, off-putting scene of the woman's death. Even the two cars making their way around the traffic circle had frozen in place.

"No way." Romeo glanced around, blinked, and sneezed.

"Remember when I told you there were witches who could manipulate people's memories?"

"Like the spell you use. Yeah."

"I can erase twelve hours. That's it. These guys, though..."

He looked at her with wide eyes. "Do you think they jumped out of those SUVs to wipe everyone's memories?"

"It seems like it. That was definitely a memory charm." She glanced across the perfectly still, silent street to see the man on the cell phone standing there, his gaze fixed on the alley. He lowered the phone from his ear, slipped it into his back pocket, and looked directly at her. "Okay, maybe that guy with the phone, too."

"He doesn't look too happy to see us still moving."

She pursed her lips and frowned. "I thought the same thing, I'm afraid."

"I mean everything, okay?" a man said and rounded the corner of the restaurant toward them as he looked over his shoulder and pointed at either the alley or his apparent partner or something the couple couldn't see. "And take some of that back to Luc so we can find out exactly what that is." The man was completely bald and wore jeans and an olive-green, collared shirt. He continued up the side-walk and turned toward the man across the street, obvi-ously the person who had alerted them, and he nodded at the bald man and raised a hand to gesture toward Lily and Romeo.

The newcomer slowed and turned to see the witch and the werewolf in front of their abandoned café table, obvi-ously unaffected by the memory-warp spell that had frozen at least two square blocks in Paris. She gave her compan-ion's wrist a little squeeze, released him, and prepared to cast whatever spell she might need next. The bald man stalked toward them, his eyes narrowed and his expression suspicious as if he wanted to know why the only other magicals in this part of the city didn't bombard him with questions.

SIX

"Who are you?" the apparent leader of what they assumed was a clean-up team of some kind asked brusquely. His eyes were now almost slits in his hard face as he made his way between the tables toward the young couple.

"Uh..." Lily glanced at Romeo. *Somehow, it doesn't seem like the right time to tell anyone anything.*

"Right." The man stopped with only two tables left between them and folded his arms. "So I'll start with who I am. Gabriel Mercier. Non-Magical Relations for the French chapter of Cadre Europa."

"Non-Magical Relations?" the werewolf asked.

Gabriel looked over his shoulder, met his gaze again, and offered a grimace of distaste. "And cleanup."

"My name's Lily. This is Romeo."

"Really?" he whispered from the corner of his mouth. "Do you think this guy—"

"Cadre Europa is another Order." She looked at him and raised her eyebrows. "Safe."

"Only if he has proof—"

"I do." The man took another step toward them and withdrew his wallet from a back pocket. He flipped it open in front of her. Before he had a chance to anticipate it, she flicked her finger quickly toward what looked more like a social security card than an Order ID. A dark-brown smudge streaked across the card displayed in his wallet, but it faded again in the next second. He glanced at his wallet before he scowled at her. "That wasn't necessary."

"Being careful is always necessary." She raised her eyebrows and offered the man a thin smile. "And it's never a waste of time to make sure you are who you say you are." Romeo folded is arms and chewed the inside of his cheek.

"Fair enough." Gabriel glanced from one to the other for a few more seconds before he tipped his head back as if he were conceding to some request they hadn't actually made. "You obviously knew what my men and I were here to do and acted accordingly. Now, I'd like you to tell me what you know about that woman in the alley."

She shook her head. "I know she's a witch. I know she was crying and looked extremely scared when she crossed the street and passed our table."

"What table?"

"We were having brunch." She pointed at the euros on the red table and the half-drunk cups of coffee. Then, she gestured toward the broken plates and spilled crepes at the restaurant's front door. "Whatever got to that woman made her scream before we had the chance to actually eat, though."

"Did you see anything else?"

"Are you with the police too?" The werewolf frowned at the man.

"No." Gabriel's face remained impassive but observant. He returned the younger man's stare. "But I might as well be. I'm the lucky bastard tasked with finding these idiots before they expose so much magic with so many dead bodies that we have to wipe every Parisian simply to keep them all sane."

"What?" Lily's eyes widened. "This has happened before?"

He nodded and his bottom lip protruded belligerently. "Over the last few months, yeah. And it's getting worse."

"So you know what that is, then." She gestured toward the alley none of them could see from the restaurant's front patio.

"Magic. That's it." The honorary detective for Cadre Europa frowned. "There's been considerable activity around here lately that I've never seen before. And that's sayin' something." He glanced at his wristwatch, sighed, and turned away from the traffic circle and toward the alley. "We only have another two minutes until everything...picks up again." His finger twirled in the air. "Come take a walk with me." The couple exchanged a glance and Gabriel pressed his lips together. "Unofficial, of course. But the way you're looking at each other makes me think you have something to say."

"Really," she told him and shook her head firmly, "we didn't see anything."

"Well, then, tell me what you have seen." He frowned and flashed a tight smile that looked way more like a grimace of distaste. "Please."

"Unofficially?" She raised her eyebrows.

"You have my word."

When she looked at Romeo, he pulled a wry face and shrugged. "Okay."

"Thank you. This way." He waved them toward the alley and the magically murdered witch and waited for them to weave through the red tables outside the restaurant to follow him. "Stay close, if you would." She moved to his right with Romeo on the other side of her, so their new acquaintance walked closest to the restaurant and the alley. "Okay, to reiterate, you've never seen anyone perform this kind of...magic before?" He nodded toward the alley as they passed.

"Oh, my God." She leaned forward for a better look of the vacillating, goo-like purple tendrils that scrambled and wove almost as high as the back of the restaurant. The dead witch's body was completely covered with them now, and the team of magical-cleaners cast their spells as carefully as they could to avoid splattering the stuff all over themselves.

"Watch that one!" someone shouted, and a silver streak of light snapped the largest stem in half before it could grab hold of the top of the restaurant to pull itself farther up.

"Are they gonna be able to clean this all up?" the werewolf asked as he stared in something close to disbelief at the scene in the narrow space between the buildings.

Gabriel paused to study the alley, then nodded and continued up the sidewalk and gestured for them to follow. "My men are the best at what they do. There's always the possibility of danger in it, yes. But I have a feeling these...leftovers are a lot less volatile than whoever cast that hex."

"Do you think it's a hex?" Lily bit her lip and studied the man's profile as they walked.

"A very powerful one, yes." He ran a hand over his bald head, the gesture one of frustration. "We've seen more and more of these lately. Not the same version, of course, but the insulting frequency of magical attacks without any attempt to hide them from the non-magical public. It started here in Paris. From what I hear, it's getting worse all over the country too."

"Yeah, I've seen it before outside of France." She grimaced at her own stupidity. *Okay, I probably shouldn't have mentioned that.*

Gabriel looked sharply at her. "Where else?"

"In the US." She shrugged. "A witch I don't know attacked me out in the open and in the middle of the day. That was a few months ago, but it still left a bad taste in my mouth." *Not the smoke and ash, but at least that comes from my mom's warnings with the shadow-bird. I think.* She glanced at her friend again, who merely raised his eyebrows and shoved his hands in his pockets.

"I see." The Frenchman nodded and pursed his lips. "I don't have much sway outside my country, but I've heard a few things about other instances elsewhere. I can't say your experience is connected to this."

"I can't either."

"What about kidnappings?" Romeo leaned forward to catch the other man's gaze.

He stopped in mid-stride and turned to face the werewolf. She stepped farther up the sidewalk to get out of the way and let them stare at each other. "What about kidnappings?"

"You said this is getting worse." He didn't break the magical's gaze. "Is it only someone killing magicals, or are people kidnapped too?"

Gabriel's eye twitched and he glanced at Lily. "Yes. We've had reports of at least two dozen magicals abducted in the last four months. They—"

"Ready to wrap up, Chief!" One of the men standing outside the alley raised his hand.

The Cadre Europa officer nodded brusquely and circled a finger in the air. His man acknowledged with a thumbs-up and shouted something to the other team across the alley. There was a bright flash of yellow light, a squelching noise, and the other two men who'd emerged from the black SUVs exited the narrow alley. They carried a black duffel bag between them, which squirmed, writhed, and jerked in their hands as if they carried a bag full of angry gremlins instead of purple goo and maybe the dead witch's body.

Lily swallowed, her throat suddenly dry. "Is that—"

"Evidence," Gabriel said curtly. They stared in silence while the men carried the kicking duffel bag out to one of the SUVs. When the doors closed again, the man with the cell phone on the other side of the street raised both hands. Gabriel nodded at Lily and Romeo. "Brace yourselves."

She barely had time to look at her companion again before a blinding-white flash exploded from the other side of the street and the other witch's outstretched hands. It caught them, the street, the cars, the pedestrians, and everything else like a brilliant shockwave to trail an electrical fizzle across her skin. When it faded, the few square blocks of Paris that had frozen in time now moved again as if nothing had happened.

The werewolf swayed where he stood and his eyelids fluttered. In the next moment, he released two violent sneezes and dragged in a huge breath.

Gabriel eyed him warily for a moment. "I have to admit I've never seen that before."

"Seen what?" Romeo's voice was nasally and clogged, his allergy to strong magic aggravated by the Cadre Europa spells that filled the streets.

"A werewolf around so many witches. And their magic."

Lily glared at the man. *If he says anything about Romeo needing to get out of town, I swear I'll give him something worse to worry about.*

"Well, it looks like a day full of firsts, doesn't it?" He merely smirked at the man. "Excuse me." He turned away slightly to dig in his back pocket and draw out two of the four purple wolfsbane flowers he'd stuck in there before they set off from the *Atlantic Maiden*, just in case.

Gabriel sent Lily a questioning glance. She shrugged

and offered him an apathetic smile. *I'll let Romeo explain that one.*

He turned back toward them, chewing slowly. He swallowed, sniffed, and shook his head. "Neither one of us are here to stir anything up," he said and slid back into his old habit of preemptively trying to clear the air before any strange witches expected him to apologize simply for being what he was. "I know my—"

"As far as I'm concerned," Gabriel cut in and studied him intently, "a werewolf having a meal with a witch in the middle of the day is none of my concern. The fact that you're willing to talk to me at all may indeed override whatever preconceived notions I have of your kind. Which is my business."

"Sure." He shrugged.

"And I have many more important things on my plate today." He nodded at him, then glanced from him to Lily. "Like why you asked me about kidnappings."

He ran a hand through his dark curls. "We were in Mexico and South America before we came out here."

"It sounds like you like to travel."

"You could say that." Lily glanced at her friend. *And here's the part where we show our hand, isn't it?* "There were many kidnappings there too. Kids, mostly. We found two of them and brought them home. That led us to Guatemala..." Romeo raised his eyebrows as asking if she really intended put all this out there in the open. She nodded and turned to the other man again. "I can't actually prove that anything over there is connected to what's happening in France, but I think it's important to tell you what we found there."

He cleared his throat. "Please do."

"Have you heard of a healing temple in Guatemala called Ichacál?"

The man frowned and shook his head. "My connections run dry beyond Europe. They're limited to mostly only the EU, at this point. I'm sure you can understand why I've kept my eye more locally focused."

"Absolutely." She took a deep breath and continued. "Ichacál was supposed to be a safe place for refugees. Magicals seeking sanctuary from...anything, really."

"Something tells me that's not the case."

"No."

"The witches running that place called themselves the temple Wiseman," Romeo added. "I have no idea how many people came to them and actually got the help they wanted. But we found a...well, dungeon is really the only word that comes to mind."

"They held magicals down there against their will." She studied Gabriel's face and noted the barely perceptible widening of his eyes in surprise. "In cages. We got them out of there too, but they told us the Wiseman had been taking their magic."

"Shit." He stared at her, then blinked quickly. "I'm sorry. That's...how's that even possible?"

"We didn't exactly take the time to ask." The werewolf shrugged.

"This was all done in secret," she added. "Magicals coming in to get help from the Wisemen or even simply visiting the temple as tourists. And, of course, it's remote so there was no one else around to see when they were abducted and held underground for weeks—or sometimes, months. We really don't know more than that."

"And you think this is what's happening here in my country?" For the first time, he looked completely baffled and his eyebrows raised so high that his forehead creased in four distinct horizontal lines.

"I don't know what to think." She tucked her hair behind her ear. "But there's so much weird activity happening in the magical community now, and whether or not it's all connected, everyone deserves to know about it. Especially if it helps you save a few more people here from getting..." She glanced at the SUVs down the street and the men seated inside, waiting for their chief.

"That doesn't help me narrow anything down, you know." He tipped his head back and scrutinized her from over the bridge of his nose. "But I appreciate the information." A group of people moved toward them down the sidewalk, talking and laughing and completely oblivious to the magical murder that had taken place less than twenty minutes before—exactly like everyone else. He said nothing else and waited until the group passed and the pedestrians moved toward the traffic circle before he turned back to the couple. "Is there anything else you can think of that might help me with this?"

Lily scrunched her face in thought. "The witch...I told you she looked upset. She cast some kind of spell or charm on an amulet." She raised a hand to her throat, where her own amulet hung from around her neck—the silver-framed mirror on a chain, her mom's first clue. "If that still exists in your...evidence, it might be worth looking into. Maybe a cast-reversal."

Gabriel narrowed his eyes at her. "You know, it's not every day that I get investigatory recommendations from civilians. Even other witches."

"Well you don't have to—"

"No, it's a very good idea. Thank you, Miss..."

"Just Lily." *I don't need to make it any easier for anyone to find us right now.*

"Lily. Sure." He reached into his back pocket to withdraw his wallet again, slipped out a business card, and handed it to her. "If anything else comes to mind, please give me a call. If you see anything else or make any more connections between what you've experienced and what's happening in either of the Americas."

"Okay." She took the card and glanced briefly at the dark-blue lettering on a white background—*Gabriel Mercier. Non-Magical Relations.* Below that, light-blue letters moved in a magically scrolling tagline. 'Defense and Unity—Cadre Europa Stands.' A phone number blinked repeatedly in the bottom right-hand corner. "Thank you."

"If you hadn't seemed surprised by my affiliation with Cadre Europa, I would have assumed you two are French as well."

"Nope." Romeo offered him a thin-lipped smile. "Merely well-traveled."

And running around under a translation spell. No big deal. She smiled at the man too.

"Well." He cleared his throat. "How long are you planning on staying in the country?"

"We're only passing through." She put the man's card in her purse and took Romeo's hand. "Finishing up a summer trip, just the two of us."

"Through the Americas and now France, huh?" He pressed his lips together.

"And more of the EU." She nodded.

"Well, I can't ask you to stay. I don't even know how that would help any of us. But please, do call me if you think of anything else to share."

"Definitely."

"All right." The man turned toward the SUV but sent them one last dubious glance. "Thanks for your time. And be careful, yeah?"

"We always are." Romeo nodded in acknowledgment, and after another quick glance at the two visitors, Gabriel jogged across the street toward the waiting vehicles.

SEVEN

"Were we actually interrogated by a magical French cop?" Romeo frowned at the two black SUVs as they cruised slowly down Rue Benjamin Franklin.

"I don't think that really qualified as an interrogation." Lily looked at him and raised her eyebrows. "That was more like grasping at straws."

"Yeah, kinda like we are. Especially when it comes to what happened to that woman." They turned together and gazed at the entrance of this side of the alley. "I kinda lost my appetite."

"Wow. That's sayin' something."

He sighed. "I know." He frowned at the rising grid of the Eiffel Tower's metal beams on the other side of the river. "Sightseeing feels a little...banal right now, honestly."

"You don't wanna still go see the Eiffel Tower?"

His eyes widened. "Oh, I see it. It looks great." A small smile lifted the corners of his mouth and he squeezed her hand. "I'm good with seeing it from right here. With you."

"Okay. So...you think we should keep passing through? We can call Gabriel if we see anything else."

"That sounds like a good plan." He nodded decisively. "I don't know how safe it is for either of us to be caught up in magical murders right now."

"I thought exactly the same thing."

They walked toward the traffic circle to move around the other side of the restaurant, which now had three filled tables on the front patio. When they passed, their server looked at them with a welcoming smile before it melted into a frown of confusion. Lily smiled in response and gave her a little wave. The woman raised her hand in return and waved slowly like she had experienced some incredibly strong déjà vu that drove her nuts because she couldn't pin it down.

"She doesn't remember us, does she?" Romeo waved at her as well before they passed out of sight down Rue de la Tour and back toward the northern part of town.

"Only enough to make her think she's seen us before. Those guys did a fairly good job with the memory sweep if she can't even remember dropping all our food."

"That's gotta be a useful tool. Wiping people's minds with so much detail like that. She looks fairly peppy for being the first person to see a dead body."

Lily shook her head. "Well, she doesn't know that now."

They walked for a few more minutes in silence and turned onto Rue de Sablons, which they'd take for most of the way back to the Winnie.

"So I know you like helping people and not leaving

anyone in the dark." He squeezed her hand again and shrugged. "And I'm not saying we shouldn't have told that European Order guy about the temple and everything. But...why'd you think that was important?"

She looked at him and raised an eyebrow. "I think it's a little weird that all these magicals have suddenly come out of the woodwork and run around without the slightest worry at all whether non-magicals see them or not. Like the witch who tried to kill me in Charleston. And those creepy women in Chihuahua—the ones who wanted me to join them so they could use my blood."

He smirked. "You know, I'd barely managed to forget about them."

"Sorry." She laughed. "Then the Wisemen at Ichacál, and now here. With all the other weird connections, Order of North pins, and the image of the black heron everywhere... I don't think it was a coincidence that the Wisemen had a whole room full of items with that symbol. It has to be a symbol, right? If it's in all these places. And I think... Well, you didn't see the shadow-bird this time, did you?"

"Uh...no. But I'm kinda partial to trusting you when you say you did."

She smirked at him but the pleasure at his expression of trust faded quickly. "Yeah, I saw it. But I don't think it was the same shadow-bird that's warned me about danger or come to help me fight. My mom's bird...or whatever it is."

"Okay, I don't know if I can handle three different

black birds in this equation." He cleared his throat. "That's...it's confusing."

"Oh, yeah. I know. I think this was something else. It didn't feel like my mom's shadow-bird. It felt like..."

"Like what?"

Lily sighed and gave him a hesitant look. "Don't laugh."

"I promise I won't. Unless you're about to tell a really bad joke, I don't think anything you could say right now would make me laugh. I'm still thinking about the purple goo."

She wrinkled her nose. "Yeah... Honestly, though, I only saw that shadow-bird for a minute as it flew over us, I guess."

"And it felt like?"

"It felt like death."

Romeo stared down the street ahead of them lined by old, incredibly tall white buildings. "You thought I'd laugh at that?" he asked after a short silence.

"Not really. But it sounds kinda ridiculous when I say it out loud."

He shook his head. "There's nothing ridiculous about it. Think about it. It's good to know, right? That what you felt was actually the real deal. Because that's what it was. Death."

"Yeah, it is good to know. It doesn't make me feel any better, though."

Two women on scooters whizzed past them down the street and left a high-pitched whine in their wake.

His sigh was so heavy, she became a little worried. "What's wrong?"

After a hasty glance at her, he closed his eyes and shook his head. "I was really excited about Paris."

"Well, try thinking about it this way." She squeezed his hand this time and smiled at him. "I bet you're the only werewolf from the US who's seen this side of it."

When he didn't respond after a few seconds, she thought he'd been so preoccupied in his own head that he hadn't heard her. Then, he snorted. "See, that qualifies as a really bad joke."

"It does, doesn't it?"

"One hundred percent."

"Did it help?"

He laughed. "A little."

"Good. 'Cause that's the only thing that makes a bad joke worth it."

They stopped at a small convenience grocery store on Rue de Sablons to stock up on food for the Winnie's fridge and whatever would conceivably last them for the rest of their road trip into Romania. "I can't believe we spent weeks on that freighter eating out of cans." Lily lifted the paper bag of produce to her face and took a deep breath through her nose. "Oh, my God. This smells amazing."

Romeo readjusted the other bag in his arms and watched her with a raised eyebrow. "In no way do I understand your attachment to vegetables."

She laughed. "Still?"

"Still."

"But you like them."

He wrinkled his nose and shrugged.

"You do. I saw the way you wolfed down everything Aluino's people fed us." She giggled when he frowned quickly at her. "Oh, yeah. Pun very much intended."

"Okay, fine. I can get behind eating all that rabbit food. If there's something actually good to go with it."

"Well, you got your steaks, didn't you?"

"I sure did." He grinned at the paper bag in his arms. "Have you ever reverse-seared steaks?"

"No. You realize we don't have a grill, right?"

"We don't need a grill." His expression turned thoughtful. "Huh. You know, I bet that's something we could install in the Winnie at some point. Pimp out the ride a little more."

"You did not actually say that."

"What? There's nothing wrong with customizing an RV, Lil. And we can take that thing anywhere. Grill out anywhere."

"Okay, tailgate parties are off the table."

He laughed. "First of all, I wasn't even thinking about tailgating."

"Good." She grinned at him and raised one shoulder in a playful shrug. "Actually, I'm fairly sure tailgating is only an American thing. As long as we're on the same page, sure. Find someone who can stick a grill in the Winnie, and we'll do it."

"Excellent." He bumped her with his shoulder. "I'm cooking tonight."

"And I'll do something with all these vegetables." She

wiggled her eyebrows and couldn't help but laugh when he rolled his eyes.

When they reached the vehicle and put away the small number of groceries, Romeo almost skipped to the front seat.

"Do you want me to drive?" Lily stepped slowly toward the front and watched him carefully.

"Nope. I'm good. I have everything I need."

She slid into the passenger seat beside him and raised an eyebrow. "Why do you look so excited?"

He shrugged, then pulled a shiny cellophane bag from the other side of the driver's seat and opened it at the top.

"What are those?"

With his face pressed almost into the top of the bag, he inhaled deeply and sighed. "Roast-chicken-flavored chips."

"What?"

"Oh, yeah. Want some?" He held the bag out toward her and she read the label and saw they were exactly what he said they were.

"I honestly don't know the answer to that." She snorted and shook her head. "Did you get those at the store?"

"Yep. I saw 'em in the chip aisle and literally had to have 'em." He tossed a few into his mouth with a loud crunch. "Oh, man. That's so good. Apparently, this is a super-French thing."

Her mouth fell open and she glanced from the bag to his face. He munched happily and wiggled it under her nose again.

"Come on..."

"That actually does smell like chicken."

"I told you."

"Okay, fine." She grabbed a handful and ate one tentatively. "Wow. That's..."

"I know, right? Chickeny."

She laughed and buckled her seatbelt with one hand while she tried not to crush the chips in the other. "I was gonna say really weird."

"But in a good way." He stuffed another handful into his mouth and started the engine. "Now, we're good to go." He grinned at her, retrieved his phone to carefully plan their route, and finally eased out of the parking lot and headed toward the highway.

Lily eyed the bag of chicken-flavored chips. *Nope. I don't need anymore.* Without looking at her, he smirked and stretched his arm out in front of her until the snack was almost under her nose. She sighed and reached in for another handful.

EIGHT

They drove for another six hours across the sunny countryside before they crossed the border from France into Germany that evening at around 5:00 pm. That was easy enough with their passports—no need to fake the information, no magical energy fields that might have blocked them, and no shadow-birds coming to intervene.

At least we have a break from that after everything in Paris.

"We could stop here." Romeo glanced at the street signs as they headed into Saarbrücken. "It seems nice enough."

"Yeah, actually." Lily smiled at the river that ran beside the highway into the city. "I bet we can find something fun here."

"Beer gardens are a thing, right?"

She snorted. "In Germany? Yeah. Probably."

He pulled over in an almost empty hotel parking lot and retrieved his phone again. "Gimme a sec."

"For what?"

"To find where we can stay for the night." He smirked at her. "Unless you have any anti-towing spells up your sleeve."

Lily rolled her eyes. "That's a last resort."

"Hey, look at that. Spicherer Mountain Camping."

"How does that only ever take you two minutes?"

He winked at her. "I'm simply that good. And they have openings for...uh, fairly cheap. I think. It's in euros."

She leaned toward him to look at his phone when he tilted it her way. "Yep. Let's do it."

"Great. We actually passed it."

"By what—like, five minutes?"

"Ten, I think." He started the Winnie again and pulled onto the street. "You know, for never having been to Europe at all, I think we're doing a decent job of navigating our way through."

"Hey, that's all you. Honestly, you're way better at working out where to go than I ever would be."

Romeo chuckled. "You made that perfectly clear when you said we should go up the east coast to Canada."

She stuck her tongue out at him and glanced out the window. "You can't blame me for sticking with the only route I know."

"It's a good thing you have me, huh?"

"Yes." She turned her head toward him and grinned. "I'm glad I have you."

He pursed his lips in an exaggerated kissing motion. "I'll take it."

The Spicherer Mountain Campsite—as her spell apparently wanted to translate it—was incredibly easy to find and even easier to enjoy. "I'm very sure this wins the gold star for the nicest campsite of this whole trip." She gazed out the window at the green lawn, the pink-flowering trees, and the neatly manicured hedges. A huge brown clubhouse building dominated the tidy rows of other RVs and a few tents, and a little pavilion had been built farther in.

"Yeah, they know how to set it up out here." He pulled up beside the clubhouse, but before he could even open the door all the way, a large, heavy man in some kind of brown jumpsuit stood from the rocking chair outside the door and hurried toward the Winnie.

His grin brought his huge, round, red cheeks squishing up into his eyes to create a perpetual squint. A bald patch encircled the top of his head, and despite the fact that his waddling toward them seemed to make him breathless, he was incredibly cheerful. "Hello, hello!" He waved vigorously at them, and Romeo rolled the window down.

"Hi. We're only wanting a campsite for the night."

"Absolutely. Yes." The man scrabbled in the pocket of his jumpsuit, didn't find what he wanted there, and gave a sheepish little giggle. "Excuse me. Everything's inside. Please wait...wait right there. I'll be back." He constantly lifted and lowered a finger as if he couldn't decide whether or not they'd take him seriously. Then, he bustled toward the clubhouse door and disappeared inside.

Lily laughed. "That's also the warmest welcome we've ever received at a campsite."

"Yeah. It's not like the place is that empty."

"Well, maybe they really like guests."

The man barreled through the door again with a handful of pamphlets and stopped at the drivers' window. "For you. These have all the information about Saar-brücken. There are great things to do here. This is your pass. Hang it on your mirror." He handed everything to Romeo, who almost had to stand straight to lean over and reach the man's hand. "I'm Noah. If you need anything at all, I live over there." He pointed to a mobile home painted a bright yellow with a dark-brown picket fence out front and an immaculate garden. "During the day, though, I'm right here."

"Thanks, Noah." Lily smiled at him from the passenger seat and waved her purse. "How much is it for only one night?"

"Oh!" He giggled and patted his cheeks. "Somehow, I always forget that part. Thirty euros for the night. That includes electric hookup for your vehicle." His unencumbered grin was contagious, and she couldn't help but return it.

"Awesome." She withdrew a number of euro bills from her purse—which she'd exchanged from Mexican pesos before they boarded the *Atlantic Maiden* in Trinidad and Tobago—and handed them to Romeo. The bills changed hands one more time, and Noah uttered another high-pitched giggle.

"Very awesome. Thank you. Your site is number eighteen, I think." He pointed to the stack of papers. "Again, if you need anything, come find me."

"Thanks." Romeo shifted the Winnie into drive and moved slowly through the campsite and down the row of parked RVs.

"Would you believe me if I said he's still standing there waving at us?"

He snorted. "Yes. Yes, I would." He glanced at her with a smirk. "My grandma used to do the same thing."

She laughed. "He reminds you of your grandma, huh?"

"Only in enthusiasm."

It was easy enough to find site eighteen, and they pulled in beside the electric hookups. He hopped out of the driver-side door and rounded the front of the Winnie to see to the connections. Fortunately, they'd thought to purchase the necessary adaptors which seemed to be readily available even at convenience stores. She remained in the passenger seat for a minute, took a deep breath of the fresh air through the window, and looked out at the well-maintained campground. "I never thought I'd say any town in Germany was better than Paris. But today...well, yeah." She sighed, unbuckled her seatbelt, and moved through the Winnie to step through the side door.

Romeo had finished hooking up by the time she joined him. "This keeps getting easier."

"What, plugging in a giant extension cord?"

He made a face at her. "Ha, ha. You're so funny."

She winked at him. "Yeah, you're gettin' the hang of it. Now, all we need is a way to fix our favorite shower problem and we're all good."

"Well, I can't help you there, Lil. You're the one who tried to change the water with magic."

She landed a playful punch on his bicep. "Keep it down, maybe, huh?" But she smiled anyway. "If that's the one thing I can't seem to get right so far, I'd say we're doing well."

"Nice rig." A dark-skinned woman with short-cropped hair and faded jean overalls stepped out from behind the RV next to them.

"Hey, thanks." She nodded at the woman and smiled. "It's a little outdated but it gets us around."

He smirked and nodded at the stranger as well. "Yep. We get around." Lily elbowed him in the ribs.

The woman stopped a few feet away from them and rubbed her chin as she studied the Winnie. "Did I overhear you guys talking about a problem with your shower?"

Romeo laughed. "Probably."

Lily's cheeks grew warm. "It's only a little issue I still can't seem to resolve."

"Well, it turns out you parked your RV next to someone who knows how to fix almost anything."

"Really?" She stepped forward and clapped enthusiastically. "That would be amazing, actually. Not that we can't handle a few problems, but shower issues get really annoying after a while."

The woman laughed. "I believe you. Too many frustrating limitations, right?" She winked at her. *What's that supposed to mean?* She stepped toward them and extended her hand. "I'm Rebecca."

"Nice to meet you. Lily." The women shook hands, then Romeo greeted her in the same way.

"Romeo."

"It's always good to meet friends at a campsite." Rebecca's eyes were wide when she said it as if she thought it was actually hilarious, and she shoved her hands into the pockets of her overalls. "Where are you guys from?"

"Kind of all over, actually," Lily said hastily before they contradicted each other with their answers again. "You?"

"Hamburg. Our cousin lives in Saarbrücken, so we're only down for a long weekend visit. I'm still tryin' to decide the—"

"Rebecca?" The woman who appeared around the same RV wore a bright yellow sundress with daisies all over it and her straight black hair was cut into a short bob. She smiled when she saw the three of them standing beside the electric hookup. "I knew it. I'm trying to get us outta here, and you're standing around making new friends. Hi. I'm Mia, Rebecca's sister." She extended a small hand toward Lily, then Romeo, and everyone shook again.

"Lily and Romeo," Rebecca said. "They're from everywhere."

Mia chuckled. "Excellent. More vagabonds."

"Do you hear that?" Romeo glanced at Lily and wiggled his eyebrows. "We're vagabonds now."

"That makes it more fun, doesn't it?" The woman stepped beside Rebecca and folded her arms. "Seriously, though. I'm starving."

Her sister ran a hand through her short-cropped hair.

"Then we better go. Hey, do you guys have any dinner plans?"

"Well…" He looked at his companion and pursed his lips. "I had planned to cook some steaks."

"What are you guys doing?" Lily asked them.

"St. Johanner Market has a number of stalls up on Fridays," Mia explained. "It's part of the main market. They offer food, beer, and whatever else you could want, basically. We'll meet our cousin and his wife there, but you're welcome to come with us."

"It sounds like something fun to do." Lily raised an eyebrow at Romeo.

"Yeah." He shrugged. "I can make steak for breakfast."

Rebecca pointed at him. "Even better."

Mia pulled away a little to shoot Rebecca a skeptical glance. "He didn't say he'd make us steak for breakfast."

"That doesn't mean I can't appreciate the idea of it."

Shaking her head, the other woman stepped away toward the entrance of the park and gestured for them to follow. "Come on. Let's get going."

Rebecca stared after her for a few seconds, then leaned toward Lily and said softly, "Back to your shower issue after the market?"

She laughed. "That sounds good to me. I gotta grab my purse."

"Okay. We're in the purple Ford in the parking lot." She nodded toward the front of the campsite. "I don't know how long she'll wait, so…"

"Yeah, I'll be fast."

"Cool." The woman spun away, stuck her hands back into her pockets, and headed toward the car.

"It looks like we'll be shown around by some locals tonight." He rubbed his hands together and grinned.

"I can't tell if you're excited about that or the idea of steak for breakfast."

He paused, then looked at her in mock surprise. "Both."

NINE

"Come on!" Mia waved at them through the driver-side window.

"Okay, she said Ford," Romeo muttered. "I definitely wasn't expecting a Ford Fiesta."

Lily snorted. "You're gonna be picky about the car? They're giving us a ride."

"Hey, I have nothing against the car or getting a ride. It's simply the legroom in the back seat."

"The Winnie's spoilt you."

"Absolutely.

They reached the car and he went to the driver's side in the back, thinking he at least had a better chance behind Mia, who was at least six inches shorter than Rebecca. "Nice car," Lily said, slid into the back behind the other woman, and shut the door.

In the passenger seat, Rebecca groaned and ran a hand over her short hair. Mia's laugh was almost a cackle. "Even if she's not serious, that's one point for me."

Rebecca turned and glanced at Lily. "I told her this was a stupid car."

"It's a good investment." Her sister started the engine.

"It's a clown car." Rebecca glanced at Romeo and barked out a laugh. "See? This poor guy's practically eating his knees over here."

Lily looked at him too and fought a laugh. "Are you gonna be okay back here?"

He grunted and buckled his seatbelt. "It's a short drive, right?"

"Super-short." Mia steered them out of the campsite parking lot and onto the street. "You won't even notice."

He shot Lily a mocking grimace and she snorted.

"So, you guys are from everywhere, huh?" The driver didn't look at them in the rearview mirror but she sounded genuinely curious.

"Yeah." Lily smiled at the rearview mirror anyway. "We like to travel a lot, you know? Having an RV makes that much easier for us."

"I bet." The woman glanced quickly at Rebecca. "See? I bet they use theirs more than twice a year."

"You don't know that."

She leaned forward. "Actually, this is our first time traveling like this."

Rebecca laughed, and Mia hummed in acknowledgment. "It looks like you're enjoying it. How long have you been traveling?"

"About two months."

"Seriously?" Rebecca whipped her head around and stared at Lily over the back of the passenger seat.

"Yep." Romeo slapped his hands on his knees, which still pressed up against the back of the driver's seat so they were at least chest-level, if not higher. "We've been through...what? Ten countries so far?"

"Eleven, I think. Counting Germany, now."

"Holy crap." Rebecca turned and stared at Mia. "That's a lot."

"Like I said, you need to get out more."

The woman snorted. "We don't hafta turn it into a competition or anything."

"Why not? Competition's fun."

"Says the woman who literally wins at everything."

Romeo poked Lily in the thigh. "Does that sound familiar?"

"Oh, whatever." She poked him back. "How's the back seat treatin' you?"

"No comment."

She laughed and focused on the others. "So, where are you guys from?"

"Hamburg, mostly." Mia drummed her fingers on the steering wheel. "That's where we grew up and that's where we're staying, I guess. I wanna move."

Rebecca puffed a sigh through her lips and shook her head. "And leave me all alone with Mom and Dad?"

Her sister snorted. "Our dad's parents are from Vienna, originally. He and his brothers moved out here and he got a job teaching English in Vietnam. That's where he met our mom."

"And they fell in love, were approved to adopt little baby me, and found out they were having their own baby at the same time. We're practically twins." Rebecca leaned toward Mia over the center console. She bumped her with her shoulder and they both snickered.

"Really?" Lily smiled at them.

"Yep. So we both grew up speaking German, English, and Vietnamese. Things get weird when Mom's parents come to visit, though."

"How often is that?" Romeo let his knees fall open against the back of Mia's seat and shoved his hands between them, trying to find a more comfortable position for the next few minutes of their drive.

"Maybe once every five years." Mia chuckled wryly. "Honestly, I don't know which they oppose more. My mom marrying my dad, or all of us speaking a few languages they don't understand."

He laughed. "Hey, being married's a good thing. Lily and I got married too."

"Romeo..." She rolled her eyes.

Rebecca turned again to smirk at him. "It sounds like only one of you is into the idea." That made them all laugh.

Lily shook her head. "We were in Mexico."

"Oh... That explains it."

Mia's hand shot out to flick the other woman's shoulder. "Let her finish."

"It wasn't a crazy party or anything." She chuckled.

"They kinda thought it was." He raised an eyebrow at her.

"Oh, my God. Okay. We were...staying with these villagers for a while in the mountains."

"Mountains where?" Mia asked.

"Chiapas. They taught us this dance..." Lily burst into laughter at this point, unable to keep going until she got it all out. "And everyone told us to 'do the dance,' so we did. It turns out—" Another explosion of laughter escaped her and drew confused chuckles from the women in the front. Romeo opened his mouth as if to say something, his smile wide, and stared at her instead. Finally, she settled into softer giggles. "It turns out it's their version of a wedding dance. So we...accidentally got married in a traditional indigenous ceremony."

"Wow." Rebecca tilted her head. "That's kinda the best story ever."

"Okay, we're not actually married." She looked at Romeo, who merely grinned at her and raised his eyebrows.

"We are in Chiapas."

She covered her face with both hands and burst into laughter again.

"Hey, most people don't get a test run like that." Mia chuckled.

When she lowered her hands and looked at him, he still merely watched her with that goofy grin. She rolled her eyes. "Stop it."

"Okay, here we go." Mia turned left into a parking garage and paused long enough to snatch the ticket from the machine before she headed through the first level and up to the second. "Huh. Look at that. More than enough open places."

"Nice." Rebecca nodded approvingly as they rolled

into a space beside the elevator. "Do you think we're early?"

"Or there's something else happening on a Friday night that we didn't know about." The driver turned the engine off and unbuckled her seatbelt. "Okay. Everyone out. Let's do this." The car emptied, four doors closed, and the Ford Fiesta chirped with flashing lights when she locked it remotely. They headed toward the elevator and didn't have to wait very long for the doors to open. When they stepped inside, the silence continued for only a few seconds longer until Mia took a sharp breath. "Did you guys have that RV with you in Mexico?"

"We sure did." Romeo smiled and put his arm around Lily's shoulders.

Rebecca looked curiously at them. "How'd you get it all the way over here?"

She chuckled. "On a boat."

"That must've been expensive."

"Well..." The couple exchanged glances. "We actually got a very good deal on it."

"Oh, yeah? Do you know someone who ferries cars or something?"

He smirked. "Not really."

"More like we made a deal with the captain of a shipping freighter." She shrugged. "You know, uh...working around the ship. Doing odd jobs."

"We were basically part of the crew."

She fixed him with a mocking frown. "Maybe you were."

Rebecca gasped and gave them a wide grin. "Did you get smuggled into Europe?"

"Uh..."

Mia waved a hand at them. "You definitely do not have to answer that question." She glanced at her sister and raised an eyebrow. "Some people like to keep their own business to themselves." The elevator stopped and the doors opened.

"Why?" Rebecca shrugged as they filtered out onto the ground floor. "It sounds like these people have an awesome story."

"And it's theirs. Let them tell it if they want to. Don't be so pushy." Mia turned and smiled at them. "It's what she does."

"It's what I do," the other woman echoed with a shrug.

Lily laughed. "It's totally okay. We've definitely been through all kinds of things together." When she looked at Romeo again, he lit up like he'd realized the same thing. *Or that me saying it to two complete strangers makes it more real, somehow.*

"Okay, the market's down here." Mia nodded to the left and they walked down the sidewalk for a short distance before they crossed the first street. "Have you guys ever been to Saarbrücken before?"

"Nope." Romeo was the last to step up on the opposite sidewalk. "It's our first time in Germany too."

"For both of you?"

Lily nodded. "Yep."

Rebecca clapped. "Excellent. You picked the right people to show you around."

Mia elbowed her in the arm. "Or the right people picked them."

"Yeah, that too."

They crossed two more streets until they reached Katholisch-Kirch-Strasse and headed toward the market. "Huh. It's usually much busier than this."

Rebecca shrugged and peered toward the market square. "Yeah, and it's not like we showed up insanely early or anything. It's not a holiday, is it?"

"Not that I know of."

When their group turned onto the market square, Mia's quick, light steps and Rebecca's long-legged stride slowed. Finally, all four of them stopped to stare at the east side of the market. Rebecca turned to the young couple, her expression confused. "So...I guess this is why it's a little slow today."

The whole east side of the St. Johanner Market was cordoned off on the other side of the white fountain. A red-and-white-striped line of tape stretched between two buildings, semi-guarded by Saarbrücken police in their navy and light-blue uniform while a handful of others worked and photographed and inspected the crime scene in the alley.

"Yeah, this definitely isn't a regular thing, guys." Mia scratched her cheek and turned toward them with a grimace and a small shrug. "Promise."

TEN

"What happened?" Saying it out loud brought Lily out of her surprise. Of course, none of them knew the answer to that.

"It beats me." Rebecca scanned the rest of the market square, which was still set up for the day with the various vendors around the fountain and against the buildings selling food and beer, pastry desserts, t-shirts, and one stall touting sunglasses and flip-flops. "It looks like they're handling it, though. And no crowd simply means shorter lines, right?"

Mia caught her sister's arm. "Hey, they have dibbe-labbes out today. You guys have to try these."

"What is it?" Romeo couldn't quite pull his gaze away from the police tape along the alley.

"Raw potatoes." Rebecca shrugged. "And some other stuff. It's the taste of the city, right?"

"Yeah, that sounds good." Lily pointed to a beer stall in

the opposite direction. "Oh, I wanna try some of that." She nudged Romeo's side with her elbow. "Drinks first?"

"What?" He looked a little confused for a moment before he realized where she was going with that. "Hey, yeah. Beer sounds great."

"We'll meet up with you guys after that," she told their new friends.

"Sure," Rebecca said over her shoulder as Mia dragged her by the wrist toward the food. "Seriously, though. Don't forget the dibbelabbes."

She chuckled. "Definitely not." When their temporary hosts were far enough away, she turned to her companion. "You okay?"

"I dunno, Lil." He sniffed and retrieved another wolfs-bane flower from his back pocket and shoved it in his mouth. "There's a ton of magic coming out of that alley."

She puffed a sigh and tucked her hair behind her ear. "I had a feeling that's what's going on. Rebecca and Mia aren't—"

"Magicals?" He shook his head. "Not even a little."

"So there's some other magical crime here too, and I have a feeling we're the only ones who know about it."

"Yep."

"Should we take a quick look?"

He glanced at her and met her gaze. "I'm way ahead of ya." He took her hand and they wandered off at a slow, leisurely pace around the outskirts of the square and headed toward the alley on their way to the closest beer stall.

A female officer stood on this side of the red-and-white

tape, her fingers pressed to her mouth as she studied the scene and the other officers who moved gingerly inside the alley. The couple made it to only a few feet away before the woman turned and saw them. She straightened, stepped forward, and shook her head. "This is a crime scene, folks. Please keep moving."

"What happened?" She peered past the officer into the alley.

"I can't tell you that, ma'am. I need you to step back."

And I need to know if this has anything to do with us. Her eyes widened and she stepped forward again and released his hand.

"Lily..."

"Is anyone hurt?" she asked the officer and her voice rose to a panicked pitch.

"Ma'am, I can't—"

"Please. Tell me. My sister works in the market, and I... I haven't been able to get hold of her all day. She won't answer her phone. I have this terrible feeling that something—" She lurched forward and stumbled over her own feet until she'd passed the officer for a few seconds. It was enough to see past the tape and the other officers. *Well, at least I can trip realistically.* "Oh, my God. What happened? That's...what is that?"

"Ma'am, please. Step back."

"You didn't find... I mean, there wasn't anyone in there, was there?"

"Come on, Lil." Romeo reached out for her wrist but she whirled and shrieked hysterically at them both.

"I need to know! That's why we came all the way

down here. There's something wrong with Andrea, and if anything happened to her—"

"Lower your voice, ma'am." The officer placed a gentle hand on her shoulder. "Let's not cause any more of a scene than what's already here, okay?"

She looked at her with as agitated an expression as she could muster. "What happened?"

"This is an open investigation and I can't tell you anything."

As she wiped imaginary tears from her eye, she moaned a little and flicked her fingers toward the officer's face. The air shimmered with the hint of her compulsion spell, which she'd dialed down to the bare minimum in case anyone stared at her now too. Which they probably did. The woman blinked and drew away slightly. "Was someone murdered?" she squeaked. As an afterthought, she swallowed thickly to make it sound like she couldn't bear to say the words.

"We didn't find a body, no." The officer's expression settled into real surprise, completely confused as to why she'd answered the question against protocol.

"Kidnapped?"

"Possibly."

She sniffed. "And you can't work out what any of that stuff is left behind, right?"

The woman frowned. "We've never seen it before, no. It's—" She shook her head abruptly and Lily wanted to curse when the weak strength of her spell wore off so quickly. "I won't ask you again to step back. Go and enjoy the market. I know the vendors were expecting a different kind of crowd today. I'm sure they'd appreciate your busin—"

"What about my sister?" She took a chance to lean toward the alley again to confirm what she'd seen.

"If you're that worried about her, I suggest walking into the station and filing a report there. I can't help you here."

"You can't even tell me that it wasn't her?" She forced herself to sound breathless, which in turn actually made her a little dizzy.

"What's her name?"

"It's—" Lily froze, shoved her hand into her purse, and withdrew her phone before she uttered a sharp laugh. "It's her! She finally called me back." She pretended to accept the call and put the phone to her ear. "Oh, my God. I've tried to get hold of you all day. Do you have any idea how worried I was? What do you mean you didn't hear the phone ring?" Without a second glance at the officer, she stormed past the alley and whispered harshly into her phone with the occasional shout.

Romeo met the officer's gaze, shrugged, and hurried to catch up with the witch who definitely didn't have a sister.

Lily stuck her phone theatrically in her purse before he reached her. He chuckled softly. "You know, I honestly had no idea you were as quick on your feet with lying to the German police as you are with solving puzzles."

She smirked. "It's merely a different kind of puzzle."

"And you knew she wouldn't look at your phone and see you didn't actually have a call?"

"No. I banked on the fact that my outburst and her confusion after that super-tiny compulsion spell would distract her enough that she wouldn't think about anything else."

He glanced quickly at the alley. The officer had turned again to face what she had no idea was a magical crime scene. "Well, it looks like it worked."

"Yeah. And it got us a look at what actually happened." Her expression was fixed in something close to horror. "Did you see what was in that alley?"

"Oh, you mean the silhouette of a person burned into the wall?" He nodded with a grimace. "Yep. I definitely saw it."

"What else?"

"I missed something, didn't I?"

She shrugged. "Only a small detail, but it definitely wasn't minor." She took a deep breath. "There was a black heron with a circle around it on the wall beside the other silhouette."

"Seriously?" He stopped and stared at her.

"Oh, come on." She caught his hand and pulled him with her toward the beer stall. "You can't stand there looking at me like that. We still have to act like everything's normal."

"It's not normal, though, is it? The black heron in four different countries now?" He lowered his voice and leaned toward her. "Like it's following us."

"Romeo, I know what it looks like. But I don't think it's following us. Whatever the black heron stands for, I think we're following it." They stopped behind the four other people waiting in line at the Wirtsbräu Brewery vendor. Unfortunately, she had to lower her voice too and wished there was a toggle switch for her magical translator. "It wasn't only the black heron, either. Whoever put it there also decided to write a little message."

"Please don't tell me it was another code of your mom's."

"What? No, it—" She frowned. "At least, I don't think it was. Honestly, there might be a chance that my translator...thing"—she did not intend to start talking about spells where everyone could hear her—"might actually work with her code. But I don't think so. I don't know what language it was in either, obviously, but it said, 'to complete the circle.'"

His green eyes narrowed with disapproval. "That's what those creepy women in Mexico told you when they asked you to join them."

"Right before they attacked us, yeah." She nodded and glanced around the market square. They moved up in the line. "I knew the guy running those illegal fights was connected to all this, but I didn't know how until I saw what's in that alley." His darkening frown made her pause. *I can't say 'the werewolf pack leader' out in the open right now, either.* "You know who I'm talking about, right?"

He responded with a slightly insulted glance. "Why would you ask me that?"

"Oh...hey, I didn't mean anything by it. I'm trying to..." She sighed. "You looked really confused."

"Of course I know who you're talking about, Lil. I won't forget that asshole's face anytime soon. He drugged me and chained me to a tree by my neck." Remembering where they were, he glanced around to make sure no one had heard that tantalizing snippet of out-of-context conversation and cleared his throat. "I'm only trying to put the pieces together. You're still much better at that than I am."

"Okay." She nodded. "Sorry. I didn't mean to make you think that I—"

"Lily." He took her hands and lowered his head toward her to hold her gaze. "It's fine. We're good. Tell me what you discovered."

"Right." She sighed and he squeezed her hand. "I had a really strong feeling that the guy who ran the fights in Mexico was connected somehow. The only way I could put it together was that he wore a pin on his shirt, right? It had the Order of North's sigil on it, so I automatically assumed he had something to do with that underground speakeasy for magicals in Montreal. The guy who ran the place had one of those same pins on his jacket."

"Yeah, and he also had a giant silhouette of a black heron painted on the wall in his office."

"Right. That seemed like only a coincidence. Or maybe I was already connecting the club owner to the black heron symbol and I hadn't realized it." The line moved again and left them with two people now between them and their beers. "And those levitating...whatever they were women who attacked us in Mexico—the ones who said they wanted my blood to 'complete the circle'—were obviously working for the pack leader."

"They were the ones who kept me chained." He chewed the inside of his cheek. "I still don't see where you're going with this."

"Romeo, it's finally all tied together in that alley." She

nodded toward the police tape behind the white fountain. "The black heron and 'completing the circle.' The club owner in Montreal had the black heron painted in his office. He wore the same pin as the pack leader in Mexico, which I assume at this point was merely both of them trying to hide behind a society that works to keep magicals safe. But he kidnapped other werewolves. He kidnapped you. The creepy women worked for the pack leader, and that's where we heard 'complete the circle' first. The Wisemen at Ichacál? They were using safety and sanctuary as a disguise too. Again, they kidnapped magicals and locked them up under the temple to siphon their magic for who knows what. But remember that guy Joseph at the temple? He showed us that book—"

"With the black heron on it." Romeo nodded, but his frown remained.

"With the black heron on it," Lily repeated. "And now, there are all these magical kidnappings in France and Germany, in broad daylight, where every non-magical who walks past can see it. Whoever's doing this doesn't care about exposing magic. They don't care about keeping everyone safe. And they left a calling card. The black heron and 'complete the circle.'" She searched his gaze and waited for all the pieces to fall into place in his mind too. The second they did, she saw it in his eyes.

"Holy shit."

"Yeah."

He blinked quickly. "You think all those people know each other?"

"I don't know. Maybe not directly, but they're all

connected to the black heron. The club owner is the only one—as far as I know—who wasn't kidnapping people, but you can't say there wasn't something seriously creepy about all those spinning rooms in the speakeasy."

"Nope. Those were definitely creepy."

"They could've been taking something from the magicals who stepped into those rooms. I don't know. Maybe even kidnapping them from the rooms. That's only a guess, though."

Romeo released her hands to scratch the back of his neck with both of his. "We didn't stay long enough to find out."

"No, we didn't. And if that club owner had actually managed to catch me outside his invisible cabin in Mont Tremblant, I'm very sure that would've counted as a kidnapping too."

"Man." He puffed out a sigh and shook his head. "And the only thing connecting them all is the black heron and that 'complete the circle' thing. Whatever that's supposed to mean."

"Right." She scowled. "That and my mom."

"Wait, what?"

"We ran into every single one of those people right before we found the clues my mom left me. She's the other connection." His eyes lit up and she nodded. *Now he's gettin' it.*

"Woah. So you think your mom—"

"I said next." The man standing at the Wirtsbräu Brewery stall waved at them.

She turned to face him. "Oh. Is that us?"

"Yep. Do you folks want beers? 'Cause you're kinda holding the line up."

"Right. Sorry." She stepped toward the table and quickly scanned the list of beer the guy had on tap. "How's the Märzen?"

"Unfiltered amber." He shrugged. "Little malty. Little sweet."

"Yeah, I'll have one of those, please."

Romeo nodded. "Make it two."

ELEVEN

They turned away from the beer stand, each with a sixteen-ounce plastic cup of dark, foaming beer in hand. Lily leaned forward to slurp at the top of hers and narrowly avoided sloshing the dripping overflow all over her pants. It splattered onto the cobbled stones of the market and a little on her shoes instead.

Romeo found the same level of difficulty with his beer, and they stood there for a few minutes and tried to keep from sloshing it all over themselves. Finally, when they'd sipped enough that they could walk without worrying about spilling, he nodded toward a few tables outside one of the restaurants facing the market square. "Do you wanna sit for a minute?"

"Yeah." They wove their way through the slightly smaller crowd than Rebecca and Mia had said normally came to the market on a Friday night. Still, for some people, the sight of a police crime scene taped off in the St.

Johanner Market wasn't enough to keep them from their night out. "I wonder how many people have even stopped to see what happened." She stepped around the table he had chosen and pulled out the black-iron patio chair.

"It's kept some people away, I guess." He chose the chair beside her and sat. "If that had happened on a highway, you know everyone would slow to get a good look. The traffic would be backed up for days."

"Well, a car wreck on the highway and a magical crime in the vicinity of non-magicals aren't exactly the same thing." She took another slow sip of her German Märzen and studied the pedestrians in the market. "Maybe it's 'cause no one understands what it actually is. The magic, that is. So they simply stay away."

"It could be." He turned to look at her and leaned forward over the table. "We never finished our brainstorming session."

She snorted. "Right. So you made all those connections I tried to lay out for you."

"I did."

"I know." She grinned at him. "I saw it. To answer the question you almost asked, yes. I think my mom left her clues for me specifically with or close to the kinds of people affiliated with that black heron. And 'complete the circle,' whatever those actually mean."

His eyes widened again and he made an odd snort that could have been a laugh but wasn't really. "Okay, now I completely understand the totally baffled look you get when I say something you were already thinking. You read my mind."

Laughing, she took another sip and shook her head. "We came to the same conclusion. That's all. It's not mind-reading."

"Okay. So why did your mom choose those people? Why leave you clues in those places where you'd run into those people?"

She set her elbow on the wire-mesh table and leaned forward. "She wrote it all down in her last message. The one I found at Ichacál. My mom already knew she would be caught when she wrote that. She was looking for something. 'Following this dark trail' is what she said. She found something that no one wanted her to see, and they took her. Maybe to keep her from finding all the answers, or maybe simply to keep her from telling anyone else." She turned to meet his gaze and smirked. "But she did anyway."

"She told you."

"Yeah. And now, all the things she saw when she was hunting for...whatever, she made sure I saw them too."

He tilted his head thoughtfully. "Whoever's connected with the black heron, right?"

"Maybe..." She frowned. "Okay, that's what I thought at first, but something still doesn't make sense. She said she'd been into this stuff for years. Melissa Bore sat on that clue in her magical vault for at least four years before we found her. But all the other stuff that we've run into—the kidnappings and the weird magical crimes in front of non-magicals... Think about it. As far as we or anyone else know, this has only been going on for...what? Four months? Six, maybe? That man Joseph went to the healing temple with my mom years ago for the first time, and they both left there perfectly fine. The really crazy stuff wasn't happening yet. He went back five or six months ago and was abducted the second time. And my mom was only gone for maybe two weeks before everyone declared her dead."

"And someone forged her will."

"There's no way she wrote that." Lily shook her head emphatically. "Not after all these clues we've found."

"Oh, I know." Romeo took another sip of his beer and nodded. "I'm right there with you." He paused and his thoughtful expression slid quickly beneath another frown. "And when your mom left that stuff with Melissa and her magical vault, Melissa still lived in Colorado. Her house had burned down maybe a few months before we found it."

"That's a big hole, then, isn't it? Either my mom somehow knew Melissa would have to flee the country from an angry vampire and she'd go straight to Mexico, or it's a really scary coincidence that her friend decided to hide with a werewolf pack in Chihuahua who somehow happened to be affiliated with the black heron somehow."

"You don't honestly believe that, do you?"

She raised her eyebrows at him. "What?"

"That any of this is a coincidence."

A wry chuckle escaped her. "Not really, no. She doesn't believe in coincidence. I guess I picked that up from her too."

"So this is really, really big." Romeo leaned back in his

chair, sighed, and ran a hand through his curls. "It's much more than finding your mom. Yeah, she wrote in her last message that she couldn't fit all the pieces together, but you could." He shook his head. "Wow. Until right now, I literally thought that it meant she didn't know how to protect herself, so she left it up to you to come find her and get her out of whatever mess she's in."

"Obviously, it's more than that." Lily drummed her fingers on the metal tabletop again. "She wanted me to see what these people are doing. Except it seems like everything we've found—all the really crazy stuff—only started happening after she disappeared. And there's another thing that's bugging me now. That witch who tried to kill me in Charleston, right before I showed up at your house?"

"What about him?"

"You mean besides the fact that he tried to kill me?"

He rolled his eyes and smirked a little. "You know what I mean. That's another way of saying, 'please, do carry on.'"

She laughed. "I know. But that's the thing. He tried to kill me and said he was only trying to clean up loose ends, right? It would make sense if he had something to do with these black heron people if all they wanted was to keep my mom quiet or make everything she found out about them simply disappear. But after that, no one else we've come across has actually tried to kill me."

"I'm reasonably sure we've been attacked plenty of times, Lil."

"No, no. Well, yeah. We've been attacked often." They

both found it impossible not to laugh at the absurdity of that truth. "But they didn't want to kill me. Outside that cabin in Canada, the club owner said he wanted to take me back and question me. Like he wanted to find out what I know. Those seriously creepy women in Mexico with the..." She wiggled her fingers at her jaw.

"The grotesquely stretching snake-jaws?"

"Ha. Yeah. They asked me to join them 'to complete the circle.' Then they said I didn't have a choice and they'd take me anyway. The Wisemen in Ichacál were obviously connected to the black heron. You'd think if my mom was such a big threat to them, they'd know who I was too. But they didn't try to kill me. Honestly, they probably would've simply locked me up too and tried to drain my magic if they had the chance. So it's... Honestly, I can't figure out why one witch in Charleston would want to kill me and everyone else would want me alive. If they're all connected, that is."

"You don't know that the witch in Charleston had anything to do with the black heron." He scratched his chin.

"No. Except for the fact that who else in the world would want to kill me? To clean up loose ends, if it wasn't because of what my mom found out about whatever they're doing?"

"Oh..." He wrinkled his nose and stared at the table. "Then we're still missing a really big piece of it."

"Now, we simply need to find out what that is."

He scoffed. "Simply. No big deal."

She met his gaze with a smile and placed her hand on

his forearm, his fingers still wrapped around the plastic beer cup. "We've come this far. None of it's been that hard, really. Except for maybe force-feeding you liquid wolfs-bane and helping Melissa exorcise a curse out of your chest."

With a snort, he nodded. "Or being trapped in a temple dungeon—that sounds weird. And trying to fight our way past a whole team of witches in blue robes."

Lily shrugged. "Yeah, that one was cutting it a little close."

"We have a necromancer to thank for that."

"Death witch. Neron said they weren't quite the same thing."

"Huh."

For a few seconds, she ran through that night again in her head. Then, she looked at him and squinted. "You know, I actually thought Neron had some kinda part in kidnapping all those kids in Mexico. That he was playing one giant act and took us down to those cages on purpose so we'd be trapped down there when the Wiseman came for us. You know, that he'd betrayed us. If someone can really betray people they've only known for a few days."

His mouth dropped open. "What?"

"I know, right? I felt a little bad about that for a while."

"Why'd you think that?"

She sighed. "He didn't fight with us. He didn't do anything, really. Until that—" She took another sip of her beer in an attempt to wash away some of the images that surfaced. "That one witch was struck with a really bad spell. She was already dying, Romeo."

"Yeah, I know. He said that was the only way he could have used his magic. With a sacrifice and a death." His nostrils flared as he remembered the other magicals he'd watched die that night and he took a sip of his own beer.

"And Neron asked the witch if she wanted to sacrifice the life she was already losing to save everyone else. And she did, which was incredible. But I didn't know that when he actually did it. All I saw was them talking to each other and her pleading, and he drew a knife." She shook her head. "I thought he was rubbing it in."

"Jeez."

"Yeah."

Romeo nodded at her in acknowledgment. "I don't know if we would've made it out of that one without him, though."

"I've thought the same thing a few times." She smirked. "It's merely more proof."

"Of what?"

"That it pays to make friends with people everyone else would rather avoid."

He chuckled. "I'm not sure that's an accurate statement across the board, Lil. Most people like to avoid the actual bad guys too."

"Okay, fine. Maybe I have a knack for seeing who's not an actual bad guy and looking past the stigma."

"And how many people have you found like that?" He grinned at her and his green eyes flecked with gold sparkled in the evening sunlight.

"Hmm. Only two, I think. So far."

"Well, Neron's definitely one of them. Who's the—" He squinted and turned his head away from her a little to eye her sideways. "Wait a minute. Are you talking about me?"

She shrugged. "I didn't say anything."

"You are. I'm the second not-actually-a-bad guy!" He folded his arms and leaned back in the patio chair, laughing. "I get it. Werewolf. Stigma. Everyone stays away from me."

"And thinks you're gonna make trouble. And throws you out of art museums. And expects you to lose it around powerful mind-wiping spells..."

"Oh, you do really like to rub that in, don't you?"

"I'm not rubbing it in, Romeo. I'm calling the rest of the magical community out on all their bull. On thinking they know who you are simply because you're a werewolf." She grinned at him and leaned forward. "I'm gonna change that."

His lips pursed, he set his forearm on the table and leaned toward her until their faces were inches apart. "You know, I distinctly remember you promising to let all that go until after we find your mom."

"No, I said I wouldn't bring it up."

"You just did."

She smirked. "No again. You brought up your werewolf-ness and the stigma. I merely said I knew two exceptions to the cliché." He chuckled and shook his head. "And even if we weren't arguing semantics right now, that kind of discrimination isn't really something I can let go. But I didn't bring it up. And right now, I'm not angry about it.

I'm simply not trying to sweep it under the rug like everyone else."

"No." He tucked her hair behind her ear before his fingers brushed her face and he settled his hand on her cheek. "Right now, you don't look anywhere near as angry as you were in front of that museum."

Smiling, she studied his face. "And what do I look like right now?"

For a few seconds, he didn't know whether or not he would actually say it. So instead, he leaned farther over the metal armrest and left a gentle kiss on her lips. The minute he pulled away and saw her eyes light up, he decided now was the time. "Lily, you look like the witch who I—"

"Oh, my God," Rebecca cooed from the other side of the table. "You guys are the cutest thing I've ever seen."

Romeo sighed and followed it with a sheepish laugh. Lily chuckled and lowered her head over the armrest so he planted another kiss on the top of her head before he straightened again and leaned back in his chair. "Perfect timing." He grinned at Rebecca and from the corner of his eye, saw Lily sit up in her chair too and brush her blonde hair back away from her face.

The woman laughed and popped another bite of the snack she held on a paper tray into her mouth. "It looked like it."

"I told you to leave them alone for a little longer, at least." Mia joined them and her bright sundress flittered around her legs in the evening breeze. She tossed her hair out of her face and offered them an apologetic shrug. "I'm sorry. My sister has zero boundaries whatsoever."

"Hey, it's not like I pulled a chair up right between them or anything."

"No, but they were obviously having a moment."

Rebecca gestured toward the couple and nodded. "And I complimented them on it."

Her sister snorted. "Sometimes, the best compliment is to give people some space." She gave Lily a sympathetic smile. "Sorry."

She laughed. "It's okay. Really."

"You know what's not okay?" The other woman slapped her paper tray of German street food down on the table and squinted at each of them in turn.

"Uh..." He chuckled. "I'm at a total loss."

"You guys didn't get any dibbelabbes."

He burst out laughing.

"Seriously?" Mia spread her arms and glared at her sister, and a few pieces of fried something toppled over the side and onto the ground.

"They've never tried them. They've never been to Germany. This is serious stuff." Rebecca turned and scanned the small crowd in the square. "I know Felix and Helen went over there to get some, so we'll share whatever he brings back."

"Okay, if it's that amazing, I can go get some right now." Romeo started to stand.

"No. No." She thrust a finger at him and narrowed her eyes. Lily couldn't tell anymore if the woman was still partially joking or if they'd crossed some kind of line into insulting her. "I've already made the offer. Now, I can't go back on it. And Felix doesn't ever eat all his food anyway."

She turned to search the square again and pumped a fist before she jammed both hands into the pockets of her over-alls. "Hey! We're over here."

A tall, incredibly skinny man with thinning blond hair whipped his head toward them and grinned. The woman beside him—equally as skinny but about a foot shorter, at least—laughed and shook her head. She balanced three cups of beer in her hands, and he carried two massive paper plates of food.

"I can't believe I'm saying this," the werewolf muttered and simply stared, "but I think that's more food than should ever be allowed on one plate."

"I know, right?" Rebecca pulled a chair from another table beside them, spun it around, and sat.

Mia did the same and sat on the other side of Lily. She waved at her cousin and his wife. "I thought maybe you guys decided not to show up."

"Why?" Still grinning, Felix set both plates on the table.

"I mean..." Mia gestured toward the red-and-white tape and the police still stationed on both sides of it.

"That's ridiculous. If it's not actually dangerous here, why would we let that ruin an awesome Friday night?"

Not dangerous for them, Lily thought. *Maybe. Who knows if non-magicals are gonna be attacked next.* But she smiled at the man when he leaned toward her.

"Hi. Felix."

"Lily."

Romeo shook the man's hand next.

"My wife Helen."

"So formal." Helen chuckled, set the beers down, and shook Romeo's hand, then Lily's. When all the introductions were made, she and her husband sat between Mia and Rebecca and scooted their chairs toward the table.

"So, how do you guys know my cousins?" Felix asked.

"We parked our RVs next to each other at the campsite, actually." Lily took another sip of her beer.

Helen looked at Rebecca with wide eyes. "You told me you guys got a hotel room."

The woman shrugged. " 'Cause you would've done exactly this if we said we were taking Dad's old RV out here."

"We have more than enough room for you at our place—"

"No, you don't. Are you kidding?" Mia laughed. "You guys haven't even been married for a month. Maybe Rebecca doesn't care about personal boundaries, but I will definitely not spend a weekend in a house with two newlyweds."

"Hey, just married," Romeo said. "Congratulations."

"Thanks." Smiling, Felix glanced at his new wife, caught her hand, and kissed it. She blushed quickly and tried to hide it behind a few huge gulps of beer.

Romeo grinned. "You know…"

Lily smacked his arm with the back of her hand and glared at him, although she had to work hard to maintain her stern expression. "Don't even start." He threw his head back and laughed.

Felix drew a handful of plastic forks from his back

pocket and dropped them in the center of the table. "I'm very sure I bought too much food for the two of us."

Rebecca snorted. "Ya think?"

Her cousin winked at her and glanced around the table. "Who's hungry?"

TWELVE

"Wait a minute. He actually wore the lederhosen?" In the back seat of Mia's Ford Fiesta, Lily stared at Rebecca, who'd sacrificed sitting shotgun so Romeo wouldn't have to sacrifice his knees on the ride back to the campground.

"Oh, yeah." She nodded solemnly. "Felix will never tell anyone that story. And he definitely won't let me tell it. I've been shut down enough times to know when it's a losing battle." She smirked. "But he definitely wore them."

Lily's mouth fell open and in the next breath, she simply cracked up. She shook her head and covered her eyes with a hand.

"Keep in mind," Mia said from the driver's seat, "these were our grandpa's traditional, formal lederhosen. Really nice. Hand-embroidered and all the buttons shined. They had the little panel thing over the chest, the braces, and everything."

Lily had a hard time getting the words out through her

laughter, which sounded more like a squeal the more she tried to hold it in. "And no one said anything?"

Rebecca threw her head back and barked a laugh.

"I don't think anyone even knew," Mia answered. "Until the next morning." She giggled. "Aunt Edith threw a fit. Remember that?"

Her sister nodded vigorously, lost in her own silent mirth for a long time before she managed to take a breath. "She was...she was running around the house. In hysterics."

The driver raised one hand from the steering wheel and repeatedly chopped the air with it. "'I'll get in bed with the devil before I bury my father naked.'" They both cracked up again. Romeo chuckled uneasily in the front seat and kept a wary eye on the road while all the women in the car lost it.

Lily gasped for breath. "But she didn't have to, right?"

"Our Aunt Edith?" Rebecca blinked at her with wide eyes. "No way. Felix's dad found our cousin passed out in the back yard under the tree. I've never seen a hungover person move that quickly." She snorted.

"And your grandpa..."

"Yep." Mia nodded. "Yep, he still got to wear the leder-hosen. And Aunt Edith never had to get in bed with anyone but her husband."

Rebecca laughed again. "Oh, man. That's an image."

"He really should start telling that story." Lily wiped the tears from her eyes and chuckled again. "It's perfect."

"Um..." Romeo scratched the back of his head. "I think I missed the joke."

She leaned toward the passenger seat, which was already close enough against her legs, and peered around the side to look at him. "What?"

"Come on. I've definitely borrowed my dad's clothes to go out and never told him. Maybe not like a fancy suit or anything." He shrugged. "I dunno. Is it like a cultural thing, or..."

"What?" Rebecca burst into laughter again.

"Oh." Lily's mouth dropped open. "Oh, you didn't... He didn't hear the first part of the story."

"He didn't?" Mia took two quick glances at him before she focused entirely on the road again. "How?"

"He was still talking to Felix when we got in the car."

Rebecca howled with laughter and pumped her legs up and down in the back seat.

"Romeo." Lily chuckled and patted him on the shoulder. "Their grandpa had just died."

He whipped his head over his shoulder to shoot her a surprised look. "It's funny that he wore his grandpa's clothes to a party right after the man died?"

Mia slammed her hand down on the top of the steering wheel. "It is when he partied in the lederhosen our grandpa was supposed to wear to his own funeral the next day."

He made a choking sound, then erupted into laughter. "Oh, no way."

Rebecca slapped the back of her sister's seat over and over and bounced in the back of the Fiesta as if she'd completely lost it. Laughing, Lily eyed the other woman and leaned a little farther toward her own side of the car.

"That's a much better story." Romeo shook his head, grinning.

"You don't say." She stretched to give his shoulder a gentle squeeze. "I was almost worried you'd lost your sense of humor."

He turned his head to shoot her a sideways glance. "No, you weren't."

"No. I wasn't." She laughed again and sat back in the seat.

Mia pulled them into the Spicherer Mountain Campsite, which was now only lit by the large floodlights on the side of the clubhouse, a few other campers in their RVs who hadn't yet put out their lights, and a campfire on the other side way beyond the parked vehicles. Once she turned the engine and the lights off, she sighed and swiped her black hair away from her face. "I'm definitely glad we're not staying with Felix and Helen. There's way more fresh air out here."

"Yep." Rebecca opened her door in the back. "If anyone's clinging to each other here, at least we have somewhere else to go and something else to look at." She scrambled out of the car and shut the door behind her.

Lily laughed and everyone else followed suit. "It got really dark." She raised her hand and had barely considered summoning her own magical orb of light when Romeo retrieved his phone and turned on the bright flashlight app.

"Voila. Instant light." He shot her a pointed look and smiled.

"Good thinking." With her raised hand, she tucked her

hair behind her ear and stepped beside him. *Did I really almost forget that we're totally surrounded by non-magicals right now?*

Mia shook her keys with a little jingle. "That was fun, guys. Thanks for coming with us."

"Hey, thanks for the invite." She nodded at Rebecca. "Like you said, it's always good to make new friends at a campsite."

The woman snorted. "Yeah, you guys are all right."

Romeo laughed. "You too."

"Well, I'm tired, actually." Mia stepped away from the parking lot toward the row of RVs. "Will you do something else or turn in? I only ask because it's still always awkward to say goodbye to someone and then keep walking in the same direction." She smirked.

"Uh, yeah. Sleep would be good. What is it? Almost ten?"

He tapped his phone. "Almost ten-thirty. Not that late, but we didn't really get much sleep last night." They all headed toward the RVs together.

"Yeah, you don't have to go into any of the gory details or anything." Rebecca stuck her hands in her pockets.

Mia nudged her sister with an elbow. "Hey, don't be weird."

Lily chuckled, and he merely smirked at her. "Actually...we didn't get any sleep last night, and that's because we were trying not to miss the all-clear signal to drive off that freighter."

Rebecca whirled toward her. "Wait, what? You guys drove off a ship last night?"

"Technically, it was super-early this morning." He shrugged.

"Wow. Where'd you guys land?"

"Brest."

"And you drove straight through France to get here?" Mia leaned forward to look past her sister and raise her eyebrows at Lily. "To Saarbrücken?"

"Well, we stopped in Paris for lunch," he said. "But other than that, yeah. Basically."

Lily glanced at him. *Yeah, we still need these little white lies.*

"But Paris is the City of Love, right?" Mia shook her head. "I think you guys are the only couple I know who's simply driven right through the city without actually stopping there for a while."

"Oh, we're not—" Lily stopped when Romeo slipped his hand into hers and grinned. *Okay, I can't actually say we're not a couple now. Can I? I don't even know what we are.*

Rebecca chuckled. "You're not what?"

"We're...not trying to visit all the romantic places. Okay, yeah. Paris is great. We've already been, though, so we figured why not use our time to look for something completely new?" *Not to mention the fact that we might actually still be in Paris if a witch wasn't magically murdered in broad daylight.*

"I can get behind that kind of adventure." Rebecca nodded slowly and studied them. "So what's next?"

Romeo uttered a non-committal hum and held Lily's gaze. "We'll work our way through the EU, I guess. It's kind of up in the air. It would be cool to get all the way to Romania. You know, coast to coast." He glanced at the sisters and shrugged. "Maybe we could make it down to Turkey or Greece. Who knows?"

"Sweet. How'd you get all the money to fund a trip like this?"

"Seriously?" Mia gave her sister a warning shove as all four of them stopped beside their respective RVs. "Again. So rude."

Lily glanced at them and grinned. "Savings."

Rebecca shook her head in disbelief. "Man. I'd have to save my entire life to put away enough for that."

"No, you wouldn't."

"Hey, we can't all run our own super-successful business, okay?"

Mia stared at her sister and flashed the couple a wide grin. "Goodnight."

They laughed. "'Night," he said.

"Thanks again," Lily added.

Rebecca jabbed her thumb toward Mia. "She knows a lot. But she thinks she knows everything."

"Oh, hey. Speaking of knowing things." Romeo nodded at the Winnie. "I know it's late now, but if you have some time in the morning to look at our shower problem..."

Mia had already opened the door to the RV she shared with her sister, but she shut it again with a loud bang. "Is that what you told them? That you'd fix their shower?"

Her sister shrugged. "Not in those words—"

"Oh, my God. It's like you're still twelve." The woman

opened the door again and stepped inside, shaking her head.

"No, it's not." She started after her, paused, and smiled at Romeo and Lily. "See ya tomorrow, I guess." Before either of them could reply, she pulled the door to her own RV open. "Hey, I'm only trying to be helpful."

"It's not helpful. It's annoying."

"Hey. Whatever."

With wide eyes, the couple exchanged a glance before she pulled the keys from her purse to unlock the side door. He opened it for her, and they didn't make a sound until he'd closed and locked the door behind him. "Wow." He ran a hand through his hair and climbed the two stairs into the living area. "Talk about sibling rivalry."

"It doesn't even have to be a genetic thing, I guess." She chuckled. "It kinda makes me glad to be an only child."

"Yeah, no kidding." He stepped toward her and put his hands on her hips. "Nice cover-up, by the way."

"For what?"

"For why we drove through France so quickly." He smirked. "Though honestly, if our brunch hadn't been interrupted by...well, that attack, and if we hadn't been questioned by a witch investigator who can freeze time and wipe people's memories to clean up a magical crime scene..." She laughed, and he lowered his head toward her as he drew her closer. "I would've liked to spend more time in Paris with you. You know, City of Love and everything."

She rolled her eyes. "You're not actually into that cliché, are you?"

He paused for a second and looked startled.

Oh, no. Was he serious?

"You got me." He grinned. "No clichés. No Paris. Who wants to spend a romantic day there when we can take this exquisite domicile"—he gestured at the Winnie with a wide, exaggerated sweep of his head—"with us anywhere we want?"

I think he was serious. She smiled at him. "Hey, I was only kidding—"

"I'm not." He pulled her closer. "Forget romance. We have danger." She laughed and threw her arms around his neck. "We have clues and secret messages. Invisible cabins. Blind seers. Werewolf fighting rings. Snake-mouth women."

"Don't forget the teleporting villagers."

"The teleporting villagers! A death witch! Temple dungeons!" She shrieked when he swept her legs out from under her and lifted her into his arms. "And none of it stopped us." He wrinkled his nose and pressed a firm kiss on her lips with a loud smack. "Who gets to say that, huh?"

She grinned. "No one."

"That's right. No one." He carried her through the Winnie's living area, past the kitchen, and almost made it down the hall. Instead, her foot thumped against the corner of the bathroom behind the kitchen table and knocked one of her flats off. "Oh, jeez." He snorted and raised his eyebrows. "That wasn't part of the speech." She burst out laughing again, and he turned to sidle sideways down the narrow hall. "We have this hallway that's not even big enough for me to carry you through like a normal person. It's incredible."

She kissed him this time and pulled back to meet his gaze. "It really is."

"It really is." Grinning, he stepped through the bedroom doorway, turned fully toward the bed, and dropped her onto it. She shrieked again, laughing, and before she'd even stopped bouncing on the mattress, he sat and turned to lean over her. "I wouldn't have it any other way, you know."

She studied his green-eyed gaze and bit her lip as she ran her fingers through the dark curls at the nape of his neck. "Me neither."

"Good." He leaned down and kissed her again as he inched slowly onto his side across the mattress so he could brush his hand against her cheek. Lily slid closer, and he pulled away a little to gaze across the room. "Okay, beyond the necessary remodeling." He shrugged. "I still need more legroom under the table. The shower could definitely be bigger. And, of course, we gotta get rid of that four-and-a-half-minute problem—"

Lily laughed. "Okay, you know what? I think it's time to stop talking."

He chuckled and looked at her, quite pleased with himself. "Oh, is it?"

"Yeah."

"I talk too much, huh?"

"Yeah."

"Well, what else did you have in mind?"

She took his face with both hands and pulled him down to kiss her. He didn't say another word.

Right. Who needs Paris?

L ily jolted awake with the feeling that something was very, very wrong.

That only grew worse when she realized the sun had barely risen and Romeo wasn't in the bed beside her. "Romeo?" She paused for a minute and listened intently, but there was no response. Then, she sniffed at the air. "Okay...smoke again." But it wasn't the acrid, burnt, sulfuric smell of the smoke and ash she always experienced whenever the shadow-bird made an appearance. "Something's actually burning. Romeo!"

She threw the covers off and pushed herself out of bed, grateful for the fact that she still slept in her pajama shorts and tank top, even after nearly two months of sleeping in the same bed with him. It meant she didn't have to waste time getting dressed.

"Hey, are you in here?" She stumbled through the bedroom doorway and down the short, narrow hallway into the tiny kitchen. A quick glance at the living area and the seats in the front confirmed that he was not. "Did he shift and go missing again? No. There were no clothes on the floor. There would be clothes if he—what the heck?"

The Winnie's side door hung wide open to the morning breeze, which brought with it another strong scent of smoke. She stepped gingerly across the living area toward the door and froze when a loud shriek came from outside.

"Romeo!" In two bounds, she reached the open door and jumped over the first stair, ready to bring her red-sparking attack spell to hand despite the fact that there were only non-magicals at this campground. If it came to protecting Romeo and herself—and anyone else—she cared about hiding her spells as little as the people who'd used theirs to murder magicals in public—not at all.

Her bare feet landed in the worn, trampled grass beside the Winnie, and she sidled around the side of the RV toward the stronger smell of smoke and the sound of something definitely burning. *Yeah, I'm ready now.* When she reached the back of the vehicle, she paused to listen. Another shriek rose, much louder this time, and she stepped quickly out from behind her home on wheels.

"Hey!" Romeo raised his hand, which glinted in the morning sunlight.

She froze and struggled to bring her panic under control. The shriek was actually Rebecca's laughter. The woman sat on the ground in long, baggy workout shorts and a white t-shirt, her legs crossed. She glanced at Lily and waved. "Morning!"

With another quick glance at Romeo, Lily swallowed.

The flashing thing in his hand was a pair of tongs. The smoke came from the grill in front of him. The only thing burning was a little char on the grill and the coals beneath it. "Awesome," she muttered and sighed.

"Is everything okay?" He flipped whatever he'd put on the grill long before normal cookout hours, glanced at her again, and frowned. "Lily?" He stuck the tongs through the rack on the side of the grill and stepped toward her. "What's going on?"

"Nothing." Her smile felt forced. "Nothing, I'm fine."

"It doesn't look like it." He stopped in front of her and brushed her hair away from her face to tuck it behind her ear. "Did something happen?"

She stared at the flattened grass. "No."

"Hey."

When she looked at him again, his gaze examined her face cautiously. "I only... I woke up with this awful feeling that something was wrong. You weren't in bed, the door was wide open, and the smoke..."

He chuckled but stopped when she couldn't bring herself to smile back. "Oh. Hey, I'm sorry. I didn't mean to freak you out—"

"I'm not freaked out." Finally, she managed a small smile. "I merely jumped to conclusions, I guess. 'Cause I do that." She shrugged.

"I..." He gestured behind him toward the grill. "I said I was gonna cook those steaks for breakfast, remember?"

"Yeah."

"And I didn't wanna wake you up going in and out all the time so I left the door open."

"Right. I get it. It's totally fine."

"Lil..."

A bigger smile came much more easily now. *I might as well be embarrassed and laugh than be all bent outta shape.* She stepped toward him and wound her arms around his waist. "I'm okay. Promise."

"Yeah?"

"Yeah." She stood on her toes to give him a quick kiss. "I probably had another bad dream or something and didn't remember. You did have me goin' there for a minute, though. I was—" Her gaze flicked over his shoulder, although she couldn't actually see Rebecca seated on the ground. She whispered anyway. "I was ready to start throwing spells around if I had to. No matter who saw me."

He hugged her tighter and chuckled. "It's a good thing you didn't."

"Well, yeah. My mind simply went right to the last time I woke up and you were gone."

"No shifting and no trespassing." He smirked. "And definitely no getting drugged and hexed."

"Well, I didn't know. Rebecca's laugh sounds like a scream. And then I smelled something burning—"

"Oh. Crap." Romeo squeezed her shoulders and darted away from her toward the grill again. He almost dropped the tongs but caught then in time and flipped two huge steaks. "That's not what I wanted." His nose wrinkled but he shrugged and snatched the plate from the picnic table a few feet away to quickly cover it with steak. With his cheeks puffed in frustration, he looked at Lily and lifted the plate. "Hungry?"

She snorted. "Well, I'm not gonna say no."

Rebecca grinned as she approached, held her knees, and rounded her back in a stretch. "I don't really sleep, but if I wasn't already awake, I think I probably would've gotten up for this steak too. It smells amazing, right?"

"Oh, yeah." Lily met his gaze and smirked. "I hopped right outta bed."

"Okay, I'm gonna go get some silverware. Hey, do you want any of this?" He turned and pointed at Rebecca.

"No, thank you." She shook her head. "Don't get me wrong. I'm sure it's good. But I don't eat meat."

He stared at her in utter astonishment and glanced at Lily. "Why?"

The woman shrugged. "It makes me sluggish and tired."

Lily chuckled. "Wouldn't that help if you can't sleep?"

"Not really, no. I still don't sleep. So I'm awake and I feel like crap."

"Huh." He shook his head and smirked. "I'll be right back." He skirted them and headed to the Winnie's open side door. Lily sat on the picnic bench and smoothed her hair from her face again with both hands, feeling tired all over again after that unexpected and completely unfounded little scare.

"So." Rebecca jerked her head back and smirked. "How long have you two been together?"

She opened her mouth, smiled, and took a quick breath. "Well, we grew up right next door to each other."

"That's super-cute." The woman wiggled her

eyebrows. "I bet you were high school sweethearts too, huh?"

"Um...not exactly—"

"Rebecca!" Mia's angry shout rose from their RV.

The woman hunched her shoulders and sent her a joking grimace. "She's gonna wake up the whole campsite, isn't she?" Before she could respond to that, her companion leaned toward the RV and shouted even louder, "What?" It made her jump on the picnic bench in surprise.

"Have you seen my hairbrush?"

Rebecca squinted, swayed on the ground as she held her knees, and muttered, "Hairbrush. Hairbrush. Oh." She leaned toward the RV again. "Yeah, I used it."

"What? You don't even have enough hair to brush."

"Not on my hair." With a snort, Rebecca shook her head and glanced at the other girl. "I'll be back. Maybe. If she doesn't kill me first." She scrambled to her feet and headed to her RV. She opened the door and peered inside. "I needed a backscratcher."

"You what?"

"Yeah. You know those really bad itches you can't reach with your hands?"

"That's disgusting."

With a sigh, she hauled herself into the RV, and while Lily heard their voices inside, she couldn't make out what they were saying. She bit back a laugh. *I've already heard enough.*

Romeo hopped out of the Winnie with two bottles of water in one hand and forks and steak knives in the other. While he walked toward her at the picnic table, he stared at the sisters' RV with wide eyes. "There's a fair amount of yelling going on."

"I know." She shook her head. "You know, if I had any siblings and if choosing siblings were an actual thing, I'm very sure I'd wanna have a brother and zero sisters."

"Well, it's either yelling all the time or fistfights, right?"

She considered that in silence for a moment and smiled in confusion. "What's that supposed to mean?"

He set a bottle of water in front of her, moved to the other side of the picnic table, and put all the silverware on the plate with two steaks. "I only mean that my dad and his brothers still fight each other. In their forties." He opened his bottled water and gulped half of it before he screwed the lid on again and shrugged. "I think that's only when they're drinking, though."

"How often is that?" She chuckled and retrieved her set of silverware as he swung his leg over the bench across from her.

"Only every time they see each other." He settled on the bench and grinned.

She snorted. "That's awful."

"I know."

With a fork and knife in each hand, she studied the steak and paused. "So, who gets what?"

"Oh, you want this one." He tapped one of the steaks with his knife.

"Because it's the smaller one?"

"No." He made a face at her and shook his head. "Because it's rarer. That's the way you want it. This one's more like medium-rare, and that was only because I didn't pay attention."

"I can eat that one, then."

"No, you can't." He shook his head firmly and smirked at her. "I cooked you steak for breakfast, so you get the better piece."

"Really, I don't mind medium-rare—"

"Lily." He raised an eyebrow and lowered his fists onto the table so his silverware protruded upward on either side of the plate. She tried not to laugh. "I eat raw meat as a wolf. I can eat"—he glanced down at the larger, slightly more blackened steak—"not so rare meat like everyone else. Like a regular person."

"Okay…" A laugh escaped her anyway.

"Except for people who order their meat anywhere between medium and well-done. There's something wrong with those people." He shook his head in disapproval and pushed the plate toward her. "Go ahead. Cut a few pieces. We can both try some of each."

She chuckled, leaned forward, and spread her arms. "Why didn't you simply bring another plate?"

" 'Cause it's fun to share." Her next laugh made him grin again. With a shrug, she set to work cutting the steak he said was better. He watched her for only about five seconds before he couldn't help himself. "Okay, what are you doing?"

"What? I'm cutting steak?"

"Seriously?"

Lily tossed her head back and glanced at the brightening sky. "Yes." Pursing her lips, she looked at him in a challenge. "Can I continue?"

"Sure." Instead of silently watching her and cringing when she resumed, he stood and leaned over the plate. "Lily, Lily, Lily. No. You have to cut against the grain."

"What grain? It's a steak, not a two-by-four."

"Well, it's not chicken, either."

She laughed. "What?"

"It's only..." With a heartfelt sigh, he glanced at her and the fork and knife poised above the steak neither one of them had actually eaten yet. "Let me show you, okay?"

"Sure."

His fork had barely pierced the top of the steak when he looked at her again. "Are you paying attention?"

"Romeo, cut the steak. Are you trying to torture me or something?"

That made him chuckle and he looked a little sheepish. "Yeah, maybe."

"Oh, my God. I'm actually really hungry now." It was true, but she had to laugh.

"Me too. Okay, watch and learn."

They had finished eating when Mia and Rebecca came outside to join them. "Wow." Rebecca peered over Lily's head at the plate. "You guys went through that really fast." She turned toward her sister. "You woulda loved this. It smelled amazing."

He tapped the plate with his fork and raised his eyebrows at Mia. "There's one bite left. Do you wanna try?"

"Oh, no thanks. I already ate." She smoothed a

different sundress—this one bright blue with tiny white polka dots—glanced at Rebecca, and rolled her eyes. "I normally wouldn't say anything because you didn't ask, but my sister literally won't stop bugging me about it."

Lily turned sideways on the picnic table to look at her. "Is everything okay?"

"What? Yeah, everything's fine. But..." She sighed. "Do you guys still want your shower fixed?"

Rebecca pumped her fist and whispered, "Yes."

"Uh, yeah." Lily grinned.

Romeo glanced from one sister to the other. "That would be really great, actually."

"Excellent!" Rebecca did a little dance and nodded toward the Winnie. "Come open the panel for us."

Mia glared at her sister and followed her quickly. "Will you chill out, already?"

"Probably not."

The couple looked at each other with shared confusion. "You heard Rebecca say we parked next to someone who could fix anything, right?" he asked.

Lily nodded. "Yep. I hope she knows what she's doing, though."

He swung his leg over the picnic bench and piled all the dishes onto the plate while she retrieved the bottled waters. "Then again, it's not like the shower can get much worse, right?"

She turned toward the Winnie and frowned. "Well, I can think of a few things." *Like no shower at all. Cold water forever.*

"I'm trying to stay positive."

They joined the sisters beside the vehicle. Rebecca clearly already knew where the maintenance panel for the water tank and the hookups was. She stared at it and rubbed her hands together in excitement. Trying not to look too skeptical, Lily stepped past her and opened the panel door. "There you go."

"Yes." The woman stepped up to the open square, took the edges of the panel with both hands, and stooped to peer into the semi-darkness. "It's lookin' good. What's wrong with your shower?"

"Uh..." When Lily glanced at Romeo, he merely shrugged. "It turns off after four and a half minutes."

"So, like, it kinda gives out after a while? Sometimes it keeps running, sometimes it doesn't. That kinda thing?"

"Nope." Lily bit her lip. "I mean literally four and a half minutes. We've...uh, timed it. Often."

"What?" Rebecca ducked, withdrew her head, and turned to shoot Lily an incredulous glance. "How does that even happen?"

Mia rolled her eyes and stepped toward the Winnie. "All right. Time's up. You're being ridiculous."

Her sister shrugged. "Hey, I'm only trying to ask the right questions."

"Okay, well, now we have our answer." The other woman moved as close to the RV as she could without pressing her dress up against it, slid her arm into the open panel, and continued all the way up to her shoulder. Her hand slapped on the inside for a while with a metallic thud until she stopped, stuck her tongue out between her teeth, and nodded. "Got it." She removed her arm and brushed it off, although she hadn't really collected any dirt. With a small smile at the very confused couple, she added, "No more shower problems."

"Um...what?" Lily tried not to let her disbelief show and allowed herself a hesitant chuckle. "That's it?"

"That's it. I had a customer once who had one of those same timers installed in his RV. It was a Newmar. Really nice and ran very clean, as far as rigs like this go. He said he put it there to keep his teenage daughter from using the whole tank after two days on the road." Mia laughed. "I haven't seen very many of these, but you definitely have one. I'm reasonably sure that's your answer."

"Just like that?" Romeo asked. She nodded.

"A timer." Lily shook her head.

"One of those little manual turning dials. Yeah. It must've been nudged somewhere along the way."

When Lily sent Romeo a blank look, he cracked up laughing. "Well...thanks, Mia."

The woman smirked and offered a little shrug, although she was obviously quite proud and satisfied with the results. "No problem."

He met Rebecca's gaze and jerked his chin up in acknowledgment. "I guess we don't need you to fix the shower after all, huh?"

"Me fix your shower?" She snorted. "No way, man. I don't know the first thing about plumbing. Especially in an RV."

"You said you could fix anything." He frowned at her.

"No, I didn't."

"Wait..." Mia glanced from Romeo to Lily, then at

her sister. Her eyes widened. "Oh—oh, you thought Rebecca was the one who..." She threw her head back and cackled.

The other snickered. "For real?"

He shrugged. "Kinda, yeah. You brought it up." He shared an unsure smile with Lily, and she shrugged. "More than once."

"Ha!" Rebecca grinned. "Nope. I'm the least handy person physically. I was talking about Mia. And that part's true. She can fix everything."

"Well, I try."

"Yeah, and I've never seen you look at something and not immediately know what was wrong." She jerked a thumb toward her sister. "She runs an auto garage in Hamburg. Didn't we tell you guys this?"

"Uh...no." Lily laughed. "I think we might've missed that part."

"Really?" The other woman shook her head, laughing. "I could've sworn I'd said something."

He shook his head. "We obviously made the wrong assumption."

"Yeah, that happens." Mia glanced at her sister with a smirk and shrugged again.

"Wait, Rebecca." Lily pointed at her. "What do you do, then?"

"Me?" Mia snorted, and Rebecca spread her arms with a grin. "I'm a writer."

The couple exchanged surprised looks. "I...wouldn't have guessed that."

"No one ever does." When she fell into another fit of

laughter, the others joined in because it was impossible not to.

Finally, Mia smoothed the hair away from her face and nodded. "You guys should still try the shower before you head out to make sure I was right."

"Oh, come on." Her sister nudged her with an elbow. "You know you're right."

"Still."

"Yeah, we will." Lily grinned. "Thank you."

"Hey, thank me when you know for sure that your timer problem's fixed." She winked and turned toward the RV she shared with her sister. "I have to make some calls and check in on things. Don't leave without saying anything, okay?"

"No problem." Romeo gave her a thumbs-up, and she laughed before she wandered away. Rebecca did him one better and gave him two thumbs-up and grinned before she swept them toward Lily and followed her sister into their RV.

For a moment, they simply stood beside the Winnie and stared. "I really like it when people don't look anything like their job." Lily looked at him and pressed her lips together in an effort not to laugh again.

"I'm not gonna argue with you. It's only..." He scratched the back of his head and wrinkled his nose. "It's really confusing."

"You know what'll clear that confusion right up?"

He squinted and raised an eyebrow. "Shower test-run?"

"Bingo."

FOURTEEN

"I gotta say, I thought I was actually starting to get used to rushing through showers." Lily ran a hand through her newly washed hair, grabbed the steering wheel with both hands again, and exhaled a huge sigh.

Romeo chuckled. "Well, it wasn't impossible."

"No. But don't tell me you didn't really enjoy being able to take your time."

"I definitely can't tell you that." With a smirk, he leaned forward to take his phone from the center console. "Do you know what would make it even better?"

She shook her head and stared at the road as they cruised down Untertürkheimer Strasse toward Highway A-6 and Vienna. "What's that?" she asked and fought a smile.

"A bigger shower."

"There's always something with you, isn't there?"

"Hey, I'm simply a guy who doesn't settle." He chuckled. "Plus, that thing can only fit one person."

"Right."

"Lily. It only fits one person."

She turned her head as much as she dared while driving and smirked at him. "Oh, I heard you."

For a minute, he merely studied her. Finally, he leaned back in the passenger seat and nodded. "Good. Next thing on the list, then."

"As long as some other more important fix doesn't crop up first."

"You mean...like your spell on the water tank somehow also sets a timer you didn't even know about to four and a half minutes?"

She laughed. "Okay, how was I supposed to know that was the issue. We already had a guy take a look. He said everything was perfect."

"Well, it's a good thing we didn't take this beast to a magical mechanic, huh?" He chuckled. "They would've said the same thing."

"And Mia said those timers aren't a common thing." A thought occurred to her. "I wonder if Bentley had it put in."

"Your mom's accountant? Yeah, he seems like the kinda guy who has a timer for everything."

"Oh, okay..." She glanced at him again, then at the phone in his hand. "You gonna put music on, or what?"

"How did you know?"

"It's what you do."

He made a face at her and snorted. "Yes, it is."

Ten seconds later, he'd chosen the first song of the day for this leg of the European road trip. The first verse of

"Sister Europe" by the Foo Fighters came through the Winnie's updated sound system, and she laughed. "Here we go."

Five hours later, they decided to take a tiny detour off A-3 and into Straubing for lunch. "Come on." She gestured at the giant banner strung across Ittlinger Strasse off the highway exit, highlighting the eleven-day date range starting the day before. "We've seen these signs for Gäuboden Folk Festival for the last hour at least. There's gotta be something good here."

"It looks like something fairly big." He gazed through the windshield and grinned. "I'm ready."

The parking signs gave her remarkably easy directions into the parking lot for the festival itself. "We might as well, right?" She turned into a dirt parking lot beside the massive collection of carnival rides, tents, booths, stages, and whatever else was inside the outdoor center for the festival. "At least the parking's free."

"It probably means we have to pay to get in, though."

"You know, we do still have a couple of bags of gold coins stashed away." She turned the engine off and unbuckled her seatbelt.

"Oh, yeah. That's a great idea. We'll roll up to a massive festival in Bavaria and hand out your mom's... what? Treasure? We'll fit right in!"

"You're so funny." She stuck her tongue out and opened the driver-side door. "I'm hungry. Let's go look."

Romeo did another quick slide across the massive center console—although it wasn't nearly as exaggerated as the first time he'd attempted that trick once they got rid of the carpet—and hopped out after her. Laughing, she shut the door, locked it, and shoved the keys in her purse. "Do you think the stuff here's anything like in Saarbrücken?"

"I have no idea. But I bet it'd be like saying you get the same kinda stuff in Oregon that you'd find in Louisiana." She nodded toward the growing crowd of people heading into the convention space.

"Fun." He stuck his elbow out, offered her his arm, and she linked her elbow with his. "To the festival."

By the time they found the entrance, there was already a fairly long line. They reached the narrow opening and simply walked through. "So they're merely bottlenecking everyone inside, huh?" She gazed at all the brightly colored tents, the flashing lights even in the middle of the day, and the bold-striped tents with brewery logos and huge, incredibly long tables and chairs inside. "I can't believe all this is free too. To get into, I mean. I wonder how— Romeo?"

He'd slowed his pace, and the minute she stopped to look at him, he stopped too. "I can't believe it."

She laughed. "What's going on?"

His mouth dropped open and he stared at a group of people who walked past them, all wearing traditional Bavarian dress and toting massive beer steins. "We walked into the summer version of Oktoberfest."

"What?" It only took her a few seconds to see what he saw. "Oh, my God. You're totally right." A man in lederhosen and a dark-green Alpine hat pushed a cart of huge, freshly baked pretzels toward the closest tent. "That guy has an actual feather in his hat."

"Yup."

"And pretzels."

"Yup."

She grabbed his arm with both hands and gazed at him. "Okay. We can't spend all day here, though." He shook his head slowly and gazed out at the festival grounds with wide, glistening eyes. "We stopped for lunch." His head-shaking shifted into a nod. "We have to get back on the road again. Today."

"Yeah, Lil. Yeah. I know." Finally, he looked at her and nodded. "We can still have fun while we're here, though."

"Of course we can."

"Good." He looked around and gestured a few tents down. "I literally see two empty chairs in the beer garden. Let's try that one first."

They almost didn't make it to the empty chairs before two huge, burly, bald men who could've been lumberjacks except for the lederhosen. Fortunately, she managed to dart away from Romeo toward the table in the tent, slip into one chair, and prop her feet on the other. She turned to grin at him as he hurried toward her before the grin shifted toward the men who'd wanted the same prize. They chuckled at her and kept walking, talking in low voices as they pointed across the festival center.

"Nice steal." He narrowly missed sitting on her feet before she removed them. "And now...this." He snatched the standing menu from the table to scan the huge list of beer. "All this is right here. In this tent."

"Food too. Remember?"

"Yeah, totally."

As it turned out, most of the tents serving food and all

the beer tents—except for the beer garden—required advanced reservations through the festival website. By the time they finally discovered that—after a woman was nice enough to tell them—all the seats basically filled up for the next year as soon as the last festival was over, they'd already given their seats up at the beer garden and were starving. Instead, they resigned themselves to hopping from small food stall to small food stall and buying little tastes from almost every snack cart that passed them.

Half an hour later, they made their way back toward the entrance to the festival grounds, a little reluctant to leave. "We gotta put this on the list of things to do again." Romeo's belch surprised even him.

When Lily shot him a look and received a wide-eyed glance of apologetic shock in return, she couldn't help but laugh. "It didn't look like you left much room for staying another twenty minutes."

"Yeah, but they have other stuff here besides food and beer." He inclined his head in acknowledgment. "Although that's admittedly the best part. Look at all the rides. I saw a sign for a local band I can't even pronounce playing later. They look cool. And there are tons of stuff I bet you can't get for real anywhere but here. Hey. You would look amazing in one of those." He pointed at a woman walking around selling cotton candy in her traditional Bavarian dirndl dress.

She snorted. "I'll wear that if you get your own lederhosen."

"Done."

"Seriously?"

He nodded sternly. "Oh, yeah. I'd rock a pair of those, no question."

Chuckling, she licked the last trace of Nutella off her fingers and tossed the thin paper wrapping into the trashcan as they exited. "Well, I've had enough bread and pretzels and cheese and meatballs for the rest of my life, I think."

"Which is why you needed a Nutella crepe too, huh?"

"It looked delicious. And it was." She smirked at him. "It was a little weird, though, that the place selling crepes here is the same place that sells them inside the Eiffel Tower, don't you think?"

"Lily, that's the least weird connection we've seen since we got off the *Atlantic Maiden* in France."

She raised a finger and opened her mouth to argue, but she couldn't. "Fair enough." With a regretful sigh, she put a hand gingerly on her stomach. "I can't believe I ate that much."

"I'm fairly sure we ate exactly the same amount."

Her playful shove made him laugh. "Yeah, and you're twice my size."

"Twice your size? Really?"

"Close enough. Hey, is there any chance you wanna drive for a while?"

He frowned. "Probably not. If I sit down now, I'm gonna end up falling asleep."

"Oh, my God. You're exactly like your dad."

"There's nothing wrong with that." He grinned. "Julian Stephens can sleep absolutely anywhere."

"I don't even understand how that's possible." She

stopped before they crossed the street to the festival parking lot. "Except for right now and being this full of... Austrian food. Do you wanna take a little walk around?"

"We were walking around in there."

"Yeah, in a huge crowd of people. And we obviously couldn't control ourselves with the food." She grunted and rubbed her stomach again. "I mean to walk it off. We don't have to go into the middle of town or anything. Oh." She turned toward the festival grounds and pointed. "The Danube River is literally a couple of blocks that way." He turned with her and fixed her with a look of total surprise. "Okay, yes. I actually looked at a map."

"Is that the first time on this trip?" He tried as hard as she did to hide a smirk.

"Maybe." Lily sidled toward him, caught his arm, and gave it a little tug. "Come on. How cool would it be to say we walked along the Danube River for a minute?"

"Not as cool as you wearing one of those Bavarian dresses."

She snorted. "Cut it out. This'll be perfect. Enough to walk off all the bread and beer, I promise. Then, we'll come back to the Winnie, and I'll keep driving."

This time, he felt the belch before it came up and clamped his mouth shut. He gasped a little when it burned through his nose and made a muffled version of the sound he tried to hold down. "That hurt."

"Gross." Lily released his arm and chuckled. "You need a walk as much as I do. Let's go."

"Okay, but if I get a cramp and fall over, are you gonna be able to carry me back to the Winnie?"

She lowered her head and eyed him from beneath raised brows. "Do you really have to ask that question?" To prove her point, she flicked her fingers through the air at him. The tiny, unseen force of her physical-compulsion spell made him stumble forward down the street as if she'd shoved him with both hands herself.

"Okay, okay." He chuckled and took her hand. "I get it. You can literally make me do whatever you want."

Lily squeezed his hand and grinned. "Only if I have to."

"You know you'll never have to, Lil."

"Yeah, I know. That's part of why I really like you." *Did I actually say that out loud?* Romeo beamed at her and squeezed her hand in return as they set off down Hagen Allee to head for the Danube only a few blocks to the east. *Doing what we're doing is one thing. Talking about it is something totally different.* She couldn't bring herself to look directly at him as they walked in the afternoon sunshine, mainly so she could avoid talking about it. For now.

About ten minutes later, a path cut from the street toward Kagerser Haupstrasse, and they could see the dark waters of the Danube glittering in the light. A few birds swooped low over the banks and squawked raucously. "Yeah." He took a deep breath. "It'll be nice to say we saw this. Part of me wishes I could tell my dad about everything we've seen and everywhere we've been, you know?"

"Yeah, I know." *But I'd rather have my mom at home, wondering what I'm doing, than out there somewhere in a cage or...whatever else.* "How'd he take it when you said he wouldn't be able to reach you for a while."

He shrugged. "He dove into this ridiculously long story about the time he spent a winter in Alaska with some high school friend. Something about how they were out of range too." He smirked. "I kinda tuned that part of the conversation out, honestly."

She laughed. "It's easy to do when it comes to all your dad's stories."

"Tell me about it. But I think he—" A frown creased his brows, and he paused on the street. "There's..." He sniffed the air and his eye twitched. "Okay. Magic, Lil, and a great deal of it. Somewhere close too."

"Wow." She turned to look behind them, but the streets seemed almost deserted. There weren't many houses or stores out here—only a few commercial buildings, a rundown-looking grocery store, and open space. "Do you know where it—"

A bright-green flash came from a building to their right, a quick flare between the partially drawn curtains.

She stared at it, her eyes narrowed. "Never mind." They focused on the small, single-story house near the river that had no neighbors to see the strange light show, but nothing else happened. "Do you really think there's a ton of magic in there?"

Romeo blinked sluggishly and raised a finger for her to wait, his nostrils flaring. But the sneeze never came. He shook his head. "Not as much as in Canada. And not nearly as much as teleporting with Aluino's people in the mountains. But..." He sniffed. "Yeah. Probably a little more than usual."

"Huh." Lily studied the oddly isolated house again. "I wonder what they're up to. Maybe it's some kinda shop?"

Right on cue, the front door burst open, and man in a light-brown business suit stormed outside. The murmur of multiple voices drifted out behind him, followed by a woman's shout. "Hey! Jonas, come back."

The man whirled toward the open door and shook a finger at whoever was inside. "No! I'm not wasting my time with this...this... These people are doing unspeakable things to our city. Who knows how much of the whole state is affected at this point? And all you can do is hold another useless meeting to talk about the issue? I want to find them, Nele, not merely talk about them."

"Jonas, we still don't know who's behind these—"

The enraged man whipped his hand through the air, slammed the door shut from four feet away, and stormed around the side of the building.

"Woah." Lily glanced at Romeo.

"It sounds like—"

The squeal of tires filled the air and seconds later, a small blue BMW barreled out of the lot beside the house and accelerated toward them on the road. They scrambled onto the thin, browning grass beside the house before the car streaked past them. Jonas screamed in his car and pounded on the steering wheel before he made a sharp left turn and obviously floored the gas pedal.

"I'm gonna assume he didn't see us," Romeo muttered at the tiny spec of BMW before it completely disappeared.

"Yeah, he wasn't looking at anything." Lily took a deep breath. "Part of me wants to say this isn't any of our business and that witches fight all the time."

"It's a really small part of you, isn't it?"

"Yeah. He said, 'unspeakable things,' Romeo."

"Okay. Let's go see what it's about."

They stepped across the lawn in front of the house and skirted the picnic table on the front porch. She looked at the wooden letters nailed to the top of the covered porch and painted a light blue. "Restaurant Boat Ride Club, huh?"

"Not always, apparently."

"Hey. Do you recognize that?" She pointed to the small oval painted on the white post. It could have fit twice in the palm of her hand and it wasn't that noticeable unless someone was either looking for it or had seen it before.

"Nope." He squinted it. "What is it?"

She dug through her purse and felt carefully for the thick edge of Gabriel Mercier's card, then brought it out for him to see. "Oh..." He glanced at the front door. "Okay, the French detective seemed like a decent guy. But the last time we walked into a building with a magical Order's sigil on it—which is supposed to mark it as a safe place—we were attacked by...what? Three different witches? Oh, yeah. And a spellcasting werewolf." He shook his head. "I almost forgot about that one."

Once she'd put the card back in her purse, she stepped farther onto the porch. "Well, that club for magicals also had a black heron painted on the door. Remember? Do you see any of those around?"

"That's another no."

"Okay." She stopped a few feet from the door and looked at him. "I'm gonna give these guys the benefit of the doubt, then, and say they're actually operating within Cadre Europa's standards."

He eyed the front door and grimaced. "I only now remembered I left all my wolfsbane in the Winnie."

"You said there was way more magic than this in that speakeasy. You handled yourself fine in there."

"Yeah, okay." With a shrug, he stepped toward her onto the faded doormat. She reached for the doorknob.

FIFTEEN

"But that's not how we do things." A short, squat woman in a bright-purple shirt spread her hands on the table. Six other witches sat around it with her. None of them had bothered to return the eighth chair to its rightful place after the disgruntled Jonas had leapt out of it. "We didn't found this chapter in Straubing to handle any investigations—"

"That's not the point, Nele, and you know it." A much younger woman seated across from her spread her arms. "This chapter wasn't founded under the assumption that we'd find ourselves in this situation, either."

"We don't have the authority."

An older man with a thin, twisting handlebar mustache beside Nele inclined his head in almost a nod. "That's a simple change."

Nele turned toward him with a scowl. "Do you really think this is a good idea? A call to arms of every witch in the city? To prepare for battle against a force we can't even name?"

"It's better than doing nothing." The man turned his head toward her but wasn't able to meet the woman's gaze. "It's been almost three months, Nel. And it's only getting worse. Honestly, I now spend my nights wondering which of my family will be taken next. I'm ready to see change, even if it's merely from being a coward to an old man who takes every precaution he can." The woman glared at him with wide eyes.

"If it's an issue of getting the Order's permission first, Nele," said a younger man, "I don't think they'd hesitate to grant it."

The head of Cadre Europa's Straubing chapter raised her chin and sighed. "Do any of you know the first thing about how to find who's behind these attacks?"

Lily pushed the door open a little wider and raised her hand. "Excuse me."

Only then did any of the witches in the house notice that two strangers—and one of them a werewolf—had let themselves into the clubhouse acting as a restaurant. Nele pressed her lips together in irritation before she forced a thin smile. "No, we're closed for the festival, dear. We won't be open again until the last week of August."

The other witches shifted uncomfortably in their chairs. Some of them stared with wide eyes at the newcomers. One thin, nervous-looking man fiddled with the collar of his shirt as if he meant to loosen his tie but had forgotten he hadn't worn one today.

"I'm sorry." She stepped fully inside and Romeo joined her before he closed the door behind them. "What I should have said is that I think I might be able to help you."

"With what, exactly?"

"With finding who's behind these attacks."

Chairs creaked again under shifting weight, and this time, the witches around the table looked far more prepared to bolt up and fight than to listen to anything she had to say.

"What are you doing here?" their apparent leader demanded.

"Honestly, we're passing through, but—"

"Then keep passing, girl." The man who'd admitted to being scared for his family had now abandoned all semblance of remorse and what he'd called cowardice. His eyes burned fiercely from beneath his thick eyebrows. "We'll handle our own problems in this city. And we don't want anyone else to step in where they don't belong. You have no idea what's happening right now."

These witches are terrified. She nodded. "Actually, I think I do. Many witches here have gone missing in the last few months, haven't they? Kidnappings someone never bothered to hide? Maybe even a few...well, lost lives?"

All the witches glanced at their chapter head in concern. Nele sputtered under all the attention and her cheeks wobbled in indignation before she stood abruptly from her chair. "How did you find us here?"

"We were merely taking a walk after the festival, actually." Lily stuck a thumb behind her. *Okay, the river's actu-*

ally in that direction. Whatever. They'll get it. "We thought we'd come take a look at the river. And here we are."

"We saw one of your other members leave," Romeo added. "And heard shouting. If there's anything we can do—"

The old man pounded a fist onto the table. "There is nothing you can do. As a general rule, I don't trust tourists. I wouldn't trust you to sweep the floors in here without trying to get something more out of it."

She glowered at him. "Excuse me?"

"Not when you let that animal run around with you."

"Okay, that's taking it way too far." She pointed a warning finger at the table of witches. "I understand that you're afraid. What's happening right now is terrifying, especially when no one really knows what's going on. And I feel for all of you who are missing friends or family." Her finger swept toward the old man, and she glared fearlessly at him. *I should send a few sparks into his bigoted mouth.* "But those kinds of hateful assumptions are gonna end up digging an even deeper hole that none of you will be able to climb out of."

"Lily..." Romeo brushed her elbow gently but she ignored him.

"Think what you want," the man grumbled. "How do we know you're not one of them?"

She gritted her teeth furiously, fighting to comprehend what he'd said. "What?"

"Is this some kind of joke, then? Toying with your victims first?" The old man stood. "Have you come here to take us away? Leave another mess behind in Straubing?"

"No." She glanced at the other witches. Their surprise and trepidation were clearly and quickly morphing into rage. "No, I'm here because I think I can help. And I actually want to."

"That's what you say." Nele placed her hands on the table and leaned forward. "But you broke into my place of business uninvited, and you brought a werewolf with you." The other members of the Straubing chapter stood from their chairs as well and faced the couple, each of them fuming with rage, stiff with terror, and definitely confused.

"Lily, we need to go."

"Are you kidding me?" She stared at the witches and the pounding of her heartbeat echoed in her head. "This is ridiculous. You really care more about that than about the fact that we might actually be able to help you protect the people who live here?"

"Oh, we'll protect them." Nele straightened and raised her hand. "Tell whoever sent you that we'll find a way to stop them. We'll fight back." The witch flicked her hand, and the door to the restaurant flew open with a bang. "We'll fight you too if we have to." Balls of green fire, swirling opalescent orbs, and crackling yellow sparks flared to life in the witches' hands.

The old man clapped his hands and drew them apart again to summon what looked disconcertingly like a bull-whip exploding with dazzling blue energy. "Get out."

Lily stared at them and her mouth worked in dumb-founded surprise. *There isn't even a reply for this level of stupidity.*

"Lily." This time, Romeo took her arm and after a few

gentle tugs, he gave up on trying to be gentle at all. "This is not the right time. Let's go."

She was so baffled she didn't try to resist his much more forceful pull on her arm toward the open door. As she all but staggered after him, she glanced at the terrified witches and their pretended bravery and took a sharp breath. For once, she'd run out of words.

He dragged her out of the little house and off the porch. The minute they stepped onto the grass again, the door slammed shut behind them. She jerked her arm out of his grasp, whirled, and finally found a target for her anger that wouldn't actually hurt anyone. She hurled a handful of red attack sparks at the blue-painted letters spelling Restaurant Boat Ride Club above the porch. The last half of the word 'Restaurant' exploded in chunks of splintered wood before they toppled into the grass and bounced off the porch. She wanted to keep going, but the sight of that small destruction made her stop. Her translation spell worked to catch up with whatever German word she'd wiped off the sign and completely changed the meaning of what she read.

"We should—"

She didn't wait for him to finish. Instead, she stormed past him toward Hagen Allee and the festival grounds and the parking lot where the Winnie waited for them.

"Lily, don't." He jogged to catch up with her but he didn't try to pull her back again.

"You know what?" She kept walking, balled her fists, and felt like she was about to explode. "If those people wanna be that closed-minded, fine. We have our own people to protect. Starting with my mom."

He offered to drive the rest of the way and she didn't argue against it. The Winnie took them through Germany and across most of Austria, where they stopped a little after 6:00 pm in Vienna. They found another relatively nice campground outside the city with low prices and fewer people than in Saarbrücken. She hadn't said a word during the four-and-a-half-hour drive, and when he pulled into their campsite and turned the engine off, he'd had enough of it.

"Okay. I know you're not gonna wanna hear this."

Lily closed her eyes and sighed as she dropped her head back against the passenger-seat headrest.

"First, let it go. It's really hard to focus on driving when I feel like there's a bomb about to go off right next to me." He smirked but she only sighed deeply through her nose. "All right. Not funny." He reached out for her hand in her lap and gave it a little shake. "Come on, Lil. Look at me."

She opened her eyes and drew her gaze slowly across the dashboard until she did what he'd asked.

"I know it's hard to get the kinda space you want after something like that when we're sitting next to each other and driving through two different countries. The only way I could think of to give you space was to not talk. But that obviously didn't help. So we're gonna talk. Right?" He focused his gaze on her and raised his eyebrows. This time, when he squeezed her limp hand gently, she returned the pressure.

"I'm so pissed off right now." Her voice trembled a

little but she wasn't anywhere close to the verge of crying. *Only the verge of blowing up. Or blowing something up.* She clenched her jaw.

"I know, Lil." He nodded. "I know. You tried to help and they weren't ready for it."

"They thought we had something to do with it. The kidnappings. Probably the murders. Who knows what else?"

"Yeah, but we both know that's not true."

She frowned and bit her lip. "How can they jump to those kinds of conclusions? Come on, you'd think that when they've run out of all their options, they'd actually be grateful for some help. They'd actually wanna listen to what someone else has to say. But they only..." Shaking her head, she withdrew her hand gently from his and smoothed her hair away from her face with both hands.

"Some people turn into assholes when they're scared, Lily." He nodded. "They don't wanna listen, so it's all on them, now. Their problem. Got it?"

Lily glanced at him again and shook her head. "But it's not only their problem. Romeo, this stuff is happening everywhere. Almost every single place we've been, and definitely everywhere we've stopped in Europe, this awful stuff is happening to people. No one knows what to do. I mean, yeah. Maybe telling them what we know and what we're guessing...maybe that wouldn't really have been that much help, but..." Her hands balled into shaking fists again before she took a deep breath, let it out, and forced herself to relax. "My mom used to tell me that knowledge and understanding were as powerful as mastering spells and casting powerful magic."

"Well, your mom's usually right." He smirked.

She stared at him for a few seconds. "You know, it's really hard to keep up this righteous indignation when you look at me like that."

"Good. That's kinda the point."

"Oh, man." Another huge sigh escaped her, and she rolled her shoulders in irritation. "I don't understand how you could stay so calm like you did after what those idiots said about you."

He shrugged. "A lifetime of hearing it, I guess."

"Don't tell me you've grown a thick skin and it all goes in one ear and out the other. There are zero clichés that would actually help the situation right now."

For a moment, he smiled and held her gaze. Then, he glanced at the center console between them and scratched the back of his neck. "Nope. I can't say any of those things. It definitely still hurts to hear, Lil. I don't expect that to ever get better." Chewing his cheek, he nodded as if someone else had said the words and he simply agreed with them. "But I've definitely come to terms with the fact that I can't control people's reactions. I can't change what anyone else thinks or says."

"That's bull." When his gaze flickered quickly to meet hers again, she uttered a chuckle. "People have their minds changed all the time. No one's born with this inherently assumed certainty that all werewolves are dangerous, violent criminals."

"Hey, tell me how you really feel."

She snorted. "No, I'm saying that whatever opinions anyone has of anything happen because they were told, or taught, or convinced. Their minds were changed, right? It's not impossible to do it again. We can change their minds."

"Not when there's so much fear, Lil." He shook his head. "No one's open to hearing anything if they're already convinced it'll really hurt them. Maybe even get them killed. Or worse." His raised his eyebrows. "Embarrass them." She responded with a sardonic huff and he chuckled. "Those witches in there were terrified even before they knew we were there. They wouldn't have heard anything you said."

"That's not an excuse for the things they said."

"No, it's not. But it's a really good excuse for us to get out of there when we did."

She rolled her eyes. "A good excuse for bashing their sign in too."

He shot her a sideways glance. "Seriously?"

"Okay, admittedly, that was not one of my finer moments. And no matter how good it felt, I probably shouldn't have done it."

"Yeah. Probably. And I thought we made a deal that you'd leave this whole 'fight the werewolf stigma' thing alone until—"

"Until after we find my mom. I know. I'm trying." Lily shook her head and stared at the center console now too. "Did you see what that sign read when we left, though?"

"Yeah, your translation spell doesn't miss a beat, does it?"

"Apparently not."

Romeo laughed and spread his arms. "Well, here's to hopin' that changing the sign from 'Restaurant Boat Ride Club' to 'Gas Trip Club' is at least a little insulting."

She laughed, covered her face with her hands, and shook her head. "It might even be funnier if we actually spoke German." She looked at him and sighed. "Okay. I'm not sure I really like admitting it right now, but even talking to you about this makes me feel better."

He chuckled. "Excellent." A grin slowly bloomed on his lips.

"What?"

"I saw a meat market about two blocks before we turned in here."

"Oh, my God. Romeo..."

"It's an Austrian meat market, Lily."

"Yeah, yeah. Okay. Fine." She unbuckled her seatbelt and stood from the passenger seat. "We can go get more food. Again."

He leapt over the center console after her as she headed to the Winnie's side door. "Do you know what this means?" He caught her around her waist from behind and pulled her toward him and wound his arms tightly around her. When he buried his face in her neck, she jerked away from his curls tickling the side of her face. "We won't have to eat another meatless meal for weeks."

She laughed as they stepped toward the Winnie's side door. "Don't act like it's for me too. I could be a vegetarian if I had to and be fine."

With a suitably horrified expression, he gasped. "I'm not even insulted by what you said. Do you know why?"

"Why?" She opened the door and pushed it open.

"It's my happy place, Lil." He picked her up around the middle and leapt out of the Winnie. She burst out laughing and dropped her head back against his shoulder. "I'm taking you to my happy place!"

SIXTEEN

Despite the fact that they did end up stocking the Winnie's relatively small freezer with sausage and wiener schnitzel, Romeo's happy-place vibes lasted only until they stopped in Budapest the next morning. At the gas station where they stopped to fill the tank and buy more bottled water, they watched a small rally of Hungarian citizens outside a nondescript building across the street.

Most people pumped signs in the air that read *We Deserve Answers* and *No More Lies*. A woman with a bull-horn stood on a bench and shouted into it. "The people of Budapest need to know the truth. We're owed the truth. Yes, it's a sad fact of reality that crime still exists. That even before all this, people were stolen from their loved ones. That before all this, so many people have lost their lives through senseless acts of violence. But that's not what we're dealing with now, is it?"

A roar of, "No!" trembled in the air.

"No! That's right. Now, there's something else going on and no one wants to tell us what's really happening. But we're not blind and we're certainly not stupid. How do they explain a schoolteacher melting through the floor in front of a classroom full of children? How do they explain a blazing light that came out of nowhere, took a musician off the stage, and left behind some deadly thing? They called it a poisonous fungus. But they can't cover up the fact that it wasn't part of the show. It wasn't a lighting accident or a magic trick. They know that, and we know that. And we deserve to know the truth."

"Oh, jeez." Romeo stared across the street until the gas handle clicked when the tank was full. He shook the nozzle, returned it, and closed the gas tank. Lily stepped around the front of the RV to stand beside him. "Did you hear all that?"

"Well, the windows are down. So, yeah. I didn't miss a word. She's definitely talking about someone's magical mess."

He turned to look at her with a darkening frown. "My guess is either Hungary doesn't have their own Non-Magical Relations department, or they can't keep up with all the memories they have to wipe."

"I honestly don't know which one is more likely." She shook her head and watched the demonstrators pump their fists and chant before they quieted again to hear the next part of the woman's speech through the bullhorn. "But it's definitely not a good thing that non-magicals are starting to notice this."

"It's way past the point of starting to notice, Lil.

They're gettin' all riled up." He grimaced. "You know, I'm not really the kind of person who roots for the government about anything, really. But I feel kinda bad for whoever these people are trying to hold responsible for this stuff."

"I'm very sure this is definitely not a government conspiracy."

"Nope." He patted the driver-side door and nodded. "We should keep going."

"Right."

Less than three hours later in Arad, just over the Hungarian border into Romania, they narrowly avoided being part of a massive—and almost inexplicable—car crash on E-75. Lily saw a huge shadow pass over the highway, headed in the same direction as the Winnie. She saw a sickly-green explosion of light beside the mud-brown sedan five car-lengths ahead of them in the left lane. Romeo saw it too. That same mud-brown sedan suddenly drifted across one, then two lanes of traffic without even a hint of a blinker or flashing brake lights.

"What the—" The werewolf braked desperately seconds before the brown car collided with a silver Volkswagon and brought them both to a slow, screeching stop on the highway. The couple both lurched forward in their seats and the RV rocked on its tires.

She took a sharp breath, puffed it out, and muttered, "That was not a regular accident."

The driver of the Volkswagon leapt out of his car and brought both hands up to his head in aggravation. The sound of his angry shouting reached them clearly, but it was too muffled to hear his words. He shouted with every step he took to the driver's side of the brown sedan, which had turned so much from its drifting and the crash that the passenger side now faced oncoming traffic, which had come to a complete stop.

They both saw what had happened to the passenger-side and driver-side windows. The man finally did too.

These had been shattered and shards spilled over the inside of the brown sedan and across the highway. Steam wafted from the broken windows, which would have been impossible and strange to anyone who didn't know that magic existed. They knew, and even they thought it was odd because both windows had been transformed into pure ice.

It melted quickly in the late-summer sun and dripped from the frame of the car. Puddles of water pooled around the scattered shards on the asphalt. Lily's mouth dropped open.

"It's only ice, right?" Romeo glanced at her with wide eyes and finally released his tense grip on the steering wheel to shift the Winnie into park.

"Well, that's what it looks like." She paused and squinted down the highway. "But I wouldn't put it in my water or anything seeing as..." She gestured at the brown sedan and the Volkswagon's enraged driver who was now far more confused than angry.

His eyes were wide as he paced a few feet in front of the sedan, which now faced the side of the highway and the shoulder where he'd stopped his own car. He scowled at the vehicle's windshield, leaned forward to peer inside, then took a few steps in another direction.

Romeo rolled his window down.

"What are you doing?" Lily asked.

"I'm only tryin' to help a little." He nodded. "Something tells me he's not thinking all that clearly." He leaned out the driver-side window. "Hey, man." The shell-shocked driver whipped his head up to search the few cars who'd witnessed the accident and stopped in time on the highway. Romeo had to stick his hand out the window to get the guy's attention. "Are you okay?"

"I think... I mean, I..." He took a few steps back toward his car while he stared at the pellets of ice on the highway and the rapidly growing puddles of steaming water. With a jerky, almost disjointed gesture, he swept his hand across the whole scene and shook his head, still staring. "What is this?"

"I have no idea." At least he could be fairly honest about that part. "But don't touch any of it, right?"

Finally, the man looked up at him again, the confusion replaced by terror. "Why?"

"It's the scene of an accident, yeah? Evidence. You don't wanna mess anything up before the police get here."

"Evidence," the man muttered and glanced at the melting ice. "Sure." For a few seconds, he seemed satisfied with that answer—until he remembered the biggest problem. "But what about the driver?" he shouted and pointed at the brown sedan. "What the hell is going on?"

The werewolf shook his head and shrugged. He couldn't explain the missing driver of the brown sedan, or the fact that there wasn't a body anywhere along E-75, or that the seatbelt was still fully buckled across an empty driver's seat. Instead, he leaned back in his seat and rolled the window up again. "This is nuts."

"Yeah." Lily sighed and put a hand to her mouth before she lowered it again. "I think it's another kidnapping, too."

He looked askance at her and shifted the Winnie into drive. "It's probably best if we—oh, crap." Blaring police sirens screamed behind them. He looked in the Winnie's side mirror and saw a line of traffic stopped behind their RV and the other eyewitnesses to the crash. Lights flashed in the mirror before not one but three police cars arrived and parked along the highway directly beside the RV. Two ambulances followed, and in less than a minute, the entire eastbound side of E-75 was sectioned off to respond to the accident. It left them trapped in the vehicle and effectively blocked in by the wrecked cars in front of them and the emergency responders.

"That was ridiculously fast." He frowned at the policeman talking to the shaken Volkswagon driver. "Like weirdly fast."

She pressed her lips together. "Well, it's not all that surprising with magical abductions and entirely unexplainable murders happening so frequently. I bet everyone's on high alert right now."

"Yeah." He ran a hand through his curls and put the Winnie back into park with a sigh. "I should've driven around it and kept going when I had the chance."

It took them over an hour to start moving again.

They'd meant to stop in Râmnicu Vâlcea for the night and make the last leg of their trip into Bucharest the next morning. But when they reached the relatively remote town in Romania—so many small white buildings with red-tiled roofs right next to the growing city landscape—they had to change their minds.

From a few miles away, they could see a dark, stormy funnel that swirled in the air outside the city limits. Like a highly concentrated tornado, it whipped in tight circles and trembled at the base where it touched the green earth.

"That's not actually a tornado, is it?" He couldn't help but stare.

"It's a magical one." She leaned forward to peer past him and out his window. "It's not moving at all."

"Oh, man... It looks like it's been there long enough for government intervention." He gestured ahead as they approached the exit off E-81 and into Râmnicu Vâlcea, Romania. Three police cars stretched across the exit to block it completely. One officer even stood outside the vehicle, waved the traffic along on the highway, and cast nervous glances at the tornado frozen in place on the other side of the highway. The same blockade had been set up on the on-ramp from the city to the highway as well. "And they don't want anyone else coming in or going out, huh?"

"It's not like that's gonna stop whoever left that storm behind." She sighed and thumped back against the passenger seat. "How far is it to Bucharest from here?"

"Uh..." He scowled. "I actually can't remember."

"Really?"

Romeo shrugged. "It's easy to forget everything else when you see something like that. Pull the map up on my phone."

Lily retrieved it from the center console's cupholder and typed in the passcode. "Okay. We're only three hours away. Are you sure you wanna keep driving?"

"Yeah, no problem. We'll get in...what? Around ten o'clock?"

"It looks like it, yeah."

"Okay. It's a little later than I wanted to be driving but it doesn't make sense to stop anywhere else after this."

She set his phone in the cupholder and nodded. "Let me know if you wanna switch."

He chuckled. "I'll be fine, Lil. Honestly, after everything we've seen in the last two days, I'm not sure there's anywhere else to go that isn't dealing with some kinda magical headache. It's better to get there, see what that key opens, and find your mom's next clue."

I really hope there isn't a next clue. I wanna find her now. "Good." She took a deep breath and closed her eyes. "We're so close."

SEVENTEEN

Bucharest was brilliantly lit by all the streetlights, building signs, marquees, and traffic headlights. "I wonder if traffic's this bad every Saturday night." Romeo frowned at the line of cars in front of them that tried to get off E-81 in the center of the city.

"Honestly, I hope that answer's a yes." Lily leaned forward to glance through her own window at the combination of old historic buildings beside much newer highrises. "That would make this a normal night in a normal city in Romania. Not like everything else we've seen."

"Yeah, that would definitely make this far easier to deal with. I can't believe I'm actually saying I prefer traffic."

With him checking the GPS on his phone intermittently, he moved the Winnie east through the heart of the city and onto DN5, which they took farther south through the edge of the commercial area and some nicer apartment complexes. These gave way to fairly decent-looking single-family homes, separated from the street for privacy by wooden, chain-link, or even chicken-wire fencing, some painted in bright, garish hues of green and blue.

Fifteen minutes later, the neighborhood feel of southern Bucharest had disappeared entirely. He now drove them through a maze of huge concrete buildings, eight and ten stories high, sometimes more, with window after window in long rows. The streetlights were few and far between, leaving them to move through pools of dark and mostly empty streets toward the address Lily's mom had written on the keychain. She took it from her purse and turned it in her hands. "This is where she wanted me to go next?"

"I guess. Olt River Alley, right? Or however it's actually written without your magical translator." He turned right onto the street with that very name, puffed out a sigh, and slowed.

"Wow." Even in the light of maybe two tall street-lamps, the Winnie's headlights, and the various apartment windows still lit up at night, there didn't seem to be enough light to really get a good look at everything. *I'm not sure I want a better look than this.*

There was so much concrete everywhere—the buildings on either side of them, the parking lot, and the seven-foot concrete walls around the outside of the apartment buildings. A few chunks of concrete and broken rebar clearly left behind from some haphazard construction project sat between parked cars in the lot. Everything was covered in graffiti and scattered trash despite the very large dumpsters in the middle of the huge lot. Even the patios squished one after another on every level of the apartment buildings were concrete, and only a few random apartments along the sprawl of them had the luxury of a patio big enough for maybe two people. As far as they could see in the low light, most of the cars were either rundown already or covered in tarps in an attempt to protect them from the same people who'd spray-painted simple but recognizably lewd images on the walls and the asphalt.

"Okay, I can appreciate an attempt to make things look a little better at one point." Lily shook her head. "But planting a handful of trees in the middle of a concrete jungle doesn't change what this is."

"Honestly, Lil, I kinda hope this is the worst neighborhood in Bucharest."

"Why?"

"I really don't wanna think about what could be worse. I was startin' to think this city wasn't such a bad place until about two minutes ago."

"Do you even see any building numbers?" She glanced at the keyring with the address written on it.

"Nope." He pulled into an empty parking space halfway between the dumpsters at the end of the block and the chest-high iron fence around browning grass and two thirsty-looking trees.

"I'm fairly sure we're looking for building five. I think. I don't even know what these other numbers are for."

"What else does it have on there, again?"

"Sc-three, Et-seven, Ap-thirty-eight. So that's gotta be apartment thirty-eight, right?"

He glanced at the keyring in her hand and smirked. "I

guess we probably shoulda figured out how to read Romanian addresses before we arrived."

She shot him an unamused glance. "That would be a lot funnier if we weren't sitting here with the engine running and no idea where to go next."

"Fair point." He turned the engine off, removed the keys, and handed them to her. Then, he took his phone out of the cupholder. "Do you feel better?"

"Well, if this takes us too long to figure out, not leaving the Winnie might be worse."

"Relax, Lil. It's too dark for anyone to watch us that closely—"

"Unless they can see in the dark." She smirked.

"You realize that we've already fought our way out of tighter spots than this, right?" He laughed. "And we were in a literal knife fight in an alley in Veracruz. With non-magicals. We're fine."

"I know we're fine." Lily unbuckled her seatbelt. "There are merely more people here than there were in that alley. More non-magicals to have to deal with if we end up in another fight. Or are attacked. Or have to use some kind of magic." She raised her eyebrows at him. "And the fact that there have been unexplained magical crimes everywhere we've driven through in the last two days makes me wonder what kinda reception we'd get if anyone here found out what we are."

He held her gaze for a moment, his expression unreadable. "Are you telling me you're scared to find the apartment that key unlocks?"

She rolled her eyes. "Of course not."

" 'Cause if you are, we can turn around, go somewhere else, and come back when things are less touchy—"

"Cut it out." She slapped the back of her hand against his arm and he chuckled. "I'm only thinking out loud, okay? You're not gonna try reading into everything I say, are you?"

"Nope." He grinned. "It looks like all your hesitation's gone, though."

"You're being ridiculous. I wasn't hesitating. Let's do this." She nodded toward the driver-side door and with another chuckle, he unbuckled his seatbelt before he opened the door and slid out.

Lily climbed over the center console and leapt down behind him. Once she'd closed the door, she locked it and stowed the keys in her purse. The keyring clue from her mom, though, she slipped over her middle finger and clutched in her hand. Music played somewhere a few blocks over. All they could really hear was the loud bass thumping repetitively, but she thought she could feel it in the asphalt beneath her feet.

"All right. Building five." Romeo glanced at his phone and turned it a few times. When he noticed Lily's questioning glance, he shrugged. "I switched the GPS to walking directions. See? It looks like we want…that building." He pointed across the parking lot at one of the four monolithic apartment buildings around them.

"Oh. Great." She looked at him and pulled a face that revealed distaste. "The one that looks like it's about to fall over. I was hoping you'd pick that one."

He snorted. "Come on."

They headed toward what his GPS told them was building five and quickly realized they had to walk back up the street to the end of the long concrete wall separating the apartments and the parking lot by maybe four feet. At the end of the wall, they found a recessed entryway beneath the second-floor apartment in front of them. "Is this the entrance?"

"Um...it doesn't look like any of the other ground-floor doors. So, maybe?"

A small tingle spread from the base of Lily's skull and down the back of her neck. She stepped closer toward him so take his arm gently with both hands. "Do you feel like someone's watching us?"

"Yeah," he whispered.

"Me too. Like I said, more people to—"

"Are you lost?" The man who watched them from beside the apartment building across the street grunted. They turned slowly to see him inside the fenced-in area with two large trees. He shifted his position against the broken refrigerator he currently used as back support and fumbled for the bottle of home-distilled Palincă beside him on the dying grass. His gaze still fixed on them, he took a large swig. "You look lost."

The couple glanced at each other. "Everything looks a little different in the dark." Lily stuck a thumb over her shoulder at the building they needed to enter. "This is building five, right?"

He grunted and nodded before he took another swig of liquor.

"My cousin lives here." She stepped across the street

and he hung back to scan the parking lot and the dark corners all around them. "He gave me a key, but I'm..." She stopped outside the fence and shrugged a little helplessly. *At least there's a fence between us. How'd he get that fridge in there?* "So it's building five, then—"

"Bah!" The man pushed himself up and swayed dangerously on the grass. With a soft burp, he shuffled toward her and flapped his hand between them. "Let me see."

By the time he stopped on the other side of the iron fence, she could already smell the horrifyingly strong fumes of alcohol on his breath and everywhere else. Instead of drawing back, she breathed through her mouth and held the keyring up for him to see in the awful light. She wasn't about to hand him the key, even though he had to squint and peer so closely at it his nose almost touched her hand through the fence.

"Eh? That's building five, entrance three, seventh floor." He nodded once and even that small movement made him stagger sideways.

"Oh, right. I knew that." She nodded. "Thanks." She turned and headed across the street toward Romeo, who watched her with his arms folded.

"Entrance three...two more down that way," the man shouted from where he leaned uncomfortably against the thin vertical fence rail in front of him. He jabbed his finger a few times in that general direction. "I'd remember for next time if I were you. Not everyone's as nice as me!" With a grunt, he thumped his own chest and turned toward the fridge that lay on its side, muttering under his breath.

Romeo raised his hand in silent thanks but the drunk no longer paid them any attention. "If he was the only person watching us, I'm sure I wouldn't still feel eyes on me right now."

"That means we need to find entrance three as fast as we can." She slipped her hand into his and they hurried along the uneven sidewalk. "You know, in a weird way, this kinda feels like walking through North Charleston at three-thirty in the morning."

He snorted. "Only if you don't live in North Charleston—wait. You've actually done that?"

She grinned. "Only one crazy night after high school. I barely remember it."

"Did your mom find out about that one?"

"Are you kidding?" She lowered her voice and took a quick glance down the street. "She would've killed me if she knew. Then again, she never told me about coming to a place like this. I'm reasonably sure that wipes the slate clean for both of us."

"Well, that's what we're about to find out, isn't it?" He pointed at what was apparently entrance three, according to a drunken Romanian's directions. They stepped into the recessed alcove beneath the second-floor apartment of this giant building. She tried the doorknob and found the door completely unlocked. It stuck a little bit on the cement floor when she pushed it, but another quick shove opened it all the way.

The hallway was dark with bare walls stained an aged

yellow. The domed light fixtures in the ceiling hung at odd angles and were covered in dust that cast a muted yellow light on everything. The first one threw mottled shadows of all the dead moths and flies that had climbed into the fixture and never quite made it out.

"Okay..." She stepped farther inside so he could follow her. The door closed with a heavy, grating click. "The elevators are conveniently placed, at least." There were two on their right and she only had to take a few steps to reach the call button. It descended through the elevator shaft from wherever it was with a rattling click. The sound echoed down the concrete hallway in front of them.

"Conveniently on their way out," Romeo muttered. "That thing sounds like it's about to break off the cables at any minute."

"It's probably only a squeaky hinge or something." When he sent her a doubtful glance, she shrugged. *I wanna believe whoever owns this place wouldn't ignore something like fixing an elevator before it breaks. But here, I'm not so sure.* She jumped when the elevator announced its arrival on the first floor with a loud thump before the doors rumbled open slowly.

"Sure. Only a squeaky hinge." He nodded and stepped inside.

"You never know." She joined him and turned to punch the button for the seventh floor. "And hey, if something does happen, I'm quite good at casting spells, remember?" She raised both hands to wiggle her fingers at him as the elevator doors squealed shut, stopped with about an inch of a gap between them, and emitted a loud series of clicks. They finally closed the rest of the way as if someone had shoved them and the mechanical box trembled.

He shook his head and stared up at the floor-counter above the doors. "I'm not worried about it."

The elevator lurched, and her hand jerked to brace herself against the wall. He chuckled. "Neither am I." She cast him a sideways glance and smirked. "I'd merely prefer to stay on my feet." It jerked again and finally ascended.

EIGHTEEN

The elevator still groaned behind them when they moved down the hallway on the seventh floor in search of apartment thirty-eight. A dog barked from one of the apartments farther down and Romeo grimaced. "Man, I hope that dog's owners walk it at least five times a day. There's no space in here." He raised his arms to spread them and his wrists slid up the walls. "I can't even stretch out all the way."

"You can't do that in the Winnie, either."

"Yeah, but at least in the Winnie, I'm not surrounded by all these other people." He gestured at the doors spaced closer together than most hotel rooms.

Apartment thirty-six on their right was missing both the door and the hinges. Lily couldn't help but peer through the gaping hole in the gray tarp used to cover the entrance. It was completely dark inside and looked empty but for a few scattered tools and discarded newspapers. A darker shape shuffled across the room beyond and uttered a hacking cough. She looked away quickly and focused on the next apartment—the very last on the right.

"This is it," she whispered. The number eight tacked to the door was skewed a little like she might knock it off simply by blowing on it. "Okay." She lifted the key in her hand and stopped when he grunted behind her. Startled, she turned to look at him. "What?"

He shook his head hastily and sniffed. "This definitely smells like the right place. Uh...it smells like magic, I mean. But not your mom." She frowned, her head tilted in confusion. "Not that I know what your mom smells like, Lil. I only..." He sighed. "Magic. It's strong and my brain's all...soupy."

She snorted and patted his arm. "Did you forget the wolfsbane?"

"Yep."

"Maybe you should set an alarm for that or something to remind yourself."

Romeo cleared his throat and offered her a tight smile. "Is this what we'll sound like when we're all old? 'How did you forget to take your medicine, Romeo? You set an alarm.' 'I can't hear my alarm.'" He squinted, hunched over, and made what she assumed was supposed to look like an elderly person's face.

She pumped her elbow against his shoulder and he straightened with a chuckle. "Can we hold off on the jokes until after we've gotten inside this apartment?"

"I'm only trying to lighten it up, Lil. Go ahead. Let's see what kinda magic's in there." He nodded at the door.

"Thank you." She started to turn but she paused and

smirked at him. "So you think we're still gonna know each other when we're old, huh?"

He grinned. "Yeah, that'd be pretty cool."

In response, she simply rolled her eyes and turned toward the apartment but couldn't help a smile. "Okay, time to focus now." The door looked like all the others except for the number. Still, she trusted Romeo's nose more than her eyes at this point. "Okay, to be safe..." She slipped the keyring over her middle finger again so the key dangled down the back of her hand and clapped her palms together. When she pulled them apart, the thin, glistening film of her illusion-revealing spell spread between her hands and grew with every inch her palms separated. With a flick of her wrists, she released it and the pink film toward the apartment door. A faded pink light encountered the door and spread across it, up and down, and out to the sides like fog curling against a rock wall. She waited in silence.

"Huh." He scratched his head. "I thought for sure there would be something there."

"Yeah, me too." She squinted at the door and shrugged. "Okay. Plan B." She shook her hand, took a deep breath in and out, and summoned the revealing charm as a yellow light in the palm of her hand.

He chuckled. "It's like a blacklight for magical residue."

"I'm thinking it's a good thing we don't have an actual blacklight with us right now." She raised her glowing palm toward the door and trailed it up and down to search closely for any sign of a hidden ward or charm—maybe even another secret message like the one they'd found in Melissa Bore's destroyed basement in Colorado. "Nothing." She retracted the spell and put a finger to her lips. "What if the magic's inside the apartment instead?"

"There's only one way to find out, right?"

She glanced quickly down the hall toward the elevators, and when she'd confirmed that it was still empty, she nodded. "Well..." As an afterthought, she brushed her fingers against the door and paused.

"Okay, I haven't seen that one before."

Lily looked over her shoulder at him. "What one?"

"Whatever you're doing." Romeo nodded at the apartment. "Petting the door or whatever."

With a snort, she shook her head. "I'm only making sure this isn't some kind of touch-activated thing. I learned that lesson the hard way with my mom's grimoire."

He tipped his head to the side and smirked. "Not in the version I heard. Didn't you keep trying to touch that book no matter how many times it threw you across the room?"

"Yeah, but I finally got it."

"Because you turned eighteen."

"Okay, mister interrogator. I'm gonna go inside this apartment now." She gave him an exaggerated grin. "Does that sound good to you?"

"I am..." Romeo's nostrils flared again in the beginning of a magically induced sneeze, but it never came. He huffed and tried to shake the tingling out of his nose. "Ready when you are. Do you think you should knock first, maybe?"

"Come on. My mom wouldn't give me a key if she wanted me to wait politely for someone else to answer the door." She swished the keyring around her fingers, caught the key, and took hold of the chipped, gold-painted doorknob with her other hand. "Here we go." The key fit perfectly in the lock, and despite the fact that it slid inside easily, she was still cautious enough to go slow.

Lily anticipated the small click of the key hitting the back wall of the lock. She definitely didn't anticipate the flash of orange light that erupted from the doorknob or the tingling heat that sparked into her fingers and up her arm.

"Woah." She jumped back but lurched forward again and almost smacked her forehead against the door. Her teeth gritted, she managed to brace herself with her other hand first and tried to release the key. She couldn't. "What the heck?" Her elbow pumped at her side as she jerked away from the doorknob, but her fingers remained clenched around the small, thin piece of metal she'd stuck in the lock.

"Uh...Lily?"

"Yeah, I know. I promise I'm not messing around. I'm... stuck." With a sigh, she gave up trying to remove her hand and stared at the doorknob.

"Lily, I think you might wanna—"

"Maybe I need to keep going and turn the key." Testing that idea didn't bring any different results. Her fingers remained around the key, which remained in the lock, and she couldn't even turn it. "Seriously?"

"Lily. Look."

With a huff of frustration, she glanced up from her

hand magically glued to the key and snapped, "What?" She meant to turn and look at him, but the shifting orange light that now covered the entire door finally caught her attention. "Oh."

The symbols of the coded language her mom had made up when Lily was a kid—seemingly on a whim, at first, but more recently to use for real-life, hidden magical messages —glowed with that orange light. At the very top, a number of symbols appeared together in two straight lines and didn't move at all. Below them, though, all the other symbols Lily had spent her entire childhood learning how to decipher drifted across the door in no recognizable pattern, swirling like a hive of seriously confused orange bees.

"Okay, what's that?" Romeo asked.

Her gaze scanned the dozens of symbols that rearranged themselves randomly, disappeared from the door when they drifted off it, and reappeared in a different place. "Oh..." She grinned. "So, playing more games, huh?"

"This is the weirdest game I've ever seen. Are these your mom's symbols?"

"Yep."

"I guess we know your translation spell doesn't apply to made-up languages, then."

"Romeo, this is almost exactly the same as one of the puzzles she used to set up for me at home."

"Oh, good. It'll be easy, then."

"Sure." She shrugged. "Same puzzle. Different words." With another experimental tug, she tried to release the key again. "Still nothing. Okay, fine."

"Does it actually say anything with all those moving pieces?"

"Well, the part up at the top doesn't move." She focused and read the single line of that didn't change. 'Always yours. A mother's muse. You carry it but did not choose the one gift you will never lose.'"

"Oh, man. I hate riddles."

"I love them." Lily's grin faded a little when she looked away from her mom's glowing orange symbols to glance briefly at her hand on the doorknob. "I like them much more when my fingers aren't magically glued to a key, though. Okay. One gift, huh?"

"What about magic?" Romeo clicked his tongue against the roof of his mouth. "That could count as a gift, right? At least for people like you who are really good at it."

She shook her head. "No. Besides the fact that it's really too obvious—"

"Well, okay, then."

Turning to look at him over her shoulder, she shrugged and gave him an apologetic smile. "It was a good guess. But even a witch born with magic can choose how to use it. Or if to use it. And magic can be lost, too."

"What?"

"Yeah. Remember that woman in New Mexico. The one who invited us to that party thing where we met the old seer woman? The storyteller?"

"Oh. You mean the witch born without magic who made us...bran muffins."

Lily snickered. "Yeah. Maybe she was born without magic, but that's a kind of loss. It won't work for this."

He sighed with obvious frustration. "Okay. So..." He tapped the toe of his sneaker against the thin, soiled carpet lining the hallway. "Hey, what about a head?"

"A head?"

"Yeah. Always yours. Mothers love to kiss their baby's heads, I guess. You can't choose your own head."

"Hmm. You can definitely lose your head, though."

"What, like set it down somewhere and forget where you put it?" He snorted.

She scanned the scrolling orange symbols and glanced from one to the other them and at the stationary lines at the top. "I'm starting to understand why you don't like riddles."

"Hey, I'm trying." He folded his arms and frowned. "Have you lost your head before?"

"I thought I did a few times." When he didn't respond, she glanced at him again. "Oh, come on. You know what losing your mind means. Going crazy?"

"Yeah. I guess that's out, then."

"Plus, people definitely used to get beheaded and lose their heads that way. So it could be literal." She stared at the symbols again until a rather unpleasant sensation made her glance at her hand. "I think we need to be fairly quick about finding the answer, though."

"Why?"

"Oh, only the small, uncomfortable burning growing in my hand right now." She sucked in a breath between her teeth and tried to ignore it.

"You're kidding." He stepped up beside her, and they both eyed the key in her hand. Both it and the doorknob now glowed with a low, red light, like an electric stove had turned on to start heating up. "Nope. Not kidding."

"Ignore that, okay? I need to find the answer."

"Maybe we need a way to get your hand off that key." He leaned forward to catch her gaze. "Are you all right?"

"The faster we think, the better I'll be." She gritted her teeth and reread the riddle. "It has to be something tied to a mother, right? So...what's that? Having kids? And a gift..."

"Okay, so not that it will, but if this goes south, I wanna know how to call a Romanian ambulance." He retrieved his phone.

"Very funny." She winced at the growing pain in her fingers. "Stop talking for a minute. I'm thinking."

He hadn't been joking at all. With the intention of hopefully picking up someone's internet service to find the number for an ambulance, he tapped the passcode into his phone—five-four-five-nine—and froze. "Lily, what about—"

"A name. That's it." She grinned despite the growing pain in her fingers and searched through the randomly swirling symbols below the riddle. As soon as she found the first letter, she snapped her fingers and a white light bloomed on their tips. She tapped that first letter and did it quickly so as not to accidentally touch any of the others, then dragged it up the door to leave it below the lines of the riddle while she searched for the next.

"So the door's like a touch-screen now, huh?"

"It doesn't have to be."

"You know, I was about to say the answer's a name too." He glanced at his phone and the numbers he'd tapped to unlock it. The corresponding letters for those numbers also spelled a name, but that wasn't the point of this magical orange riddle on the door. He shoved the phone into his pocket and simply watched her. Lily's hand attached to the key looked like it was glowing now too and her entire arm trembled. "How are you doin'?" Stepping toward her, he saw that she'd placed two symbols below the riddle now.

"I'm trying to find the—oh." Her left hand stretched down to pin another orange symbol against the door, and she slid it up to rest beside the other two.

"Uh, are you sure that's the right one?" He pointed. "It's not like I can read these or anything, but if those are letters, the first one and the third one shouldn't be the same."

"What are you talking about?" Lily muttered, more focused on finding the final symbol anyway.

"Name. N-A-M-E. They're all different."

"Oh..." Finally, she saw it at the very bottom of the door, spinning in tight little circles. She eased into a squat with her other hand still agonizingly attached to the red-hot key, tapped the final symbol, and pulled it up. A little grunt escaped her when she stood again, careful not to release that symbol from beneath her finger or the white light that allowed her to do this. "No, I know how to spell name. And yeah, the general answer is a name. But this riddle wasn't made for everyone in general." She positioned the fourth symbol beside the others and held it there as she glanced at Romeo and grinned. "It was made for me. My name."

"Lily..."

"I know I'm right." The minute she took her finger off the symbol and the surface, all the orange-glowing magic trembled for a second before everything surged toward the center of the door. The letters and light converged, and another brilliant orange flash of light burst in the hallway. A needle-sharp pain pierced her index finger, and she jerked her hand away from the key and the doorknob. "Ow! Come on…" Then, she stopped and cradled her burning and recently freed hand against her chest with the other. "Hey, look at that." She turned toward Romeo and raised an eyebrow. "Tada."

"You didn't know a hundred percent that that was the right answer, did you?" He bit his lip.

She shrugged. "More like ninety-eight percent, probably. Very good odds, I think."

"How's your hand?"

Slowly, she lowered it from her chest and opened her fist as far as it would go, which wasn't much. Bright-red burn marks lined her thumb, index finger, and middle finger—everywhere she'd been forced to hold the dangerously hot key. A tiny drop of blood beaded at the tip of her index finger. "It's fine."

"It doesn't look like it."

"It will be fine. Right now, I'm more focused on what's inside this apartment."

He frowned at her and really wanted to tell her this counted as pushing things a little too far. But, of course, he didn't.

"Hey, I promise. I'm okay. A little pain can be a good incentive for quick thinking." She turned toward him and patted his chest with her uninjured hand. "It's not the first time. Let's do this, huh?"

"As long as you let me put something on that burn when we're done." He nodded at her hand.

"No problem." Finding the key and the doorknob returned to their cool, dull-gold color again, she turned the key with her good hand, felt the deadbolt slide open, and turned the knob. "I'm sure there's a First-Aid kit in the Winnie." With a wink, she opened the door and took the first step inside. Then, she froze.

Behind her, he cleared his throat. "Something tells me we're not going back to the Winnie anytime soon."

NINETEEN

"Holy crap." Lily's hand slipped from the doorknob and she took another slow, baffled step into the apartment. "What did we walk into?"

Romeo slipped through the door and stopped beside her to gape at the walls, the bookshelves, the one uncomfortable-looking couch, and the floor. "I thought this kinda thing was only in psycho movies. Or maybe crime dramas or whatever."

"Well, many people think magic's only in the movies too." Lily shook her head in amazement. "And yet, here we are."

The entire apartment was covered from floor to ceiling in newspaper clippings, magazine articles, handwritten notes, rough sketches, and photographs. All of them included, in one form or another, the black silhouette of a heron, the word heron, or the same phrase that had surfaced more and more for the couple as their journey progressed—to complete the circle. The couch stood along the back wall and also had various paper scraps covered in scribbled writing scattered across it. Beyond the walls and most of the floor that were plastered with someone else's attempt to discover or prove something, a large, flimsy bookcase took up the far right wall inside the door. This, though, was stuffed with huge, leather-bound books and dusty trinkets, artifacts that pulsed with barely visible magical energy. Some of them looked completely harmless and mundane like the gold-handled magnifying glass propped against two of the tomes.

There is no way even that thing's not dangerous somehow. She was reasonably sure of that because every single item on that shelf, whether clearly magical or otherwise, had the silhouette of the black heron—its wings spread in flight and neck curved in the telltale U-shape—stamped, painted, etched, drawn, or carved upon it.

"This is insane." She stepped toward the bookshelf. "I bet the Wisemen's reliquary at Ichacál looked something like this. These are all spellbooks and..." She narrowed her eyes as she focused on an object and gestured vaguely at it. "Well, that looks like some kind of ceremonial mask."

"So either your mom sent us to one of the black heron's biggest fans, or we walked right into those people's...what? Storage apartments? Trophy rooms?" He ducked under a few pieces of red, shimmering string on the other end of the small living room beside the kitchen, where someone's spell had started stringing various newspaper clippings together.

"Actually, this looks more like someone who's trying to

find the people connected to the black heron. Like they're looking for clues and—oh, my God."

Romeo whirled to face her. "What's up?"

"That's exactly what this is." Lily brushed her hand against a scribbled note magically tacked to the wall beside a newspaper article titled *Local Venezuelan Taxidermist Claims Attack by his Stuffed Figures.* The note, while written as hastily as the other scrawled messages on almost everything in this apartment, had the same unmistakable handwriting she'd recognize anywhere. "Romeo, my mom was here."

"How do you know?" He joined her at the wall between the bookshelf and the couch.

"This is her handwriting. Right here. This is her." She poked the note.

"What does that say?" He squinted and leaned closer. "'They have...'"

"'They have wings. So do I.' I know this was her."

"It makes sense if the shadow-bird has more to do with your mom than we think." He nodded at another article on the wall. "That looks like hers too." This came from a magazine she thought looked like National Geographic, but there were no identifying titles. There was, however, a picture in vivid color of a white-walled temple rising high through the canopy of a jungle. The courtyard in front and the open entryway looked all too familiar.

"That's Ichacál." She leaned closer to see the light scribble of her mom's writing again on the magazine page. "'What's happening in the dark? Find the endgame. Maybe here.' What's that supposed to mean?"

"I dunno. She already found the cages under the temple. She knew something was going on. I guess maybe she thought she hadn't worked it all out yet?"

With a deep breath, she looked away from the message and scanned the cluttered, chaotically assembled documentation. "Yeah, this...this doesn't look like a collection someone would put together if they'd already found all the answers. Romeo, I was right." She turned toward him and grinned. "My mom was following the people connected to this black heron, whatever it is. Maybe she did find the truth before they took her. And I think... I think this is everything else she wanted me to see so I can find these people. And find her." She took a few more deep breaths when she realized how incredibly close they actually were to doing exactly that and immediately felt a little dizzy.

Romeo stepped toward her and steadied her with gentle hands on her shoulders. "Okay. Let's assume for a minute that you're right and all this stuff can help us. We're not done yet, Lil. We still hafta understand what all this"—he swept his gaze across the wall in front of them—"really means. And how to make sure that the people who took your mom don't take you too. Right?"

She sighed, gazed intently into his eyes, and forced herself to slow her breathing. Finally, she nodded. "Right. I'm jumping way too far ahead of myself, huh?"

"Maybe a little." He smiled. "We only need to decide on the next step." After he rubbed her arms gently a few times, he released her and ran a hand through his curls. "Honestly, I have no clue where we'd even start."

"How 'bout you start by telling me who you are and

what the hell you're doing in my apartment?" The man who'd watched them for the last two minutes from the doorway folded his arms and grunted.

The couple spun away from the wall to face the stranger who leaned against the doorframe. Romeo crouched a little and uttered a low growl of warning, although he didn't go so far as to flash his eyes their bright-silver color as he did immediately before a shift.

The man stood at least six and a half feet tall and had to duck his head low over his hulking, muscular shoulders to avoid catching the top of the doorway. His dark eyebrows and wild, dark-brown beard matched the color of the long ponytail haphazardly tied back away from his face. His folded arms bulged beneath the tight blue t-shirt that had to have been size XXL at least, if not bigger. With his lips pressed tightly together in disapproval, he stared at them and raised his eyebrows.

"Um..." Lily glanced at Romeo and decided to play nice for now. *He didn't whip out a spell and threaten us with it. So at least there's that.* "My name's Lily. And this—"

"Lily?" He unfolded his arms, leaned back to dart a quick glance down the hall, and jerked the key out of the doorknob. Hastily, he ducked inside and yanked the door quickly and quietly shut behind him. "Where did you get this?" The keyring jingled when he shook it.

She straightened and steeled herself. "I found it." *Well, that's not technically a lie.*

"By luck, or someone gave it to you?" The man

stormed toward them and his footsteps actually made the apartment floor shake. "What's your last name?"

"Hey, that's close enough." Romeo stepped a few inches in front of Lily and growled again. This time, he did let his eyes flash silver. "You only get one warning."

The giant of a man pulled his gaze away from her to study the silver-ringed werewolf eyes. He blinked in surprise, then chuckled. "Well, that makes sense, now, doesn't it? It's a little ironic, though, a werewolf coming to join the cause. If that's why you're really here." He spread his arms in submission and took two slow steps back before he met her gaze again. "Does the name Greta Antony ring a bell for you?"

She swallowed. "What about her?"

He smirked and shook his head slowly while he studied her in amazement. "You look exactly like your mother, girl."

TWENTY

Lily frowned at the stranger, both astounded and a little annoyed to hear someone she'd never seen or heard about tell her the same thing everyone else had said on this trip. *Of course I look like her. Why is everyone so surprised?* "You know my mom?"

"Oh, yeah. Very well." He sniffed and looked at the werewolf. "Relax, kid. There's no need to shift. It's not like there's any room for it in this rathole anyway, is there?"

Romeo snorted and glared at the stranger who still hadn't explained himself, but he released the energy that quivered demandingly before a shift. His eyes melted to their usual green but he kept his eye on the man in case.

"Where is she?" she asked.

"Um…" The man jerked his head and his ponytail drifted over his shoulder. "We should sit for this, I think. I'd offer a few chairs, but we got rid of the whole set a few months ago to make space."

Lily clenched her jaw and barely managed to keep herself from screaming. "Tell me where she is."

In response, he gave her a sympathetic frown and his large, dark eyebrows twitched together as he studied her face. "If you're anything like your mother, I know it's better to cut to the chase. Bottom line? I don't know where she is."

Lily sighed and closed her eyes for a few seconds. *I really thought this was it.* The feeling of Romeo's fingers brushing against hers gently, only for a moment, made her open her eyes again and meet the stranger's gaze. "Then tell me what you do know."

He glanced from the witch to the werewolf who stood in his crowded apartment. "That's a long story."

"I don't care how many chairs you have or how long it takes. I'll stand all night if I have to."

The giant chuckled in disbelief and muttered, "God, it's like she cloned herself." Then, he stepped aside and made a sweeping survey of the cluttered space. "All right. Well, I need to sit, so we're gonna do that anyway." In two massive steps, he was at the thin, lopsided couch, and quickly stacked the scattered piles of news clippings, old photos, and pages torn from books and magazines and shoved into notebooks with worn edges. He dropped all this rather unceremoniously on the floor beside the couch and gestured for his unexpected guests to sit. "Please."

The couple shared a glance, and he told her it was her decision to make simply by raising his eyebrows. "This is Romeo." She gestured toward him as she stepped toward the couch and dropped quickly onto the hardest, most uncomfortable couch cushion in existence.

The man nodded as the werewolf took a seat beside the young witch. "Darius. I'm a friend of your mother's, Lily. I have been for a long time." With another grunt, he hunkered into a squat with his back against the wall, careless of the various notes and drawings that fluttered around him when he slid down and sat. "Almost since the beginning, we've been looking into this together."

She sent him a skeptical glance. "The beginning of what?"

Darius regarded her dubiously and frowned. "The transference artifact. You know about that, surely."

Lily felt Romeo staring at her but held the man's gaze and shook her head slowly. "No, I don't, actually. Do you mind explaining it to me?"

He snorted. "That's funny." But when he realized she wasn't kidding, his smile faded and he regarded her with cautious surprise. "You really don't know?" She shook her head again. "That's...wow." He stroked his beard and stared at the floor between his feet, his huge knees drawn up to his chest. "The discovery that skyrocketed your mom's career, girl. The artifact that changed everything."

"Wait, what?" She froze for a moment and tried to put those pieces together. "You're saying the huge discovery that made my mom a professor of antiquities and got her all that attention and fame—"

"And money, yeah." He nodded.

"You're telling me that's connected to all this?" She gestured at the mess of an apartment and tried not to think too hard about the fact that there were black heron symbols literally everywhere.

"Of course it's connected. I can't believe she never told you that. It seems like a massive oversight, given everything else you know."

Lily glanced at Romeo finally, who'd tried to make himself comfortable by propping an elbow on the couch's armrest and laying his cheek on his fist. He merely gave her a clueless glance and nodded toward Darius. She frowned at the man. "I don't know anything."

"Oh, come on." He looked incredulously from one to the other, on the verge of laughing. "If you don't know anything, how'd you get a key to my apartment?"

"I already told you. I found it."

Darius assumed a scornful expression. "In your mom's jewelry box? Maybe her purse?"

"What? No." She leaned forward on the couch and pointed toward the magazine photo of Ichacál magically tacked to the wall. "I found it there. Actually, I dug it out of a hole in the ground." Still pointing, she fixed the man with a burning gaze. "I'm not messing around here."

He glanced at the photo, then turned slowly toward Lily and narrowed his eyes. "You dug up a key to my apartment at—"

"Ichacál. Yeah."

"If Greta didn't tell you what's happening, how'd you get here?"

She managed to resist the urge to roll her eyes. *What do I hafta do to get this guy to believe me?* "Check the keyring."

The man lifted the key, which looked humorously small in his giant hand, and studied it. "You found a key with Greta's handwriting in a hole in the ground at the healing temple."

"Yeah, and as far as I know, she left it there specifically for me to find. She buried it under rocks with a lily—look." She leaned forward on the couch and spread her hands, ready to stand and walk out of this apartment if he didn't begin to take her seriously. "I didn't come all this way to have everything I say questioned by a stranger. I choose to believe that you are who you say you are and that you know my mom. If you can't do the same with me and choose to believe that I really don't have the time to make up stories merely for fun, I'll stop wasting both our time." At that point, she did stand, fully intending to walk out. *Let him sit on it. He doesn't know this is the only option I have. I can come back and try again—*

"Wait." Darius' low command made her pause. "Lily, please sit." He stared at her right hand and the burn marks on her fingers, which throbbed now with her racing heart and her anger. "What happened to your hand?"

Slowly, she lowered herself onto the couch and took a deep breath.

Romeo growled. "She burned it on that damn key trying to solve the ward around your front door."

His gaze flickered quickly toward the werewolf. "That's not my ward."

"Yeah, I know." Lily slumped against the corner of the couch and the armrest. "My mom put it there. Knowing that is probably the only reason I still have a hand. Okay, yeah. I know one thing. She wanted me to come here. To see this and maybe to meet you. Other than that and the fact that every single place her clues led me brought us face to face with the worst kind of magicals imaginable, I'm still completely in the dark. So if you can shed some light on anything about all this"—she flicked her hand toward the cluttered walls—"or what she was up to or how the hell I find her, I would really appreciate some insight." Her nostrils flared as she glared at the giant man sitting on the floor. Beside her, Romeo puffed out a tiny, tense breath of surprise.

Darius cleared his throat. "She sent you on a...treasure hunt, for lack of a better term. Didn't she?"

"The best puzzle she ever left for me, Darius. And I need to finish it."

He took a deep breath and nodded. "Okay, Lily. I completely misunderstood what was happening, and I apologize. Greta..." He cleared his throat again. "She's not the kind of person who lays all her cards on the table."

She snorted. "Yeah, that's one way to put it."

The man shook his head in amazement and uttered a wry chuckle. "She talked about you all the time, you know. Everything you were learning. High school. Friends. Your training with her. It never once occurred to me that she hadn't told you about any of this. I asked her once, yeah? How she planned to keep you safe from the Pandora's Box we opened. Do you know what she told me?"

Lily rolled her eyes and couldn't help the tiny flicker of a smile that broke through her scowl. "Well, I know it wasn't that she and I had a very specific plan in case anything went wrong."

"No." He studied her face and a kind, warm, genuine smile bloomed on his lips. "No, she told me, 'Lily's fine. She's more prepared to deal with the consequences than I will ever be.'"

A lump formed in her throat and her nose burned a little with the first tingle of tears. She pushed them down. "She really said that?"

"Verbatim. That was a little over four months ago, Lily. only a few weeks before all the trouble she had stirred up for the wrong kinda people caught up with her." Darius nodded gravely.

She pulled her legs up onto the couch and crossed them beneath her. Then, she shrugged. "I'm not so sure I'm as prepared as she made me out to be."

"Seriously?" Romeo's voice was so soft, it was almost a whisper. "All the puzzles, Lil? Her code language? Your training? Your mom's right. You're the most prepared witch I've ever met."

She inclined her head in half-hearted acknowledgment but couldn't look at him. "Not when it comes to information and knowing what I'm getting into. She should've told me."

Darius chuckled and she directed a scathing glance at him. "Hey, don't be angry with her, girl. Greta Antony doesn't ever lie. She merely doesn't always tell the whole truth." He scoffed. "And she didn't lie to me that day, either. The things she taught you... How to fight. How to protect yourself and those around you. How to see through the fog"—he chuckled again—"of her vaguest clues. Solving those puzzles. Hell, I bet your spells and wards are almost as powerful as hers—"

"They're better," her friend interjected. He still watched the huge man with wary reservation but he glanced quickly at her and smirked.

"They could be." Darius nodded. "That's what Greta thought, too. And it looks like that was her plan the whole time. She wasn't trying to keep you in the dark or hold you at arm's length with this to keep you safe, Lily. Your mom was teaching you how to protect yourself. Preparing you for the moment when she wouldn't be around to do it for you."

Lily folded her arms. "She could've done that and told me what she'd found here. What she was doing with you." When Romeo snickered, she whipped her head toward him with a warning look.

"Sorry, Lil." He smirked and shook his head. "It's only...she knew exactly what you'd do if she told you about all this before she went missing."

"Oh, yeah?" *Why is this so funny?* "Go on. What would I have done? Since you seem to think you know the answer too."

He leaned away from her a little, still smiling but beneath a frown now. "Hey. Lily, I—"

"Lily Antony," Darius cut in. "Greta Antony's only daughter. I've never seen two people who look and think and act more alike." She turned to frown at the man on the floor, who raised a hand for her to wait. "For a moment, let go of being angry with her, huh? You can use that later if you have to. Which you might." With a sigh, she leaned back against the couch and pulled her crossed legs farther beneath her. "Can you honestly say, when you look deep enough, that you would've paid as much attention to Greta's puzzles and her games—to your training—if you knew what it was for?"

"Of course I would have." She frowned at him. "If I knew she was doing...this, whatever this is, I would've still paid attention. It would've made everything she taught me that much more real 'cause then I'd be going with her to help—"

"Ah." He lifted a finger and pointed it slowly at her. "You would have wanted to help."

"I don't see what's wrong with that."

"There's nothing wrong with it, Lily. Not at all. But you would have been learning only to reach an end goal, yeah?"

She frowned, started to shake her head, and paused. "Yeah...and the end goal would've been to make sure she didn't get snatched by whoever took her. Like she did because I wasn't there to help."

Darius smiled. "And the whole time, while you were training and solving her puzzles and strengthening your magic, half your mind would've been filled with all the various ways you'd help her. If you'd known...whoops." His thick fingers flittered through the air in front of his face. "There goes your focus. Not all of it, no. Merely enough to keep you from truly understanding the things Greta wanted you to know."

Again, she opened her mouth to argue but couldn't find anything to say. *Oh, my God. He's right.*

"Woah." Romeo puffed a breath out and nodded quickly. "This guy doesn't even know you, Lil, and he still knows you."

She eyed him sideways and pursed her lips.

"Well, I know Greta," the man added. "And in all my years, I've never met another witch like her. Until you, girl."

"Okay, so exactly how well do you know my mom?" She frowned at the man. "You keep saying you know her. But she's gone—is somewhere else—and you're still here." His smile faded into a frown of curiosity mixed with a little pain. "So how exactly were you helping her?"

"Me?" He raised his eyebrows. "Your mom and I fought together more times than I can count. We followed this trail and exchanged ideas and theories about what all this really is." He glanced at the papers and notes and photos cluttering his apartment. "Mostly, I did this with her."

"What?"

"Talked things through, girl. Slowed down to really look at all the pieces before jumping to conclusions. A sounding board, I guess."

Romeo smirked. "It sounds like Darius is your mom's version of me, Lil."

Lily froze and closed her eyes. *God, I hope not. That would make this...way more awkward.* She tried to shake the image of her mom and this giant man doing everything that she and Romeo did out of her mind completely.

Finally, she looked at Darius again. "So hypothetically, you know everything she knows about this black heron...thing, right?"

"Not hypothetically. As far as I know, the only information I don't have is whatever she discovered after they took her."

"Why'd they take her and not you?"

Darius took a deep breath, held her gaze, and released in a long sigh. "Because I couldn't keep going. And much like you, I imagine, your mother doesn't let anyone or anything scare her away from doing what's right."

Lily glanced at Romeo. He shifted forward over his knees and propped his forearms on his thighs before he nodded at her. "Okay." She looked at Darius and fixed him with a stern look. "So tell me what you guys found."

TWENTY-ONE

"When Greta discovered the transference artifact, it turned the non-magical archaeological community almost on its head. She dug that thing up—"

"In Egypt." Lily nodded. "I know that much."

"Right. It's a magical artifact, of course, from the ancient Egyptian witches who helped build the pyramids. Something like it was also used for the standing stones like Stonehenge. A few of the original statues on Easter Island. One or two Mayan temples. Those artifacts...drew certain energies from the people in those long-gone communities—magicals and non-magicals both—and funneled it into the creation of these wondrous pieces of architecture and history."

Romeo frowned. "It's not something the whole non-magical world would be very happy to hear about."

"No. Definitely not. And Greta..." Darius laughed. "She was brilliant. I'm sure there was some compulsion charm woven into every interview and public event she gave when she found it. No one seemed to question the fact that this first-time archaeologist no one had ever heard of before knew exactly what she'd found. She told the world that this artifact tied the ancient Egyptians directly to ancient Mesopotamia, the first and oldest documented civilization in the world. I don't remember the specifics of it, but your mother could convince a blind man that he can actually see."

"Yeah. If she ever wanted to."

He smirked at her. "It brought her a lot of fame, this discovery, as you know. It got her tenured at College of Charleston. And that fame spread through the archeological community all over the world. And, of course, the rest of us magicals couldn't stop hearing about it. You turned on the TV or the radio, and there was Greta, talking about her discovery and her plans to find more artifacts like that one. I was intrigued, actually. I'd heard some things from a few colleagues of mine who'd seen her on dig sites. They all knew she was a witch and hid the magical part of herself from the world with such a glaring spotlight on her. I wanted to know more from her, magical to magical, you might say. So I set up an interview."

"And she told you what she'd really found." Lily stuck her hands in her lap and leaned over her crossed legs.

"Not during the interview, no. She gave a fantastic interview, I have to say, and then she wanted to go completely off the record. So, I agreed. That's when she told me what it really was. What that artifact had done for the ancient Egyptians and that others like it existed elsewhere around the world. The first time I met her in person, Lily, she somehow trusted me enough to tell me, that very day, that she thought someone was trying to find the other transference artifacts. Not to illuminate more knowledge within the magical community about our past or to document the world we know for posterity. Your mother thought these people wanted what she'd found to use it. In our day and age, with technology and video and the internet, can you imagine the repercussions of summoning strong magic with something like that."

"Not good." Romeo pursed his lips.

Darius snorted. "That's an understatement."

"How'd she know someone was looking for the other artifacts?" she asked, nibbling on her bottom lip.

"Apparently, someone broke into her hotel room in Egypt and went through all her things. From what she told me, they tore the place apart. She'd taken the artifact with her to a peer dinner that night, and that was the only reason she was able to take it back home with her and... well, it made her famous."

"Okay..." She frowned. "And how did that lead to all this?"

"Honestly, Lily, I've had to chalk it up to Greta's inability to let something go once she's curious enough to be suspicious. I think she had to know why someone would want to use one of these artifacts. Whoever it was stopped following her once she donated her find to the Smithsonian, but she kept digging—into them. Of course, her money and her new prestige funded all of it. And when she found out that it wasn't only one person or one group in an isolated location, she reached out to me again and asked for my help."

"She found the black heron."

"Yes." Darius nodded. "Five years ago. Greta tracked down the witch who'd broken into her hotel room and discovered his affiliation with them. She never told me what happened to the man, and I never asked. But she kept digging. We kept digging together. When one question was answered, three more appeared in its place." The man shook his head and his long, thick ponytail swished across his back. "I swear, it was like trying to run up an avalanche—"

"Darius." Lily pressed her lips together while she waited for him to pull himself out of his reverie. When he finally looked at her, she nodded. "What did you find?"

He took a sharp, hesitant breath. His nose twitched in a quick grimace before he swallowed. "The Black Heron."

"Obviously." She gestured toward everything in his apartment. "What is it?"

"That's a capital B and a Capital H, girl. The Black Heron Society."

"What is it with all these secret societies and magical Orders?" Romeo grunted with annoyance. "As far as we've seen, they don't actually do anything but loan out their sigils."

"No." Darius shook his head. "The Black Heron Society isn't sanctioned by the Council. As far as any of us could determine, the only people who know about the Black Heron are its members...and us."

She drummed her fingers on her crossed legs. "I'm

gonna take a wild guess here and say that this society isn't contained to a single continent like the Order of North or Cadre Europa, is it?"

"They're all over the world, Lily."

"And the black heron we've seen everywhere is their sigil then. The heron on all of this stuff you have in here." He merely nodded and she sighed. "So how often do they leave that sigil behind after they kidnap someone or murder witches in broad daylight?"

Romeo reached out and put a gentle hand on her shoulder. "Lily—"

"I know." She closed her eyes. "I know. That part of this whole thing really pisses me off, though."

"They didn't use to." Darius stared at her with wide eyes. "Your mom and I spent years on a trail that was already cold more often than not. But yes, they now seem to be leaving their sigil everywhere like some kind of sick, gloating signature. And I know it's getting worse."

"A lot worse." The werewolf grimaced. "Quickly."

"You've seen it, then?"

"Seen it. Heard of it. Tried to stop it. Yeah." Lily shook her head. "We fought the Wisemen at Ichacál—"

"You what?"

Romeo nodded. "They were keeping magicals in cages beneath the temple. Not only witches, either."

"We got them out. And then we had to fight the Wisemen, which I didn't really have a problem with after hearing they'd been sucking the magic out of all the people they'd locked up down there."

Darius cleared his throat. "And how'd you manage that?"

The couple exchanged a quick glance. "We had a necromancer with us." She shrugged. "Well, a little different. Neron called himself a death witch."

His mouth dropped open. "Unbelievable."

Romeo leaned forward with wide eyes. "It was awesome."

"But it wouldn't have even been necessary without the Wisemen or what they were doing to those prisoners. Or the Black Heron." She returned her focus to the other man. "What are they doing?"

He sighed. "The timing couldn't have been more fragile. I still can't decide which one caused the other. Our discovery or Greta's...disappearance. The day we found the answer to your question was the last day I saw your mother. Right here, before she left Romania and went back to Ichacál." The man leaned his head back against the wall and stared at the ceiling—the only place in his apartment that hadn't been touched by the notes and clippings and scribbles.

I really wish he'd get to the point already. Lily bit her lip and stared at him. *If it hurts him this much to think about her going missing, he has to tell us.* Rather than voice her impatience, she waited.

The huge man grunted and shook his head. "The Black Heron is behind all the kidnappings and unexplained murders of magicals over the last year, as far as we can tell. We think they found one of those transference artifacts—or something like it. It could be only a spell, but it's powerful enough to turn the entire world inside out. And it needs to be powered by insane amounts of magic in turn."

"That's what the Wisemen were doing to those people under the temple," she whispered. "Stealing their magic to power a bigger spell?"

"Essentially, yes. The murders are the same, mind you. Only those magicals who lost their lives lost their magic in the process. There's a..." Darius scowled. "A nasty process to draw someone's magic from their very existence before they die. There's more than one way to do it, but it always leaves a...toxic signature behind, if you will."

Lily glanced at Romeo. "That purple...stuff. In Paris."

"And the fungus." He nodded. "That woman at the rally went on and on about the fungus."

"So they need all this extra magic to do what? What's the spell?"

Darius gritted his teeth and swallowed, his nostrils flaring. "Transference."

"What?"

"All that magic will power the spell that will directly... redistribute it."

The werewolf snorted impatiently. "Into what?"

"The Black Heron. All its members. Anyone magical who can shell out enough money to make it worth the society's troubles. Who knows? Maybe even non-magicals, if this makes enough waves."

"That's why they don't care about who sees them, isn't it?" She smoothed the hair away from her face.

"It's possible. Although I don't think they care about

anything but getting what they need to finish the job. Whether or not non-magicals are involved might as well be irrelevant. And this isn't only a magical boost, either. If the Black Heron completes this spell, it's all magic available to all magicals."

Romeo took a breath, paused, and looked confused once again. "You lost me with that one."

"Imagine Lily using the same death magic as the witch who fought with you at the temple. Or a warlock who could shift into any shape he chose at will. Or even you, Romeo. A werewolf with the ability to cast spells as powerful as any witch."

"Jeez."

Lily glanced quickly at him again. "We saw that, though. Didn't we?"

"Saw what?"

"A werewolf with magic."

His eyes widened. "Holy shit, we did!" He leaned past her to gape at Darius. "Did these people already learn how to do that?"

The man shrugged. "I wouldn't be surprised if they managed it in bits and pieces. Trial runs, right? Was the werewolf you saw connected at all with the Black Heron?"

"Oh, yeah." His upper lip twitched in a snarl. "He worked for a man with a giant black heron painted in his office."

"Well, then, it makes sense."

"Wait." Lily glanced at all the drawings and articles and scribble notes on the walls. "Why did my mom go back to Ichacál?"

"She thought that was where the Black Heron was taking all their kidnapped magicals. That they were planning to cast the final spell there. She'd found the cages below the temple already. When we realized what was happening, she was dead set on going back. I tried to convince her to stay here and to wait until we knew more." Darius closed his eyes. "Even when I knew it was impossible."

"Well, that's what got her caught, then." She sighed. "It's the first time I've ever known my mom to be wrong. I know she was there. One of the witches we helped escape said he knew her. That he'd seen her there before they... took her somewhere else."

"I see." The man pressed his lips together. "So wherever the Black Heron is gathering right now, it's not in Guatemala."

"Not at Ichacál, at least." Her shoulders sagged when she realized what that meant. "So you don't have any idea where they took her then, do you?"

"No, Lily. I'm sorry."

She scoffed. "Don't be sorry. Help me find her."

The huge man's eyes glistened beneath his dark brows, and he shook his head very slowly. "I can't."

"Why not? You helped her get where she is now. I'm not blaming you, but you're as responsible for finding her and getting her away from these people as I am."

"It's too much, girl." He frowned at her although he still looked like he might cry. "They're everywhere. It's so much worse than any of us thought. We had six other people tracking them with us, do you understand? I'm the only one who ever came back to this apartment. And I'm not anywhere near as powerful a witch as your mother. If Greta couldn't stop them, I..." He shook his head again. "There's nothing I can do."

"There is always something you can do." Lily stared at him in disbelief. "It might be easier and safer to try to convince yourself otherwise, but that's simply being a coward."

"Yeah." Darius stared at the carpet beneath his feet. "I realized that a while ago."

I should drag him with us. Make him fight to find her. She had to force her anger down again before she accepted that wouldn't solve anything. "Well, if you're not gonna come with us and at least try to look for my mom, the least you can do is answer my other questions."

"If I have any answers at all, Lily, they're yours." He didn't look at her and his cheeks reddened slightly above his beard.

She looked at Romeo, who chewed on the inside of his cheek and had absolutely no idea where she was headed. "Okay." She pointed at the picture of Ichacál on the wall again. "What does that mean?"

"What?"

"What she wrote. 'They have wings. So do I.'"

The man shook his head. "That first part is the Black Heron. I think. The rest of it... Lily, I don't know what wings she's talking about. I'm sorry."

Tense and frustrated, she stood from the couch and paced a few times over the worn carpet and the scattered notes scattered across it. Her gaze landed on another note with her mom's handwriting. *What circle?* Those two words reminded her of the last note her mom had left her at the healing temple, sealed in a Ziplock bag in the hole with the key to Darius' apartment. She turned to face him. "Then I really hope this rings some kinda bell for you, 'cause it's all I have left."

Darius nodded but didn't say another word.

"Every time I found what she wanted me to see, my mom left me a message. A note that wouldn't make sense to anyone else—except maybe you. The last one was basically a dead giveaway that she knew she was gonna be caught. But the end? She wrote..." She closed her eyes and pulled up the memory of the note she'd stuffed under old t-shirts in her shirt drawer in the Winnie. In all honesty, she didn't need the real thing to remember. "'Don't judge anyone by who they say they are. You can find everything you need to know by looking into the eyes.' That part I can't work out." Opening her eyes, she looked at him and found his eyes widening as he stared at the floor. "Does that mean anything to you?"

Slowly, he looked up at her with a startled expression. "Actually...I think it might."

TWENTY-TWO

"There's a tribe here in Romania. Witches." Darius lowered his head. "And Romani."

"What's that?" Romeo asked.

"Well, you'd call 'em gypsies."

He frowned. "Those still exist?"

"Oh, very much so. When they're witches too, they operate a little differently than non-magical Romani. Some things are the same but many other things aren't." He glanced at Lily who stood in front of him. "They call themselves the Ochiului. The Eye."

"Okay. I definitely see the connection to what my mom wrote."

"She spoke to them at least once. Maybe twice. I, uh...I couldn't go with her." He forced out a cough. "And yes, before you feel compelled to say it, I couldn't go because I honestly didn't want to run the risk of finding myself speared through the gut with Ochiului magic. I know what my limits are when it comes to bravery."

Lily licked her lips and frowned. *It's so weird to see a guy as big as this openly admit something like that.* "So, where are they?"

"A few brothers run a convenience store on the south end of District Five. But they...wait. No." He shook his head. "Lily, do not go looking for answers with these people. I don't know what your mother was able to offer them in exchange for their time, but they always have a price. It's not worth it."

"Yes, it is." She turned toward him head-on and clenched her fists. Her burned fingers erupted in sharp pain at the pressure and she hissed in a breath before she loosened that hand a little. "I have no problem paying them if they can help me find my mom."

Darius glanced at the werewolf with an almost desperate expression. "You can't let her go after these people."

"No one lets Lily do anything." Romeo stood from the couch. "Especially not me. But I'll be with her if you're that worried about what happens."

"Of course I'm worried." The huge man glanced away from them and shook his head, completely overwhelmed as his fear and his loyalty to Greta Antony battled for his attention. "You don't—" He looked at them and sighed. "You'll do it anyway with or without me, won't you?"

"Well, I don't want to." Lily offered him the only smile she could, which was small and strained. "But yeah. If I have to."

He took a deep breath. "Fine. I'll give you the address

to their store. But they don't know me, so I can't help you with introductions."

"We don't need introductions."

Romeo pulled his phone from his back pocket and nodded. "What's the address?" The man gave it to them and he typed it in.

"Thank you," she said and held the man's gaze. "We'll find her."

"Oh, I have no doubt of that, girl. I can't get right with what might happen when you do." They turned to head to the door. "Wait." He grunted and pushed himself up from the floor. "Let me take a look at your hand before you go. A burn like that will only slow you down."

"I'll be fine." She smiled. "We have a First-Aid kit."

"Well, I promise it can't do what I can for you." Darius nodded. "Please. It's the least I can do." He beckoned her toward him.

She shrugged. "Okay...thanks."

When she stopped only a few feet in front of him, he wiggled his fingers and nodded at her hand. "Let's see." She raised her hand and gritted her teeth against the pain of it when she uncurled her fingers as far as she could. The man took it in both of his and looked at her with a tender smile. "It might feel a little...odd. But I promise it won't hurt."

"I'd be fine if it did." She smirked.

He nodded, set the back of her hand in one palm, and covered her burns with the other. As he lifted her hand toward his lowered head—he had to bend considerably to get low enough—he whispered an incantation she couldn't hear. Then, he brought her hand inches away from his lips and the whispered words became an altogether different sound.

Lily stared at the man's mouth, which didn't seem to move at all now despite the sound coming from it. *Is he... purring?* A yellow glow flecked with green sparks brightened between his hands and a wave of energy pulsed through her fingers. *It feels like bees. Yeah, that's a weird connection.* The purring sound from his mouth grew a little louder—or from within his throat, she couldn't tell. When he stopped, the light faded.

Darius closed his eyes and took a deep breath. He opened them again, looked at her, and released her hand. "It may be another few hours until it's...well, as good as new, I suppose."

"What did you—oh, my God."

"Are you okay?" Romeo asked warily and stared at the huge man who'd let her go.

"Yeah, I'm...I'm fine." She opened her burned hand fully. It wasn't burned at all and only faint pink patches of healed skin remained where she'd been magically held by the key in the lock. She gave a few experimental wiggles and grinned at the man in front of her. "You're a healer."

He chuckled. "It's that surprising, huh?"

"Well." She leaned back and couldn't help scrutinizing his massive frame. "You look more like a Viking, honestly."

"Ha! That's still a compliment."

"A purring healer." Romeo folded his arms and smirked.

"I've learned a thing or two from really big cats, yes." He raised his eyebrows at the skeptical werewolf. "They're actually remarkable healers themselves, too."

"Okay..." He tilted his head at the man and raised his eyebrows. "Next time I see a...big cat, I'll hafta say thanks."

"Yeah, me too." Lily stuck her healed hand out toward him and nodded. "Thank you. For everything."

"I'm glad Greta led you here." He took her hand and shook it once. "For however hard the journey was."

"It's nothing we can't handle."

He hummed and squinted at her with the barest hint of another smile. "I believe you. Good luck, girl." They released their handshake, and she turned toward her friend. "When you find your mom—"

"Don't worry." She glanced at him over her shoulder and grinned. "She'll hear how much you helped us." Darius laughed before they stepped out of his cramped apartment and into the equally cramped hallway beyond.

Romeo closed the door behind them and sighed. "That was...interesting."

"Yep. I wish he could've told us more, but we definitely have enough to keep going." They headed down the hallway toward the elevators.

"So. Let's go back to the Winnie and get a few hours' sleep. We can head out to this Romani convenience store in the morning."

"What?" She sent him an incredulous glance and shook her head vehemently. "No."

"It's almost eleven-thirty, Lil—"

"And that convenience store's...what? Twenty minutes

away? There's no way I'll sleep without talking to these people first. I'm not tired, anyway."

Merely the mention of being tired made him yawn. "Not even a little."

"Nope." She chuckled. "You know, I haven't actually had an energy drink since we first headed to Canada."

"Oh, yeah." He shrugged. "It's been a while."

They stopped at the rickety, most likely failing elevator and she punched the call button to go down. "We can always stop and buy you something if you feel like you're fading too much to handle a quick talk with a couple of gypsy witches."

"No. I'll be fine." He smirked at her as the elevator clanked toward them. "I'm not sure I wanna test energy drinks in Romania for the first time this late at night."

"Okay. I'm gonna hold you to it. No falling asleep in a convenience store." The elevator doors shrieked open and shuddered the whole way when they slid open.

Romeo stepped inside first and held the doors open for her, just in case. "Hey, this'll be way too exciting to fall asleep, right? Gypsies." He shook his head as she pressed the button for the first floor, then released the doors. They stuck again a few inches away from each other before they banged shut. "I can't believe it."

"Really?" she scoffed at him and couldn't help but laugh. "Out of everything Darius told us, that's what you can't believe?"

"Come on. It's the only thing I haven't actually seen with my own eyes yet."

She folded her arms and smirked at the closed elevator doors as they lurched into their descent through building five. "That's about to change."

TWENTY-THREE

"Okay, admittedly, I'm a little surprised." Lily frowned at him as she pulled the keys from her purse to unlock the Winnie's driver-side door. "By what?"

"That no one tried to...you know." He nodded at the RV. "Mess with our killer adventuremobile."

She laughed and opened the door. "That's probably 'cause she doesn't look like a killer adventuremobile."

"Not yet." He smirked.

"And really, how tempted would you be to try to steal something out of an RV with dents and char marks on the outside?"

"That's a good point." He caught hold of the side of the door and hoisted himself up. With a quick hop, he skirted the driver's seat and scrambled over the center console. "Hey, why haven't you fixed those up, anyway?"

"Maybe so no one thinks there's anything in here

worth stealing." She pulled herself up into the driver's seat and shut the door.

He laughed. "Except for a few slightly diminished bags of gold coins."

"Well, I'm not gonna broadcast that fun fact." She stuck the keys in the ignition and started the engine. "Honestly, there's been so much going on, I didn't even think about it until you brought it up."

"It is one...okay, two or three upgrades we can make for absolutely free." She chuckled and shook her head. He leaned toward her over the back of the driver's seat. "Do you want me to drive?"

"Uh...no. No, I think I'm good. I'm feeling a little antsy, honestly. Driving's a good thing to focus on."

"Okay..." He slid into the passenger seat and sighed at all the new space for his legs to enjoy. "But if you start feeling too antsy, lemme know."

"We're merely driving somewhere else in the same city. And you look way too comfortable there anyway."

"I am." He grinned. "Sure, we had that guy cut all this space out a week ago, but I've only been able to enjoy it on the road for two days. I'm gonna enjoy it a little longer before I start takin' it for granted."

Lily sighed as she buckled her seatbelt. "I can't believe it's only been two days in Europe. It honestly feels like two weeks."

"Well, maybe that's a good sign." Romeo buckled his seatbelt too and smiled at her. "We're getting close."

"Yeah. We're not done yet, though." She turned the

headlights on and put the Winnie in drive. "Okay, naviga-tor. I need your skills again for our next short trip."

He laughed. "Aw. You haven't called me that in a while."

"Supply and demand, Romeo. Three weeks on a freighter doesn't leave much demand for navigators."

"It's a good thing I stuck around, then. Otherwise, you'd be out of supply too."

She snorted. "Yeah. That's the reason I'm glad you stuck around." Slowly, she pulled the Winnie through the parking lot and out of Olt River Alley toward Strada Tiparnitei.

The drive to the address Darius had given them took only about ten minutes. "Oh, man." She squinted at the storefront as they approached down the street. "I didn't even think to check if they were open, first."

"Huh. I should've thought of that."

"I guess operating hours kinda go out the window on trips like this." She pulled into the parking lot outside the conve-nience store and grinned when she saw the bright yellow-and-red *Open* sign in the front window. "Maybe they don't matter for Romani witches running a convenience store, either."

"Or maybe they're simply a twenty-four-hour store, Lil. Those exist."

She shot him a warning glance, then smirked. "Let's go check it out."

They got out and headed to the door. "Perfect Grocery, huh?" Romeo squinted at the marquee sign in dark-green letters. "It's probably a much better name in Romanian."

"It still gets the point across." Lily opened the door and a string of tiny brass bells tinkled at the movement. "Is there anything you want to get? We should probably also buy something, right?"

"Right." He gazed around at the short, low aisles found in convenience stores across the board. "I wonder what kinda beer they have."

"Well, if nothing else, I hope it's the beer-flavored kind."

He huffed out a laugh and shook his head as they headed toward the back of the store and the beer cooler. "I literally have no idea what any of this is."

"Pick one." She glanced around to see if anyone was watching them. *Yeah, that's not suspicious-looking at all.* No one else at midnight had come to the Perfect Grocery for last-minute needs. *At least we won't freak anyone else out when we try to talk to the owners.*

"Okay. This...Zaganu looks good. Let's give it a shot."

"Great. Come on." She took his arm and steered him toward the register at the door. He let her pull him along and studied the six-pack in his hand, hoping it was something he could stomach.

A man with dark hair, dark eyes, and incredibly pale skin sat in a cheap, folding metal chair behind the register counter, his feet crossed and propped up on another chair exactly like it. He didn't look up from the comic book in his hands, even when Romeo set the beers down on the counter.

Lily cleared her throat but still, they received no response. "Excuse me?"

The man lowered the comic book slowly and glanced at her.

"Um...hi. We'd like to..." She pointed at the beer.

"Buy some beer," Romeo finished and exchanged a confused glance with her.

He sniffed and turned his attention to his comic book. "Twenty lei."

"Okay." She withdrew her wallet from her purse and covertly tapped her finger against the euro bills she hadn't exchanged anywhere. The bills quadrupled and almost spilled from her wallet but she caught them and counted out the twenty. "Here." When the man still ignored her, she put them on the counter and slid them toward him. He grunted but didn't lift a finger to take her money. *Great business practice, guy.* She put her wallet in her purse and leaned forward over the counter. "I'd also like to talk to the owner. Are they here tonight?"

"Yeah."

"Can you tell him—or her—that I'd like to speak to them? Please."

His eyes moved over the frames in his comic book and nowhere else. "So, talk."

"Oh, you're the owner?"

He grunted.

"Great." She glanced at Romeo, who could only offer her a clueless shrug. Finally, she put both hands on the counter, leaned forward again, and lowered her voice in what felt like exactly the right amount of mystery and force. "Then I'd like to talk to you about the Ochiului."

If the man hadn't been as unresponsive this whole

time, it would've been far easier to see him pause in his reading. But she caught the way his eyes stopped abruptly and his hands tightened their hold on the comic book. *Huh. I hit the nail right on the head, apparently.*

Finally, he lowered his feet from the second chair and set the comic book on it instead. Slowly, he stood, approached her, and mirrored her stance when he placed both hands on the counter and leaned much farther forward than she did. His face was so close to hers—only mere inches—that she could see the odd streaks of yellow in his dark-brown eyes. "Do you have an appointment?"

"No."

"Then who gave you that name?"

Despite the awful attempt to mask his really bad breath with something bubblegum-flavored, she held her ground and met his gaze. "A friend."

The man scowled at her. "Friends make introductions to other friends. But there's no one here to introduce us. Explain that."

"Well, this friend is a little indisposed right now." Lily pursed her lips and let that sink in a moment. "Her name's Margaret Antony."

The man's gaze flicked from one of hers to the other before he slapped a hand on the lei bills she'd set there for their beer, slid them toward him, and stood fully. Still staring at her, he pocketed the money and glanced briefly at Romeo. "Wait." He walked away toward the open office behind the counter, stepped inside, and closed the door.

"That was easy."

He glanced at her companion. "Yeah, right."

They waited for perhaps two minutes before the office door opened again. The man emerged to stand against the far wall behind the counter and a short, rail-thin woman with a ridiculous amount of black hair piled atop her head in a mess of wild curls followed him. She stepped up to the counter and studied her newest customers. For a few seconds, she picked at her teeth with a long, gold-painted fingernail, then smacked her lips and jerked her chin at Lily. "Margaret Antony sent you to us, huh?"

I'd better be careful with what I say here. And how I say it. "I heard she came to talk to you a few months ago. You and your people."

"My people." The woman nodded. "We are very open with each other, of course. Strangers? Not so much. What do you want from us?"

"Only information."

"The same information your mother sought?"

She blinked and forced herself to swallow the sudden lump in her throat. *So much for anonymity.*

The woman chuckled, her voice low and dark and menacing. "It doesn't take magic of any kind to see who you are, child."

"My name is Lily."

"Lily. Yes. And you?" Her dark eyes settled unnaturally on the werewolf.

"Romeo."

"Hmm. I can't give you the information you seek, Lily. Nor can my people. But we can take you to a place where you might succeed in finding answers."

"I would be really grateful if you took me there." She

nodded at the woman although she couldn't even pretend to smile. Still, she had a feeling she wouldn't have been able to even if she could feel that now was definitely not the right time for it.

"Yes. Gratitude is...nice." The woman spread her arms. "But it won't be enough to get you where you want to go. That requires a different kind of payment."

"Like what?"

"Ah. Things being as they are around here nowadays..." The woman shrugged and raised a finger. Its long, gold-painted nail glinted in the harsh lights of the convenience store. "You must agree to pay before I can tell you the price."

"Then I agree." Lily nodded. "Whatever your price is, I'll pay it."

"Lily," Romeo whispered and stepped toward her, "are you sure that's—"

"Done." The woman grinned. "We'll leave in the morning."

"I don't need to wait." She took a deep breath. "I can leave now."

"No, you can't. You need to sleep." She flung her hands in the air. "I need to sleep. Everyone needs sleep, don't they? Especially you, Lily. Andrei!"

The man, who now leaned against the wall with his arms folded, straightened. "Yeah."

"Go tell Mihai that he's behind the counter until Tuesday. You're coming with us." She didn't once break away from Lily's gaze.

Andrei nodded. "Yeah, okay."

The woman nodded at Lily, and her upper lip curled in not quite a grin and not quite a snarl. "You can call me Loana. Meet us here at seven o'clock tomorrow morning. I'll take you to the rest of my people."

"Thank you."

"You too, Romeo."

He looked startled. "I'm sorry?"

"Don't be. Verbal agreements are very important, yes? I'm inviting you too." Loana inclined her head toward Lily in a very clear warning. "No one else."

"Agreed."

"Good. Now get out." She laughed and her black curls flopped on her head when she threw it back.

Finally allowing herself a small smile, Lily nudged Romeo with her elbow and turned toward the door. He took the six-pack off the counter, raised it at Loana with a nod, and followed.

"Wait." They both turned at the harsh bark of the woman's voice. "Did you two come here in that giant thing out there?" She nodded out the window at the Winnie parked outside.

He raised his eyebrows. "We sure did."

Loana shook her head and gave them a dismissive wave. "Stay here. Pull around back. We don't have any hookups, but you already bought something. Bathrooms and parking lots are for customers only." With a chuckle, the woman stepped into the office and left the door wide open.

Andrei sat on the metal chair, retrieved his comic book, and propped his feet up to resume reading without another word.

The couple left without saying anything else, either. The bells jingled on the door when it opened and closed again behind them, and they climbed into the Winnie.

When Lily pulled it around to the parking lot behind the Perfect Grocery, she finally felt like talking again. "That was one of the weirdest conversations I've ever had."

"I know." Romeo scratched his head. "And I feel like we've had countless weird conversations with people."

"That woman is...I dunno."

"Terrifying?"

She laughed. "Yeah, I guess that's one way to put it. Where am I even supposed to park here?"

"I'd go with as far away from the building as possible. I think these people live here."

"What?"

He pointed out his window at the two-story building attached to the other side of the convenience store. "She didn't say anything about going home. But I bet it's that house."

"Oh, good. We're camping out at a terrifying gypsy woman's house attached to her business. What a fun night." She parked the Winnie in front of the neon-orange mesh fence at the back of the lot and locked the doors before she turned off the engine, just in case.

"Hey, I can think of at least one good thing about it." He smirked at her. "Besides the fact that we don't have to drive any more today."

"And what's that?"

"I bet the rest of the neighborhood thinks she's even more terrifying. No one's gonna mess with us."

She unbuckled her seatbelt. "Yeah. I guess there's that."

TWENTY-FOUR

A car horn blared from somewhere really far away—followed by loud, fast, unintelligible yelling—and woke Lily the next morning. She groaned, rolled over to flop her arm over Romeo's waist, and his phone alarm went off. It took her a minute to remember why he'd set an alarm in the first place.

"Hey." She nudged him in the back. "Romeo. Your alarm." After shaking him a little more vigorously, he finally stirred and rolled onto his back.

"My alarm," he muttered.

"Turn it off." She shook him again.

"Yeah, yeah, yeah..." His hand slapped down on the built-in bedside table, and he fumbled sleepily with his phone for a few seconds before he finally managed to turn the alarm off. He groaned and dragged his hands down his face. "Not enough sleep."

"What time is it?"

"Six-thirty."

"Okay. Let's get up. I do not wanna ruin this chance with the Ochiului by being late. Like, at all." She pushed herself off the pillow and sat there for a few seconds, her eyelids heavy.

"Oh, yeah." He rolled over again to face her. "Romani witches taking us to see their people." A huge yawn overtook him before he stretched all the way out on the bed and made a noise that sounded more like a growl than anything else. "Let's do this." He slapped the covers and bolted upright to shake his head vigorously.

She stared at him. "I don't know how you wake up that fast."

"Hey, I'm excited." He snorted and crawled toward the foot of the bed. Then, he came around to her side and tossed the covers off her. "This helps too. Get up. Let's go. You said it yourself. We do not want to be late."

"Okay, okay. You don't—hey." She glared at him but couldn't help but laugh when he struck an unusually comical pose of surrender. "You don't have to pick me up out of bed. I got it."

"All right." He rifled through the wardrobe and grabbed a shirt and a pair of jeans to get dressed. "I'm gonna go see if I can buy energy drinks from our lovely hosts. And maybe something to eat. Ooh. Maybe they have coffee."

Lily stood and yawned. "Maybe."

"I'm literally more excited than you are about everything right now, aren't I?"

She chuckled. "Go. I'll be more awake when you get back."

At 6:55, he opened the Winnie's side door. "Sorry!" he shouted.

Startled, she leapt up from where she'd knelt beside the kitchen table. Her head cracked against the underside of it, and she grunted and covered her head with both hands.

"Oh, ouch. Sorry for that too." He moved quickly across the Winnie and emptied everything he'd bought from Perfect Grocery onto the table. "Are you okay?"

Lily stuck the blue stone she'd pulled from behind the loose slat in the bench into the front pocket of her jean shorts. That done, she crawled out from under the table, scowled, and rubbed her head. "Yeah, I will be."

"Coffee might help." He offered her one, and she grinned.

"You found some."

"I did. Sorry about the wait time, though. That Mihai guy? He's slower at the counter than Andrei if that's even possible. And much creepier."

She took a sip of the coffee and sighed. "That's it. Why was he creepy?"

"He kept staring at me for a really long time before he'd answer any questions or ring me up or anything. And he kept leaving to help Andrei and Loana with random stuff. I think they're packing."

"Huh."

"Are you okay?"

"Yeah. My brain hasn't turned on completely yet. What time is it?"

"Oh!" He snatched his coffee off the table and took her

hand. "It's almost seven. Come on." They hurried out the Winnie's side door and found both Andrei and Loana emerging from the Perfect Grocery's back door. "What were you doing under the table?"

She sent him a sideways glance. "I found a new panel under the bench. It comes up easily, actually."

"For the"—he leaned toward her and whispered—"bags of gold?"

"Yep. That thing we probably shouldn't mention in public." *And the one valuable thing I have that didn't come from my mom.* Her hand went briefly to her front pocket. "So we have a new hiding place, by the way."

"Okay. That's good to know."

"And I counted it." She glanced at him and mouthed, "The gold."

He snorted. "You did, huh?"

"Hey, only for an idea of how much we actually have left. She said there was a price for their information. I wanna make sure it's enough."

"It had better be. We've barely used a fifth of it to get us this far." He held his coffee cup toward her.

"To thrifty boondocking." She tapped her cup against his.

"Oh, now it's boondocking?"

She smirked. "Hush. I'm fairly sure we're about to be given detailed instructions on what not to do." Loana and Andrei met them in the middle of the back parking lot, and Lily took a final sip of coffee before the conversation started. *Something tells me she doesn't appreciate not having everyone's full attention.*

"Good morning." The woman smiled and spread her arms. "You two are right on time. So we're off to a good start, aren't we?" Standing slightly behind her, Andrei squinted at their pseudo-guests.

"Thanks for letting us park here overnight." Lily nodded at her. "It made things a little easier for us."

"Yes, it did. There are so many great things about taking your home with you wherever you go. The rest of it's simply crap." She stuck her tongue out and blew a raspberry at them. Lily blinked in surprise, and she roared with laughter. It cut off abruptly, and she fixed her with a level gaze. "You'll follow us. Three hours tops. Don't pull over. Don't stop for anyone. Stay close behind us. We like to go fast. Got it?" They both nodded. "Good. We'll make... another kind of caravan, won't we?" Loana glanced at the still expressionless Andrei, barked out a laugh, and patted her stomach. "Wait for us to get all our things out here. Then, we'll leave." The woman walked away toward the two-story building attached to her convenience store, leaving Andrei with their guests.

The man folded his arms and stared blankly at them.

Romeo cleared his throat. "When she says caravan... does she mean like actual wagons, or..."

Andrei sniggered and shook his head. "You outsiders are all the same. Hung up on all your outdated stories."

"I was only—" He shrugged. "Only wondering. Because we have actually driven behind a wagon caravan before."

His eyes widened. "What?"

"Yeah."

Lily bit back a smirk. "In Mexico."

The man raised his eyebrow and glanced from one to the other before he gave them a feral grin that exposed a quick flash of a gold-capped tooth. "Well, we drive cars." Right on cue, a bright-blue Dacia Logan reversed into the parking lot from the other side of Loana's home. The woman pressed the horn twice, and he nodded toward the Winnie. "Time to go." He turned and walked toward the Dacia, apparently unaffected by Loana's urgency with the horn.

"That's our cue."

"I still wanna drive," Lily said as they hurried toward the Winnie's side door and tried not to spill her coffee all over herself.

"Are you sure?"

"Yeah." She opened the door and scrambled up the steps. "I drive fast too."

The Romani woman hadn't exaggerated at all about her speed. The minute they reached E-85 and headed south out of Bucharest, her blue Dacia accelerated a little over ninety miles an hour. Lily floored the gas pedal and still had a little trouble getting the Winnie up to speed. She'd never taken it that fast before, so the one minute of bumpy driving surprised her until the highway evened out again. When the RV settled again, she accelerated a little more to catch up with their guide through Romania.

"Do either one of us know if ol' Winnie here can handle going this fast for three hours?" Romeo sucked in a weary breath through his teeth.

"I guess we'll find out, won't we?" She snorted at his wide-eyed concern. "I'm fairly sure she can handle it."

"Okay..."

"What's the speed limit here, anyway?"

"Um..." They both searched the highway for a sign. "Oh. There. A hundred and thirty kilometers an hour." Romeo clenched his eyes shut to think. "I think it's like one point six kilometers for every mile, so..." He gave up and grabbed his phone instead. "Probably eighty miles an hour."

She glanced at the speedometer, which had barely poked above the ninety-miles-an-hour line. "So, not too fast." She kept her foot poised over the gas pedal and tried to keep the same two-car-lengths distance between them and Loana's car. "This feels much faster than ninety."

"We're in a Winnebago, Lil."

"I know. Cross your fingers that she doesn't start doing something weird on the highway. I wouldn't put it past her, honestly."

"Fingers crossed." He glanced at his phone again. "Do you wanna put some music on?"

"Uh...yeah. Something fast and furious. No death metal or anything."

Chuckling, he rolled his eyes and pulled his music up.

"Like a chill, high-speed car chase that'll keep me focused but not nervous."

"Right..."

She glanced at him and smirked. "Do you have something like that?"

"It's a tough request, my friend. But yeah, I think I got it."

A second later, the opening lines of "The Distance" by Cake came through the Winnie's speakers. Lily barked a laugh and readjusted her grip on the steering wheel. "That'll do. Now your real mission, should you choose to accept it, is keeping this up for the next three hours without repeating anything."

"Challenge accepted."

"Okay, then." She took a quick sip of her coffee. "Here we go."

TWENTY-FIVE

A t 9:45, Loana's car altered speed and course for the first time. "Oh!" Lily tightened her hold on the steering wheel, tapped the brake, and sighed. "Jeez."

"Are you okay?"

"Yeah." She loosened her grasp a little and turned her right blinker on as she slowed behind the blue Dacia. "Your focus playlist was really effective. The woman's blinker made me jumpy."

Romeo snorted. "But we're almost there."

She breathed deeply and shifted a little in the seat. "Yep. I'm gonna need to stretch after this one."

"You're doin' great."

She flashed him a quick look before taking the exit behind Loana. "You too, mister DJ."

They followed the other vehicle down a few side streets before they reached a rural dirt road. He peered through the window at the Romanian countryside around them. The mountains rose to the east and south and the tall trees gave way to drier climates in the distance. "Normally, I would've asked where we're going so I could look it up on a map. But..."

"I have a feeling that where we're going might not actually be on a map. Or at least not all of it."

He shrugged. "You're probably right."

After another ten minutes or so, the dirt road disappeared entirely. She didn't notice what lay ahead until Leona's car bumped wildly over the grass and shrubs, followed quickly by the Winnie, which jostled and jarred the occupants. "Woah!" She tapped the brakes a little and narrowly missed a few large rocks the woman in front of her had swerved to avoid. "What is she thinking?"

"I'd say she's probably laughing at us and going this fast simply for fun." He clutched the passenger seat's armrests and bounced uncomfortably in the seat beside her. "Yeah, this is nuts."

"Oh, my God." The abrupt appearance of red taillights was the only warning and she reacted accordingly. This time, she had to apply the brakes in a somewhat desperate need to stop because Loana had apparently done the same thing. Dirt and rocks and thick bushes juddered beneath the Winnie's tires as it skidded to a halt and stopped maybe two feet behind the Dacia. "She's crazy, Romeo. She's crazy."

"Yep."

"That woman should not get behind the wheel of anything."

"Agreed."

"What's wrong with—"

Loana leapt out of the driver-side door and spun to face them, grinning and waving like best friends seeing each other again after years apart. Lily plastered a smile on her face and tried not to look as flustered as she felt. Finally, she raised a hand and waved back slowly. Romeo managed to do the same. "She is totally nuts," he muttered from the side of his mouth.

"Totally."

"Get out," she shouted, still grinning. "Come on!" She beckoned them toward her with an urgent wave. Andrei opened the passenger-side door slowly and clung to the top of it to pull himself out.

"It looks like we're not the only ones who think she shouldn't drive." Despite his shaken look, the werewolf managed a smirk

She shook her head and tried to keep her expression blank. "I'm glad it's not only us." She turned the engine off and unbuckled her seatbelt. "I hope I can still walk after this."

"Well, I'll try to catch you."

With a soft chuckle—the only alternative to screaming, at that point—she opened the door and slid onto the dry ground. He followed quickly and shut the door behind them.

Leona stood beside her blue car with her long-nailed hands on her hips and nodded. "Come, come." She waved them toward her again. "We're almost there." Before they caught up with her, she spun, lifted her skirts a little, and marched across the ground toward what appeared to be absolutely nothing at all.

Andrei stared blankly at the couple. *At least he's waiting for us.* The man looked almost green and didn't say a word as they moved together after the over-aggressive driver who led them forward without looking back.

"So." Romeo glanced at Andrei beside him. "What exactly are we looking for out here?"

The man shook his head. "The payment is for answers from the Ochiului. Not from me. And you're not the one paying to ask questions, wolf."

He frowned at the man and cleared his throat. Then, he stared ahead at the surprisingly swift pace Loana set ahead of them. "I only tried to make a little conversation."

"I don't like conversation."

"Clearly." He glanced at Lily and nodded at the man beside him. She responded with an irritated look and focused on following their guide.

After another five minutes of walking with no clear direction, they passed between a few trees and Loana stopped and stood perfectly still. When the others reached her, the couple stepped to the woman's left, while Andrei sidled beside her on the right. Her hands jerked straight out beside her, and with a deep, hissing breath in, she raised her arms like she tried to hug a wall. In the next moment, she closed her eyes and mumbled a tuneless chant. Lily tried to hear what it was but she couldn't be sure the woman was using real words at all.

"Okay!" Their guide's shout startled all three people beside her. Lily fought the instinctive laugh in response. "Now. This is very important." The woman turned toward them and raised an eyebrow. "No talking. That's for both of you. Lily, you will have your turn to speak but know that what you say also serves as a contract in this place. Do you understand?"

"Yes." She nodded.

"You." Leona pointed at the werewolf. "You will want to, but you will not be allowed to help her."

"What?"

"Ah. Should I tell you to wait outside?"

He swept a confused glance over their surroundings— trees, hills, bushes. They were definitely outside. When he looked at his friend, all she could do was nod and let him make his own decision. "No. You don't need to tell me that."

"I must hear that you understand."

"I will not be allowed to help her. Sure. I understand."

"Good." She turned toward the nothingness in front of them.

"It doesn't mean I like it," he mumbled.

The Romani woman either didn't hear him or chose not to dignify his quip with any response at all. "Andrei?" The man whistled a complicated tune, and Loana released a terrifying hiss of a breath. Her hands jerked up in front of her again, and she flicked all ten fingers through the air. Pink and orange light erupted from her fingertips and crackled against the unseen wall in front of them. Her spell crawled in jagged streaks up and out to the left and right to illuminate an enormous dome. From where Lily stood, it looked at least four times the size of the fighting arena her mom's friend Melissa Bore had constructed with wards in the Mexican desert. This one sparkled and crackled like highly contained fireworks until the pink and orange light had engulfed it entirely.

Loana lowered her hands and turned to grin at the Ochiului's newest visitors. "It's time to see for yourself." She stepped through the shimmering light and disappeared beyond it. Andrei smirked at them before he followed in her footsteps.

Romeo grabbed Lily's hand and gave it a quick squeeze. "I said I agreed not to help you." He swallowed thickly. "I can't believe I did that."

She squeezed his hand in return and smiled. "I'm really glad you did. Now, I can finally get the answers I want. And I'll be fine. I promise."

"I know you will. If anything happens to you, though, I won't be."

Her face calm, she stepped onto her tiptoes and gave him a quick kiss. "Let's go." Together, they stepped through the flashing dome of light.

TWENTY-SIX

Lily felt the air squeezed out of her lungs and thought she'd released Romeo's hand somewhere between that first step and the next. When they were through the dome in the middle of the Romanian countryside, she felt the pressure of his fingers tighten around hers.

He noticed it at the same time and loosened his hold quickly. "Sorry." He grunted. "That was weird."

"It's okay," she whispered. "So is this."

Stretched ahead of them for as far as she could see were rows upon rows of exactly the kind of caravan wagons Romeo had envisioned when he'd asked Andrei about it. They weren't quite as long or as tall as the Winnie, but they were definitely large enough to serve as homes on wheels, which they quite obviously were.

The rows of these wooden wagons—painted in bright reds, purples, yellows, and greens with all manner of bright and garish patterns—were separated into two main columns. The space between extended ahead toward the barely visible pink and orange light that glowed on the opposite side of the dome. The Ochiului people moved in and out of these wagons, the windows covered with draped silks and velvet curtains. The smell of cooking meat was unmistakable. Children ran between the wagons, playing and screaming at each other. A few of the younger ones were naked. Members of this Romani tribe were seated on the back steps of their homes or walked toward their neighbors. Some sat on benches and rough-hewn logs in whatever open space they could find. Most of them had the same black hair and darker skin as Loana but a few were as pale as Andrei. Lily was the only blonde head among them.

"Don't stop now," their guide commanded cheerfully and beckoned them forward again. "You've already come this far." She chuckled and stepped purposefully down the open area of trampled dirt between the main columns of wagons. Lily couldn't say she'd seen anyone truly swagger until that moment.

When the couple stepped forward to follow her, the Ochiului closest to them stopped what they were doing and stared at them in silence. None of them looked surprised or particularly suspicious, but a few narrowed their eyes in curiosity or pursed their lips as the outsiders passed their homes and the clotheslines strung between them. Two children darted into the open communal space and almost barreled into Lily. The first stopped at the last second, and the much smaller girl behind him bumped into his back. Both drew in sharp, quick breaths and stared, not at her face but at her hair.

"Hi." She smiled.

The boy snatched the girl by the arm and pushed her across toward the other side. "Are you crazy?" he shouted after her, and they raced away again, screaming and laughing before they disappeared between the other wagons.

Romeo squeezed her hand. "Come on."

As soon as they passed the people who'd stopped what they were doing to study the strangers, those same people simply resumed where they'd left off as if nothing at all had interrupted their everyday routine. It was as if, when they followed Loana and Andrei, they brought with them a wave of frozen onlookers who only stopped at their approach and went on with their normal lives again the minute the strangers had passed.

"I begin to understand why Darius didn't want to come out here," she whispered.

"Mm-hmm."

Finally, Loana stopped ahead of them and spread her arms. "Hurry. Hurry. You're wasting your own time." The sound of her chuckle echoed eerily around them, although there were only wooden wagons and dirt and a few patches of drying grass. She pointed to her right as she faced them, and they immediately glanced left.

"What?" The same scene stretched before them virtually forever—two columns of more wagons in endless rows, and Lily couldn't even guess where they ended.

"We are so close." The woman nodded. "Keep up." She resumed her rapid pace down this wide aisle, and her very confused guests followed.

A person could get seriously lost in here. Probably only someone like us, though. Outsiders. What if we—nope. I'm not even gonna think about it. She shook her head and gave Romeo's hand another squeeze. Mostly, it was to reassure herself that he really was there beside her.

On the other side of Romeo, Andrei strolled along while he kicked at the dirt with his boots and scraped beneath his fingernails. It was only when he looked up in anticipation that she noticed that Loana had finally stopped again.

The woman turned to face them and gestured to their right. "Now, we will name our price."

Beside them, the long rows of Ochiului wagons gave way to a huge semi-circle of open space. Twelve sanded, lacquered logs were placed around this half-moon shape on the ground, with a ring of stones and an unlit fire in the center. She clapped her hands four times and the sharp sound of it echoed again as if they stood in a stone cavern underground instead of out in this huge, endless expanse beneath the pink and orange dome. "They're here!" she shouted and uttered a high-pitched whoop.

The doors of six wagons gathered around the semi-circle opened at the same time. A man and a woman stepped out of each wagon. Some of them bounded down the stairs while others took their own sweet time. They all fixed the newcomers with dark, curious gazes. A man wearing a tailcoat of dark-purple velvet chuckled when he saw Romeo. A few of the others smiled, and some offered no expressions whatsoever. The twelve tribespeople took their seats on the polished tree stumps and waited.

"Romeo..." Loana's lilting voice made them both look at her. She raised one finger and flicked it to point at the ground right beside her. He eyed her warily and took a deep breath.

"Hey," Lily whispered with another squeeze of his hand. His green eyes twitched in concern when he looked at her. "It's okay." She slipped her hand out of his and nodded. He hesitated for only a moment before he did as their guide commanded and moved to stand beside her in the wide avenue of dirt.

The woman nodded curtly, grinned at Lily, and addressed the twelve seated beside them. "Lily Antony. Daughter of Margaret Antony. Both women of the people."

She blinked at this. *It might be time to update my translation spell to include casual sayings. That has to mean something else.*

Loana stepped toward her and gestured with an open hand from the young witch's head to her feet. "She comes to pay the price of seeking answers from the Ochiului, to which she has already agreed."

A woman with thick smears of kohl lining her eyelids and bright, cherry-red lipstick tilted her chin at the visitor. "What have you brought as payment?"

Lily glanced at their guide, who nodded. "You may speak now."

I should have asked if I needed to bring it with me before we stepped through that dome. She looked at the twelve tribespeople and tried to assume a calm expression. "I have money. More than enough."

A few chuckles rose at that. The woman with the bright lipstick offered a rather condescending smile. "That's quite thoughtful. But that is not the price."

"What of the wolf with you, eh?" The man in the purple velvet jacket nodded at Romeo. "Do you offer him?"

"No." She said it quickly and perhaps a little too loudly. *I'm not gonna play that game.* "Romeo came with me, and he'll leave with me too."

"Hmm. If that is what you believe." The man inclined his head toward her and straightened on his tree stump to cross one shiny leather boot over his knee.

A few tense, rather confusing moments followed. Finally, a man with streaks of gray in his long black beard leaned forward over his lap and extended a hand toward her. "Have you brought anything to offer as payment?"

Lily swallowed. "Other than money? No." *Now, I have no idea what they want.* She glanced at each of the twelve and nodded. "But I agreed to offer payment for information, and that hasn't changed."

"Then we will choose for you," said the man with the graying beard. "Do you agree to this?" She glanced at Romeo, and the man laughed. "No, we do not want your friend. We will accept your payment when it reveals itself. Yes?"

"Okay."

"Mothers! Fathers!" The woman with bright lipstick stood and straightened her skirts. "It's time to discover Lily Antony's price." Her voice echoed with the same eerie ring as Loana's, and the eleven other tribespeople around her stood. Four of them clapped their hands with a sharp, unified crack, and the rest threw their hands into the air with rising howls that made Lily's hair stand on end.

She whirled to face Romeo, but a split second before she found him, the ground beneath her feet trembled. In the next moment, she stood in a much larger ring of open ground with only a few wagons scattered yards apart around her. The twelve all remained where they had stood, and Loana and Romeo were still there too. All the rows of Ochiului wagons and the other tribespeople had vanished, however.

A door creaked open somewhere behind her, and she turned away from the Romani people who smiled at her. Across the huge ring of open space was a single wagon all on its own. It's mottled, gray-white hue made her think immediately of ash fluttering from a still-burning fire. From behind the door stepped an elderly woman, hunched with age and her skin darkened by years in the sun and the shadow of so many wrinkles. Her long white hair was piled high atop her head in billowing curls and a few thin locks of it had fallen free to curl around her shoulders.

For a moment, Lily thought the Ochiului people had brought her another storyteller. *No. She had white hair, but this woman's simply really old.*

The woman clutched the railing built beside the stairs at the back of her wagon and shuffled down slowly, one step at a time. She moved across the flat, trampled dirt toward the visitor with far more speed than seemed possible for her old age, though. When she stopped in the center of the large ring around them, she clasped her hands in front of her.

"Go to her." Loana nodded. "She will find it."

With a final glance at Romeo, she steeled herself and stepped forward toward the old woman.

TWENTY-SEVEN

Every footfall seemed as loud as if she'd stamped across the packed dirt in heavy boots. She would have drawn closer, but the woman raised a hand for her to stop where she was.

"You will protect yourself, of course." She fixed her with a dark, unwavering gaze. "And I will find the value you have placed on knowledge and wisdom."

She opened her mouth to reply but she could only think of more questions. "What do I have to do?"

The words had barely left her lips when the old woman's hand lashed out toward her and unleashed a crackling green spark of an attack spell.

Lily jerked her hand up and summoned a warded shield barely in time, and the spell deflected and hurtled away into the nothingness around them. She frowned. "I will not fight you—"

The woman stepped forward and struck with her other hand to direct a blast of wind and force that tossed the dirt toward her face and made her stagger back. It didn't cease until the young witch raised a fist, twisted it, and shoved the minor ward aside. The dirt fell to the earth again, and she stared at the Romani woman. "What are you doing?"

"I am searching." One hand jerked out toward her, rapidly followed by the other, to cast attack after attack of red sparks, slicing yellow energy, and a swirling darkness that coalesced into hot, sizzling pellets before they struck.

Of course, her warded shields deflected every one of the woman's calculated spells. Some of them she avoided simply by stepping quickly to the side. *What is this?* Her unexpected adversary bared her teeth and constantly released spell after spell. It wasn't enough to put her in any serious danger, and they both knew it. But it was definitely enough to irritate the hell out of the young witch who simply looked for answers.

"This is ridiculous!" Coiling tendrils of hard-packed dirt rose from the ground at her feet and lashed at her ankles. Lily stamped on one and blasted another with a handful of red sparks, and with her attention diverted, the old woman's next spell glanced off her shoulder. A sharp, intense pain sliced through her flesh, and she leapt away from the tendrils with a grunt. A thin streak of red, raw skin showed through the rip in her t-shirt, which quickly darkened with a few drops of blood. "Okay." She looked at the Romani woman who attacked her for no apparent reason and summoned a roaring ball of flame in her hand. "Is this the price? Do you want me to fight you?" She looked over her shoulder at Loana and Romeo and the twelve other tribespeople who watched this display. "You couldn't have told me I had to enter a... witch's duel?"

"Where is it?" the old woman hissed.

She whipped her head toward the elder in time to be blinded by a brilliant, strobing green light. The intensity of it pulsed behind her eyelids, and she saw absolutely nothing but green.

Until a dark shadow swooped past her and flitted between her and the old woman and blocked the spell for a few seconds. She drew a sharp breath when she saw it—the shadow-bird had appeared again at the last second to warn her or help her or offer something she hadn't yet thought of on her own. "What—"

A howling funnel of blazing yellow light hurtled through the air from behind her toward the shadow-bird. The black, winged shadow dove at the old Ochiului witch, but the spell someone else had cast followed it. The yellow funnel struck the shadow-bird with a crack like thunder, and Lily screamed.

Her side erupted in agonizing pain, and the whole world spun around her. The next thing she knew, she was on her knees in the dirt with one hand clutching her side. The other barely kept her face from impacting the hardened earth. A thick, heavy darkness threatened to overwhelm her, and her ears rang with an obnoxiously high pitch. She couldn't even hear herself breathe, and she wondered if she even could breathe through the pain. As her senses tried to focus, she tasted the same acrid smoke and ash that always came with the shadow-bird and thought she tasted blood.

The ringing began to fade, and through the darkness, she heard whooping cries of satisfaction coming from the twelve behind her.

"Lily!" Romeo shouted. "Hey, what the hell did you do to her? You can't—"

"I'm okay." She'd tried to shout it but couldn't tell if it came out louder than a grunt. Her teeth gritted, she swallowed and took a deep breath. "Romeo, I'm okay." Slowly, she released her agonized hold on her ribcage and raised a hand to give him a half-hearted thumbs-up. She heard him growl but he didn't say anything else.

Slowly, shuffling footsteps approached and she stared at the toes of two worn leather boots while she tried to catch her breath. The old Romani woman defied the laws of age and time for most mortals who'd lived as long as she had as she crouched to then kneel in front of the outsider witch who'd come looking for answers. A cold, paper-thin finger slipped under her chin and forced her to look at her.

Her teeth still gritted against the fading pain in her side, Lily found the blackness in her vision melting away as she met the other witch's gaze. The woman's lips pulled back to reveal yellow-stained teeth as she studied Lily's face. "Yes. I found your price, Lily Antony. And you have paid it."

"What..." She grunted and raised her hand from the ground and forced herself to kneel fully upright. "What was the price?"

The woman's eyes grew wide with a terrifying, joyful excitement, and her grin only grew. "That bird of smoke and shadow and what it means to you." She removed her finger from beneath her chin and gazed over the young witch's head. "It is finished." More footsteps came to join them, and two tribespeople stopped beside the old woman to help her up from her knees. She clutched their arms with claw-like hands and let them pull her shakily to her feet. Finally, she licked her lips and cackled. "It is finished. Lily Antony has paid, and the Ochiului accept."

Lily's shoulders hunched, and she hung her head as she tried to fight the dizziness that swept over her when her hearing returned fully and the darkness disappeared completely from the corners of her vision. Her side still ached, but the worst of the pain had left her.

"Go," someone said firmly from behind her, and after more quick, pounding footsteps, Romeo slid through the dirt on his knees to stop beside her.

"Lily. Lily? Hey, it's me."

She grasped his arm, all her senses now fully returned. Simply feeling him there beside her seemed to clear her head, and she looked at him with wide eyes. "What happened?"

"You screamed and fell, Lil. I don't even...are you okay?"

When she glanced down at her side, she fully expected to see her t-shirt soaked with her own blood, but there was none. "I think so..." She sighed. "Who attacked me?"

He frowned at her. "Who... Okay, that seriously old lady who can barely walk on her own." He looked over his shoulder at the two men guiding the Romani elder gently back toward the others, who gathered around her and spoke amongst themselves in lowered voices. "Come on. Let me help you up."

She leaned on him a little and staggered to her feet. "No, I mean the last one. Whatever spell hit me...Romeo, it was awful. Who did that?"

His lips pressed together, he studied her eyes for a few seconds. "No one. The only attack you didn't fight off was the one that did this." His fingers settled lightly on her shoulder beside the grazed flesh beneath her torn t-shirt. She grimaced. "Sorry. That was it, though."

"And you saw the shadow-bird?"

Romeo paused. "Yeah. It came outta nowhere, like it always does. One of those men back there tossed some kinda spell at it. And hit it, I think, however that's possible." He closed his eyes and tried to shake the confusion out of his head.

"What happened to the bird?"

"What?"

"The shadow-bird." She looked at him with wide eyes. "What did the spell do?"

"I mean, it kinda, uh... disintegrated." He puffed a breath out through his lips and mimed an explosion with his hand. She closed her eyes and swallowed. "What's wrong?"

"She said that was my price." When she opened her eyes again, she felt the tears welling there but forced them not to fall. "The bird and what it means to me. That's what she said."

His mouth gaped but he couldn't find any words.

"Romeo, I felt it. That attack. I think...somehow... I

think my mom's been sending the shadow-bird to look after me. And now—" She stumbled a little with her next step and he slipped his arm around her waist to help keep her standing. "I don't think it's coming back."

Together, they walked toward the Romani gathered around their elder, who accepted all the help they offered in lowering her onto one of the polished tree stumps. "Well, from what I watched you do, Lil, I don't think you need it."

"Maybe." She gazed at the Ochiului and grimaced. "Unless it was supposed to help me get the answers I need."

TWENTY-EIGHT

W hen they reached the half-circle of waiting
Romani, Lily looked up to see Loana grinning at
her. The short woman gave her curt nod of acknowledgment, and all she could do in reply was incline her head
slightly.

Another woman with a bright green scarf wound
around her head to completely cover her hair beneath it
stepped forward. "Lily?" She straightened and released
Romeo's arm.

"Hey, are you—"

"Yep." She looked at him and offered a small smile.
"All good." She met the scarfed woman's gaze and nodded.

"We are prepared to open the door into the knowledge
you seek. Are you prepared to step through it?"

"Yes."

"Good."

One of the older men standing behind them lifted a
long, polished, curved can and thumped it into the dirt.

The ground trembled beneath them again, and a few of the Romani nodded toward something across the open arena where she'd fought the old woman.

She turned again, and in the center of the huge circle of open ground, a massive sarcophagus now rested. The rectangle of stone was far larger than any one person's body needed. *Even Darius would rattle around in there.* The lid was made of the same dark-gray rock, as jagged-looking as if it had only recently been cut. From the top of the lid rose a thin stone pillar, above which rested an incredibly detailed image of a carved stone eye the size of a basketball.

"That is where you must go to seek your answers." The woman with the bright lipstick nodded. "Be warned, though, Lily Antony. Some who pass through this doorway re-emerge...changed. If they do so at all."

"If you are not as prepared as you have claimed," the man in the purple tailcoat added, "if you do not know where to look, you may lose more inside that place than you will ever find."

Lily nodded resolutely. "I'm ready."

"Hey, wait a minute." Romeo caught her arm and pulled her gently toward him. "You don't have to do this, Lil."

"Yes, I do."

"No, I know you want to. But these people..." He glanced at the Romani, all of whom watched the strangers intently but didn't interfere. "You heard what she said, right? That people come out changed? It sounds like the kinda thing you're smart enough to stay away from."

She tilted her head at him and searched his gaze. "This is where I find my answers. We learn where my mom is and how to get her out. How to stop the people who took her. I'll be fine."

"Can we maybe...wait for a minute?" He turned to look at the tribespeople. "What is she walking into?" They only replied with silence. "Seriously. Is this another kind of test? Can she get hurt down there?"

"That is for Lily to discover on her own." The woman with the green headscarf gestured vaguely.

"That's not an answer."

"Romeo." She took his hand. "It's okay."

"And it's time for you to step inside." Loana came up beside her and gestured toward the sarcophagus. "Now."

She squeezed his hand and winked. "I'll see you when I find out everything I need to know."

"I—" He sighed. "I'll be right here."

Her hand slipped out of his and she looked at him for a few moments longer until she turned to walk with Loana toward the huge stone coffin. At their approach, the lid slid back on its own with a growled rumble. It grated and stopped with an echoing thud, and she peered into a long, dark stairwell lit with torches on the walls.

"This is what you came to find," Loana said.

"I know."

"Good."

With a final smile at Romeo, Lily climbed up over the lip of the tomb entry and put her foot down on the first stone step. "Please...take care of him until I come back, okay?"

"Your friend is perfectly safe here, Lily. You have my word."

"Thank you." She gazed into the stairwell with fluttering torches and flickering shadows and steeled herself for whatever might lie ahead. "Here we go." With purposeful steps, she walked down and disappeared into the gaping hole beneath the Ochiului earth.

Romeo and the other tribespeople watched her for about a minute after the top of her head descended into the open crypt. He turned to look at those standing closest to him. "If anything happens to her—"

"That falls on Lily's shoulders, young man," the man in the purple coat reminded him. "I think you know that."

"I'm not worried about whatever choices she's gonna make." He made no effort to hide his wariness from the gathered Romani. "But I don't know if I trust—" The loud rumble of stone sliding against stone echoed around the emptiness of the open ground around them. "What's that?" He jerked his head toward the sarcophagus to see the lid begin to slide into place as Loana headed toward her people. "Are you kidding me?" He moved swiftly toward the woman. "Hey. Open that thing again."

"That's not how this works, Romeo." She smiled politely and nodded at those gathered behind him. "Come and wait with us."

"No. No one said anything about shutting her inside that thing. How the hell is she supposed to get back out?"

She stopped and blinked at him. "She will if she's meant to do so. I said come—"

He ignored her and sprinted toward the quickly

closing tomb. "Lily! Don't—" The final crunch as it locked home seemed to echo mockingly, and he barreled into the sarcophagus to put all his weight behind the lid in an attempt to open it again. It wouldn't budge. "Lily? Lily, can you hear me?" He shoved on the heavy stone again with a grunt, then pounded urgently on it with his fists. "Answer me."

"Step back." The man with the purple coat and the other with the long, graying beard had joined him now. They gestured for him to step away.

"No. Open this thing now. You didn't say anything about this. Lily!"

"We'd rather not use force on a guest." The second man put a surprisingly strong hand on his shoulder. "But we will."

Romeo glared at the hand. "Let go of me and open the damn lid."

"Come on—"

Jerking away from the man's grasp, he backed away and hunched his shoulders. "Open it!" he roared. A furious growl escaped him and he let the magic of his wolf course through him to shine in the flash of his eyes that now glowed bright silver.

The men paused but only watched him with condescension. "Don't."

He snarled, and for the first time since he'd learned to control his wolf in middle school, he lost that all over again. His skin erupted with a sharp, prickling sting and in the next moment, he was on all fours, shaking the clothes he hadn't had time to remove from his shaggy black fur.

"This will not help anyone," the man in the purple coat warned.

The black wolf snapped his jaws at the Romani's legs and he leapt away with a chuckle. Someone shouted something from the open semi-circle of tribespeople, and he turned his head toward them and sniffed the air. His werewolf's vision illuminated eleven other magical bodies waiting there for him, and he darted across the dirt, his paws pounding against the earth as rapidly as the rage pounded through his veins.

"That's quite enough." The old woman who'd fought a joke of a duel with Lily lurched to her feet and pointed at the black wolf who race toward her. No visible spell left her hand and no magic streaked to stop him. All the same, he felt an undeniable compulsion to stop. His paws skidded into the dirt to obey the old witch's command, and he waited there, panting. "Come here." She pointed at the ground beside her. The black wolf padded toward the very spot. "You're being very rude, young man. If you learn nothing else today, you will learn the manners you should have brought with you. Now sit."

With a long, high-pitched whine, he sat on his haunches. He couldn't have fought it even if he could think clearly enough to try.

"Very good." The old woman groaned and settled slowly onto the polished tree stump. "Your fears are misplaced, my boy. She won't be in there nearly as long as you think."

TWENTY-NINE

L ily walked down one stone step after another. They seemed to stretch on and on below her, much farther than she could have imagined. Only once did she turn to look behind her toward the surface, but at that point, she'd already gone too far to see anything but more stone and lit torches. The only sound was the occasional crackle of a torch and the slow, cautious echo of her own footsteps.

After what felt like at least half an hour of unending descent, she finally reached the bottom. The only direction to take was a left turn from the stairwell, which opened into a large circular cavern the size of the living room she'd shared with her mom only four months before. More torches lined the walls there too, spaced out every few feet. "Okay," she muttered, stepped toward the center of the room, and gazed around. "I'm ready for some answers."

A gust of cold wind blasted her from every direction at the same time, and she brought her hands up to cover her face. The air roared and buffeted her and every single torch in the cavern was snuffed out completely. The torches along the staircase went next, and she was plunged into the thickest, most complete darkness she'd ever known.

"Huh. That's not very helpful." She opened her hand and summoned her orb of white light. "What?" There was no response—no spell, no white glow, and no pulse of magic coursed through her to take the shape she wanted. "Um..." She tried to summon the light again, but absolutely nothing happened. A confused chuckle escaped her. "I haven't had this much trouble casting a spell since...what? First grade? Maybe a light like that breaks some kinda rule down here or something."

This time, she twitched her fingers to pull up a whirling ball of flame. Again, it did not appear.

"No way..." She ran through all her easier spells first, then the more difficult ones she could remember that would help her. She even clapped her hands and pulled them apart to cast the pink glow for a revealing charm, but she couldn't even feel the humming energy of her magic between her palms. She dropped her hands against her thighs and sighed, still completely unable to see a thing. "This is definitely unexpected. No casting spells, huh? Great."

She took a few steps forward in the unforgiving black-ness and paused. "It's not such a good idea to walk around blindly, either. I guess...literally, right now." Instead, she lowered herself slowly to the cold stone floor, crossed her legs beneath her, and waited. "Hello? Is anyone in here?" Her voice echoed and repeated far more than it should have in a cavern this size. *If I'm even still in the same cavern.* "Can I...can I have a little help in here, please? Maybe a little light?" Her only reply was the same question in her own voice, over and over again.

"So how am I supposed to find answers if I'm all alone and can't see a thing?" she muttered. For what felt like another minute or two, she waited, but that was about as long as she could manage. "Okay, Lily. No one's gonna hand you what you want. Let's go get it." She stood and turned in the direction of the staircase. "I bet there's another torch that didn't go out somewhere near the top." Feeling ahead with her hands, she took slow, cautious steps toward the staircase and waited for the cold brush of stone against her fingertips.

The wall should have been six or seven steps ahead of her, but she didn't feel anything at all, even after counting her steps to twenty. "Okay, I'm definitely not in the same cavern. That is not good." She closed her eyes tightly, squeezed them harder, and opened them again, but there was no change. Just in case, she tried to cast another half-dozen spells and the result was always the same—nothing.

Her heart thudded in her chest.

"Okay. Okay, calm down. There is definitely a way out of this." The urge to pace was overwhelming, but it was also a fairly stupid choice. Instead, she sat on the ground again and closed her eyes because it helped her to focus. "All right. What can I do without being able to see or use my magic?" It felt a little absurd, but the question made her chuckle. "Not a whole lot. Even blind people without magic can—oh." She took a deep breath. "Like the blind storyteller and her gift. Oh, my God." Lily reached quickly into the front pocket of her shorts, where her fingers wound around the cold, smooth reality of the lapis lazuli stone. She withdrew it and clenched it in a tight fist. "That's it. What did she tell me? 'When you see only darkness, use this gift.' I honestly thought that would be more metaphorical."

She rolled the stone over and over in her hand and tried to discover how to activate it. "She said it would show me what I was always meant to see. That seems like virtually much everything at this point."

There was no way to tell when she'd stopped talking out loud to herself in the darkness, but after what felt like a dangerously long time, she realized vaguely in the back of her mind that she'd fallen into a semi-meditative state. *It's easy to do when there's literally nothing else. I'm supposed to see something. To see...see...*

That repeated itself constantly in her head without any effort on her part to keep the thought going. *I see nothing with my eyes. My eyes don't see. There is only darkness. Looking into the—* She sucked in a huge, gasping breath. "You can find everything you need to know by looking in the eyes!" Those were the words in her mom's last note. "I don't really know how that applies at all right now, but okay. Let's give it a try." She opened her eyes and brought the lapis lazuli from Amal the storyteller up to her face. It felt like she had it right in front of one eye, but there was no way to be sure other than touching it to her eye. She drew the stone toward her other eye and almost fell over backward.

The entire cavern around her flashed with a ghostly blue light. She sat exactly where she'd been the first time before she'd tried to walk toward the staircase as if nothing had existed between the moment the torches went out and the moment the stone from the blind seer had illuminated this new type of sight. And there was the staircase, right where it should have been.

"Woah." Her voice was muted and hollow like it didn't quite exist. Lily turned to view the circular chamber once again and now found herself dazzled by a massive blue orb that floated in midair in the center of the room. "No, that's... Okay, that's an actual eye."

It hovered in the same shape as the carved statue she'd seen on the lid of the sarcophagus aboveground. only this one was made of blue flames instead of stone.

She pushed herself to her feet and maintained a tight grasp on the lapis lazuli while she stared at the glowing blue flames. "Okay, Mom. Is this the eye I'm supposed to look into right now?" Slowly and cautiously, she stepped toward the huge, floating eye. The closer she came, the louder the whispers around her grew—so many voices echoed against the stone walls around her, rising and falling with the flickering blue flames.

She stopped directly in front of it and a single voice called out to her. "Everything you need to know."

"I hope we're both right." Before she could change her mind, she stretched her free hand out and brushed her fingertips against the blue flames.

The entire world lurched and spun, sucked her both forward and backward, ripped her through the ground, and hurled her into the sky. She thought she'd be torn apart and maybe she screamed, but she suddenly couldn't hear a thing. And finally, all her answers came in the form she never expected.

Visions flashed in front of her, one after the other—the shadow-bird gliding over mountains, valleys, rivers, villages and towns and cities; thin, malnourished, terrified people locked in metal cages, screaming in agony and fear as bright, glistening trails of magic were drawn from their bodies; hooded figures with the sigil of the Black Heron printed on their shoulders, all of them shouting, "More! It's not enough!"

She saw a brief glimpse of her mother, her wrists secure with shackles, kneeling in front of a wall with angry, faceless beings standing behind her. One of them hissed, "We cannot take it from you."

Greta Antony smirked, although her head still hung toward her chest. "It looks like you failed, then, doesn't it?"

And finally, Lily saw herself. She spread her hands apart in one long, continuous arc, and the black cloud she'd only really used once spread between her palms. It billowed and grew and crackled with magical power and a force more terrible than she could even begin to conceive. This wasn't her as she knew herself. This was her as she would one day become, as the witch who would master the power of the black cloud she didn't yet understand. And when she did, nothing would ever stand in her way again.

The blue light she had forgotten she could see flashed even brighter all around her before it vanished and was replaced by a darkness not nearly as complete as what she'd left.

A single candle flickered on a table that hadn't been there before. Lily tried to walk toward it but found she couldn't move at all. She couldn't even feel her body, let alone control where she went. Her eyes adjusted to the one source of light quickly enough, though, and she realized she was most definitely not in the cavern now.

The shadows had a muted, blurry quality to them, like a photograph of a swiftly moving object taken at low shutter speed. There was nothing else there but dark walls, that single table, and the candle upon it. As she frowned and tried to see beyond the obvious, something shifted on the floor behind the table. Someone else in the room uttered a sharp gasp, and a dark form rose from the floor. She wanted to back away but again, she couldn't move.

The person who sat from where they'd stretched on the floor faced away from her and raised a hand to scratch a head of matted, colorless hair. The stranger turned slowly—so slowly—toward the table and the candle and Lily herself while she watched from within this vision.

For a moment, she thought she was imagining it—that the blurred images of this apparition only made her think she saw what she saw. But the face that gazed sleepily at her now, however gaunt and smeared with dirt, was a face Lily Antony would know anywhere.

"Mom?" Her voice rippled away from her in this vividly real dreamscape.

Greta Antony gave her daughter a slow, tired smile. "Hi, sweets. I knew you'd find me."

THIRTY

Lily thought she'd stopped breathing until her next words left her in a muted whisper. "It's really you."

"Well, as much as it's really you right now talking to me." Greta's gaze flicked over her daughter's face for a few moments. "I can hardly see you, sweets. I can barely hear you. We... I don't think we have much time."

"Then tell me where you are, Mom." Her heart leapt in her chest toward her mother, who looked like she hadn't been washed or fed more than a few bites at a time for weeks. "Tell me how to find you. I'll come get you right now."

Her mother's tired smile faded a little, and she closed her eyes. "I don't know where they have me, sweets. Underground somewhere, obviously. There is no light. But it doesn't matter anyway, Lily. They move me all the time. You need a way to find me wherever I am."

"Like how you've found me?"

Her mom hummed in approval, her eyes still closed as

if she could better pull up the image of her daughter through this blurry, muted dream-tunnel. "Good girl."

"You've been sending the shadow-bird for me, haven't you?"

"My totem, sweets. The raven gives me eyes and wings when everything else has been taken from me."

"I think... Mom, I think the Romani destroyed it." Lily swallowed the lump in her throat, although it couldn't have been physical when her body wasn't actually there.

"The spirit can't be broken with any one spell, my love. I'm still here. The raven is still here."

"Then why did I—"

"You're my daughter, Lily. As much a part of my spirit as any totem. The Romani deal in truths. It sounds like they found a part of yours."

Lily studied her mom's ratty, matted hair and the dark circles under the woman's eyes, even in the small light of one candle. "How do I find you? I mean, for real."

Greta reached into the folds of the dark cloth draped over her shoulders. It could have been a cloak or a rough blanket, for all she could tell. She withdrew a round, glistening silver object. It flashed in the candlelight, and even with the blurred edges of this dreamlike vision, she clearly saw what it was. A silver circle around the silhouette of the heron, its wings outstretched in flight.

"I've been saving this for you, sweets." Her mother opened her eyes and smiled. "You'll discover what it means like you've worked out everything else."

She reached for the silver coin-like object but of

course, she couldn't actually move because she wasn't really here. Neither was her mom. "I can't—"

"Shh, Lily. You can." Greta set the heron coin on the cold stone floor in front of her and tried to look at the apparition of her daughter. By now, though, she couldn't see anything. Her gaze drifted around the entire room but never settled on Lily.

"Mom, I'm still here. Can you hear me?"

"I am so proud of you, Lily. Keep going. Keep fighting. I'll wait for you."

"Wait— Mom?" The single candle on the table in front of Greta Antony faded and all the edges of Lily's vision blurred into darkness. "Only a little longer, please. I'm not done—*Mom!*"

The vision vanished completely to be replaced by the blazing blue light of the flaming eye and the illuminated cavern in the Romani crypt. For a fraction of a second, she saw herself from very far away—saw the back of her own body standing beside the floating eye of blue flames and reaching toward it. Then, all the blue light blinked out.

The torches within the circular stone chamber burst aflame again with a whip-like crack. Blinded by the sudden intensity, she ducked and covered her eyes with her hands before she realized she sat on the floor again, her legs crossed beneath her. When she opened her eyes and blinked against the now incredibly bright light of the torches, she was halfway across the room again and only a few steps away from the staircase where she'd sat for the very first time.

Opening her hand, she glanced down at the smooth

blue shimmer of the lapis lazuli in her palm. "Yeah, now I'm convinced that blind storyteller can see the future." Something else glinted and reflected the firelight on the crypt floor ahead of her. "What—oh, my God..." She hesitated to reach for the shining silver object. *Is this even real?* But her hand moved toward the round silver coin with the silhouette of the outstretched heron engraved upon its surface. Her fingers touched the cold metal, and she picked up the same gift Greta Antony had left her in the dreamscape. "It was all real," she whispered. "All of it."

She let that sink in for a few more seconds, pushed herself off the ground, and stood. The lapis lazuli from the seer Amal went into her right pocket and the coin with the Black Heron's sigil went into her left. With a final glance around the empty chamber, she turned toward the staircase that would take her to the surface and all the Ochiului people who waited for her. And Romeo.

"I'm coming, Mom. Hold on a little longer."

THIRTY-ONE

The stone lid of the sarcophagus in the bare ring of trampled dirt rumbled open again and slid fully aside. Another loud crack echoed through the clearing. The Ochiului Romani turned from their conversation to focus on the keeper of their sacred knowledge. Beside the woman elder, Romeo still sat on his haunches as the shaggy black wolf. A low whine rose from his throat.

The old woman cast him a sideways glance. "I told you she'd be quick. And I don't think she's lost a thing."

Lily's blonde head emerged from the darkness in the open crypt. She moved quickly up the final few stairs and blinked against the muted sunlight beneath the orange-pink Romani dome before she clambered over the edge.

No one said a word as she looked across the clearing. She searched for Romeo's face and his dark, curly hair among those watching her, and her gaze settled on the shaggy black wolf seated beside the elderly Ochiului woman. "Huh." She studied him cautiously and walked across the dirt toward them. *Loana said he was safe here. So why the wolf?*

He whined again and lurched forward without moving like he waited for someone's permission. The old woman on the tree stump beside him snapped her fingers and flicked her hand toward him. He shifted immediately onto two legs and was pummeled a second later by his clothes that swirled from the dust and smacked him in the chest.

"Lily!" He jumped from one foot to the other as she hauled his boxers and pants on. His t-shirt fell again with a puff of dirt before he headed toward her at a slow jog and turned only once to shoot the old woman a skeptical glance. She cackled on the tree stump and slapped a knee. "I'm so sorry." He pulled her into a tight embrace, and the force of his hug made her squeak in surprise. "I tried to open it. I would've gone with you if I could. They wouldn't let me do anything."

She chuckled against his chest. "So you shifted?"

He pulled away from her, took her face in both hands, and kissed her fiercely. "I couldn't help it, Lily. I thought... I thought they'd locked you in there."

A tiny frown of confusion creased her brow. "I went down there by choice. They didn't lock me up."

"They closed that...coffin thing." He glanced over her shoulder at the sarcophagus, which now slid shut again with a grumble and another final snapping thud.

Lily stared at him. "They did?" He nodded, and she gave him a careless smile. "I didn't even notice." The concern still hadn't left his face, and she took him by his bare shoulders to hold his gaze. "I know I was in there for a while but it must've been longer than I thought. I'm sorry I made you wait so long."

He tilted his head and glanced at the Romani, who all moved toward them now. The old woman approached at the rear, holding the arm of the woman with the green headscarf. "It was only a few minutes."

"What?"

"Yeah, I... That old witch said you'd be fast. I didn't think she meant this fast."

She chuckled. "Wow. It was at least a couple hours for me. But..." She directed a quick frown at the tomb behind her. "Time and space are really funny down there."

"What happened?"

"So much, actually. I..." She grinned at him and slid her hands down his arms to take his hands. "Romeo, I saw my mom. I talked to her."

His eyes lit up. "Really?"

"Yeah. I mean, in a vision or something. She—"

"Did you find the answers you seek?" The man in the purple jacket stopped beside them as the rest of his people fanned out around their visitors.

"I did." She nodded. "Most of them, at least. Thank you."

"We're always glad to help those who know their own value in this world, Lily Antony." He put a hand over his heart and bowed his head. The other Romani around them echoed the gesture, and she could only stare at them in confusion.

What does that mean?

"Oh." She released Romeo's hand to dig in her left

pocket. Her fingers brushed the cold silver coin. *It's definitely real.* She took it out and held it in her open palm. "She gave me this. Through the vision, somehow."

He frowned at the silver disk in her hand. "That's the—"

"No!" The man with the long graying beard sneered at the coin. "We don't speak any of their names here." He turned his head and spat into the dirt. All around them, the Romani echoed the action.

"But you know who they are?" She scanned their faces and for the first time, found anger behind their eyes—and definitely fear.

"Of course we know." The old woman shuffled forward through the small gathering of her people. The others moved aside to let her approach the couple, and her bright, clear eyes within so many folds of ancient skin studied the sigil of the Black Heron in the young witch's hand. "We know what they seek, just as you now know the truth, Lily. That token is one of theirs. It sleeps for now."

"My mom..." She paused to take a deep breath. "She said I have to activate it to find her. Do you know how to do that?"

The old woman turned and spat twice onto the ground. "We don't want to know. Do not use it here in our home." Her dark gaze raised toward Lily's face, and the young witch saw tears glistening there. "The Ochiului and its people have always been safe here. Protected. Not even our magic can keep at bay what that thing summons once it's awakened."

Frowning, Lily glanced quickly at Romeo. "What does it do?"

"It calls to its brethren, Lily." The old woman's wrinkled lips trembled a little. "Use that, and yes, you will find your mother. But once you release its voice into space and time again, you yourself will stand out to the others of its kind like a bonfire in the darkness. Be very careful how and when you use it."

"I will." She tucked the coin into her pocket again, and the Romani gathered around her relaxed visibly. *So the coin will show me where Mom is...and the rest of the Black Heron will know where I am too. Nice trick.*

Loana stepped forward and inclined her head toward them. "You've been here long enough. Are you ready to be on your way?"

Lily nodded. "Yeah. I'm ready."

Romeo turned and scanned the half-circle with the tree stumps behind them. "Wait. I need my—"

His sneakers tumbled into the dirt at his feet, and Loana whipped his shirt in both hands before she pressed it to his chest with a chuckle. "You are a hasty wolf."

"Um...thanks." He took his shirt and pulled it quickly over his head before he hastily shoved his feet into his shoes and straightened.

"You two are lucky to have each other now." The woman nodded. "Come with me." She headed off in a completely new direction toward nothing at all on the other side of the dirt clearing. They followed, and the Ochiului people pressed their hands to their hearts again and bowed their heads. She didn't think about it at all before she returned the gesture, and he quickly repeated it as well, although his was a little less heartfelt.

"Lily," the old woman called. She turned to look at her with raised eyebrows. "Don't hold back. You know your greatest power now. Use it when you have to. Use all of it."

The only thing she could do was nod before they followed Loana again into the sprawling expanse of dirt and muted light from the huge Romani dome overhead. They walked in silence for a few minutes, and she turned once, thinking she might wave to the people who'd let her into their secrets so she might uncover her own. But there was absolutely nothing behind her—no ring of dirt, no stone sarcophagus, and no scattered wooden wagons or half-circle of tree stumps. The Ochiului were gone. Only a thin mist trailed behind them to reflect the gray and orange light of the dome.

With a word, their guide stopped in the middle of the nothingness and flung her arms out to her sides. She snapped her fingers with both hands, and the tingling pinch returned to Lily's lungs. In the next second, they stood in front of the Winnie and the blue Dacia again with a few trees around them, the scattered rock, the course bushes, and browning grass. Two birds flittered from one set of branches to another, and the pink dome of the Romani wards was gone completely.

The older witch turned and grinned at them. Her gold-painted fingernails glinted in the morning sunlight as she beckoned them forward and gestured toward the Winnie. "You were lucky this time. My people are not always this close to my nephews and me." A wheezing laugh escaped her. "At least you know where to find us."

"Thank you," she said.

"Bah." Loana waved a hand in dismissal and folded her arms. "Get out of here. And don't come back, huh? I hope you never have to." Her piercing cackle sent the birds fluttering from the few trees around them.

"Yeah, so do I," Romeo muttered.

Smirking, Lily grabbed his hand and walked with him back to the Winnie.

They stopped that afternoon at the smaller town of Brestak. Neither one of them were hungry yet, and it felt odd not to have an immediate destination this time. "I won't know where we need to go next until I find out how to...wake it up." She turned the silver heron coin over and over in her hand. She'd spent the last few hours telling him everything she could remember about the Ochiului crypt, the visions she'd seen, and the brief but very real conversation with her mom.

Beside her on the bed in the Winnie, he placed his hand on hers. "Maybe put that thing away for a little while, huh?" He eyed it warily. "It creeps me out more than that stone head from Guatemala."

She smirked and retrieved the wooden box with the lily flower carved into the lid—the second clue her mom had left in Melissa Bore's magical vault. "Sure. It's—"

"Not—" Romeo sighed. "Not in the box. I won't be able to sleep with it, like...right over my head."

"Oh. Yeah, okay. Sure. Give me a sec." She stood from the bed and walked out to the Winnie's kitchen. There, she knelt beneath the kitchen table and scooted aside the large red pot with the constantly blooming wolfsbane flowers inside. Her fingers easily found the loose slat beneath the bench, and she tucked the heron coin beneath one of the brown bags of her mom's gold coins. She crawled slowly out again, eyed the purple wolfsbane flowers, and stood and returned to the bedroom.

"Did you stock up on wolfsbane before we went to see the Romani?"

He opened his eyes and looked at her, a little surprised. "Yeah. Why?"

"I'm curious. I only now realized you hardly reacted to all the magic inside that dome."

"Well, I assumed I should stay on top of my meds if I'm gonna be useful to you...like at all." He shrugged.

She climbed back onto the bed beside him and leaned against the propped pillows. "You're always useful to me. Even when you're stumbling around and sneezing."

Romeo snorted and shook his head. "Yeah, I ate some before we went in. It still didn't..." A dark frown creased his brows. "It didn't stop me from losing control of myself, though. And it didn't stop that old witch, either."

"What do you mean?"

His expression a little sheepish, he scratched the back of his head and sighed. "I thought they were locking you up in that tomb thing, Lil. And no one thought it was a big deal. I...I lost it. I shifted without even thinking about it. The only thing I could think about was ripping those people apart for lying to you. I know. I know they didn't. They didn't tell me what was going on, either. And that old woman?" He shook his head. "I dunno. She used some kinda compulsion spell, maybe. Or something about the way she talked to me. I couldn't fight it. I would've done whatever she told me to."

"Woah." She caught his hand. "I'm sorry, Romeo. I didn't know they'd do anything to you."

"Hey, you had nothing to do with it. Technically. You were simply walking down hundreds of stairs." He smiled at her and squeezed her hand. "But I hated losing control like that. Not being able to think, you know?"

"It totally makes sense."

"Well, good." Lily chuckled, and he stared at their interlaced fingers. "And I think I know why I lost it. If anything ever happened to you, Lil—"

"Nothing happened to me. I'm fine. And nothing will happen to me. I have you."

He smiled again and squeezed her hand a little more tightly. "I have to tell you something, so please...hear me out for a minute, okay?"

Her eyes widened. "Yeah. Okay."

"Okay." He took a deep breath and rubbed his thumb over the back of her hand. "If anything happened to you, Lily, I wouldn't...be myself anymore. You went down those stairs, and that lid shut, and I couldn't feel you anymore. I didn't even know I could until I couldn't, right? And it was the worst thing I've ever felt in my life."

"Oh." Her heart fluttered in her chest.

When he looked at her, his green eyes studied hers with more intensity than she'd ever seen—and a little more fear. "I need you, Lil. I can't do any of this without you. I love you."

For a few seconds, she couldn't do anything but stare into his eyes. Then, she pushed herself up and swung her leg over his lap to straddle him. She took his face in both her hands and kissed him slowly, and he relaxed beneath her as he sighed and wound his arms around her. When she pulled back a little, she bit her lip and smiled. "I love you too."

Romeo pulled her down quickly for another kiss and held her against him like she might slip away at any minute. She giggled through their lips pressed together, and he pulled away with wide eyes. "I mean I'm in love with you—"

Lily laughed. "I know what you mean. It's completely different now than when we used to say it in first grade."

He chuckled and released a massive sigh. "Okay, good."

"Okay."

He sat up to kiss her again and held her against him as he rolled them both over onto the bed. She draped her arms around his neck and let everything else ahead of them disappear. For now, they had one more night alone before who knew what came for them next.

THIRTY-TWO

Greta Antony stirred when the heavy iron door groaned open. Slowly, she pushed herself up and sat on the cold stone floor. The iron manacles around her wrists clinked against their chains when she swept her soiled hair out of her eyes.

Two men stepped into her stone prison. None of them knew how long she'd be there before they moved her again.

"You're wasting your time," she whispered with a smirk. "Nothing's changed. You're still as useless as—"

Both men raised their hands toward her and released ice-cold funnels of black, crackling magic into her chest. She screamed, her head thrown back, and the manacles prevented her from moving any more than rising onto her knees in agony. Where the tendrils of the Black Heron's siphoning spell usually flared with bright light to steal their other prisoners' magic from the very core of their being, the gaunt witch—the bane of their final plan—gave them nothing.

They allowed the spell to continue a little longer than usual, if for no other reason than that it made the woman stop talking. Finally, the first man ended the spell, and the second dropped his shortly after.

She sank back onto her heels with a groan and knelt there with slumped shoulders, her head lowered all the way to her chest. The chains tied to her manacles clinked against the stone. Her chest heaved as she fought to catch her breath before a wheezing but still entirely defiant chuckle escaped her. "I tried to tell you..." She shook her head and swayed on the floor. "You'll never get what you want from me. And you still have no idea what's coming for you."

The men shared a wary glance. One of them cleared his throat. "You'll break, witch. We know it. You know it too. It's merely a matter of time."

Greta chuckled again. "Time you don't have." Slowly, she raised her heavy head to look at first one of them and then the other. She took a few deep, heavy breaths before her cracked and bleeding lips parted in a devious grin. "You're in deep shit now, boys."

The road trip doesn't end in Romania. They are now heading toward Greece. Will they find her mother there or are they being led on a wild goose chase? Find out in To Find A Witch.

Get sneak peeks, exclusive giveaways, behind the scenes content, and more.
PLUS you'll be notified of special **one day only fan pricing** on new releases.

Sign up today to get free stories.

For Hire: Teachers for special school in Virginia countryside.

Must be able to handle teenagers with special abilities.

Cannot be afraid to discipline werewolves, wizards, elves and other assorted hormonal teens.

Apply at the School of Necessary Magic.

AVAILABLE AT AMAZON RETAILERS

AUTHOR NOTES - MARTHA CARR & MICHAEL ANDERLE

SEPTEMBER 18, 2019

I was talking to Michael Anderle on the phone today, and I told him I was working on author notes. He started riffing on what I could say about him so... Why waste a good idea like that? Here, dear Readers and Super Fans (kinda one and the same) are some MA factoids...

• For some reason, when he calls me from his car, he always drives past the exit or takes a wrong turn till he's very lost – Every Time (like today). I like to think it's my witty and charismatic conversation especially since I've seen the dude multi-task like a wizard. <<Mike Add: She's right – I miss my turn off all the time! It's freaky it happens so often. One time, I almost went the wrong way on a one-way street. (It's in Vegas, a two-way turned into a one way, and I had to take a left. In order to get it right, I had to drive across the road and turn around in a parking lot of a motel to get going the right direction. I actually DON'T multi-task well during conversations. Two people talking at the same time completely shuts down my brain.>>

• He hates it when I mention Surviving Cancer in the Author Notes because he figures, no one is reading any farther in his notes. Too many triumphant fist pumps instead. <<Mike: Yeah, what the shiznit are you supposed to talk about after someone plays the cancer card? It's not like you can then say 'So, I was eating at Burger King...' She freaking beat cancer HOW many times... I need to ask her if she is going to recite an eighth time just to screw with me?>>

• Whenever I mentioned still doing something that an admin could do – he cackles... loudly. He's amused that I choose to overwork myself for no good reason. It's really super effective behavior modification and especially since I have such a great admin – Hello Grace! <<Mike: Yeah, this is kinda true - I do cackle like Jack Nicholson playing the Joker. It was the only way I could get her to see the issue for what it is. When you work ninety hour weeks for a year, at some point, you need to look around and spend a few dollars to get your life back (if you are making some money after that year.) Not only does she enjoy the fruit of working hard, but someone else is able to put the money together to make their own life a bit better and reading is helping Martha, who is helping others. It's a nice cycle of life.>>

• We were on a zoom call once, and both forgot to turn off our computers and walked away. Perhaps we were a teensy bit overworked that week? Anyway, I came back three hours later and wondered what I was looking at – someone's living room? Right at that moment, Michael walked across the room drinking a Coke. He was on brand!

Should have seen the look on his face when he heard me yelling, "Hello... hello!" Priceless. <<Mike: I don't have much to add, it was embarrassing to know I had screwed that up so bad. I don't find THIS particular story so funny. LOL>>

• He swears no one else can write the troll (you know, that troll) but me because my personality is exactly like the troll's – one part snarky, one part swearing, and one part Zen. He may be right. He usually is. I can own that one. (Is the troll coming back? Will you see more of Leira and the gang? Stay tuned... Wonder how many readers notice this...). <<Mike: If someone is willing to tap their inner Martha, they can write the troll. But, the problem is Martha is an older woman (this is important) who has the heart of a teenager still. So, she has decades of experience to place the troll in silly situations to play within.>>

• My swearing makes him laugh. I am very Zen and sort through what I can change and what I need to let go and trust the universe, but a good Aloha in just the right place... <<Mike: I find cursing hilarious. Proper use of an expletive at the right time is an art form.>>

• He believes in the abilities and dreams of absolutely everyone. Legit. I've seen it on way too many occasions – and often it's people who a lot of others might have overlooked. Introverted, stumbled in life, and yet, you ready to work hard? You have a good idea? It comes without conditions or expectations, and it's amazing and such an honor and a blessing just to watch over his shoulder when another author blossoms into their dreams. Note – it's always their dreams – their design. That's an amazing ability. It's as advertised, for real and universally offered. It's why I chose to write with him and why I trust him without question. It's an amazing ride. More adventures to follow. <<Mike: Awwww! This is without a doubt the nicest thing you have ever mentioned, Martha. I'm sure your wings are waiting for you in thirty or fifty years when you finally decide to step into the next adventure off Earth.>>

PS Go read his Author Notes anyway... even if I did mention that whole survived cancer seven times thing... <<Mike: Martha, Heaven called - they want their wings back for author-note blocking me AGAIN!. Fooled you, I put my notes up there ^^ LOL.>>

THANK YOU, EVERYONE, FOR READING OUR STORIES! – Mike (and Martha – but she's out enjoying herself in Los Angeles tonight and won't get to see these notes before they release... BWAHAHAHAHAHA...(Yes, I know, no Angel wings for me, either.))

OTHER BOOKS BY MARTHA CARR

Series in the Oriceran Universe:

Other series:

THE LAST VAMPIRE
THE WITCH NEXT DOOR

OTHER BOOKS BY JUDITH BERENS

OTHER BOOKS BY MARTHA CARR

JOIN THE ORICERAN UNIVERSE FAN GROUP ON FACEBOOK!

CONNECT WITH THE AUTHORS

Martha Carr Social

Website: http://www.marthacarr.com

Facebook: https://www.facebook.com/
groups/MarthaCarrFans/

Michael Anderle Social

Michael Anderle Social
Website:
http://www.lmbpn.com

Email List:
http://lmbpn.com/email/

Facebook Here: https://www.
facebook.com/TheKurtherianGambitBooks/

www.ingramcontent.com/pod-product-compliance
Lightning Source LLC
Chambersburg PA
CBHW031624100726
47898CB00006B/1934